FIGHT
TO
SURVIVE

ALSO BY ALAN McDERMOTT

Tom Gray Novels

Gray Justice
Gray Resurrection
Gray Redemption
Gray Retribution
Gray Vengeance
Gray Salvation

Trojan
Run and Hide
Seek and Destroy

FIGHT
TO
SURVIVE

ALAN
McDermott

THOMAS & MERCER

Text copyright © 2019 by Alan McDermott
All rights reserved.

Published by Thomas & Mercer, Seattle

www.apub.com

Amazon, the Amazon logo, and Thomas & Mercer are trademarks of Amazon.com, Inc., or its affiliates.

ISBN-13: 9781542006637
ISBN-10: 1542006635

Cover design by Tom Sanderson

Printed in the United States of America

For Ed Stackler

The only thing necessary for the triumph of evil is for good men to do nothing.

—Edmund Burke

CHAPTER 1

January 2020

As Eva Driscoll arrived home from the restaurant, violence was the last thing on her mind.

She could still taste the buttery lobster and fruity wine she'd had for dinner, and all she wanted to do was curl up on the couch with a box set and a cup of hot cocoa.

The screams coming from the house next door put paid to those plans.

Eva had lived next to Sally and Jake for three months, ever since arriving in Melbourne, Australia. Raised voices had become a regular occurrence. Based on what she'd observed, they seemed like a normal couple most of the time, but when the sun went down it was a different story. Eva didn't know if it was alcohol-related, or the stress of Jake's job as a cop, but most evenings she had to turn up the television to drown out the shouting.

But the sounds currently coming from the neighboring house were on a whole new level.

As Eva locked her car and got her key ready to open the front door, a female scream made her pause.

Eva had had coffee with Sally a few times, but the state of the marriage had never come up in conversation. She'd delicately probed, but Sally had dodged the issue like a pro. That in itself told Eva that something wasn't right within the Holman residence.

Jake was a big man, at least six-two and 230 pounds, with a physique that told of an athletic youth. Sally was built like Eva, a few inches shorter than Jake with a lean body. Hardly a fair match if things got physical.

Leave it, Eva told herself as she put her key in the door. It wasn't her fight, and she didn't need the aggravation. She was lying low, staying off the radar, and that meant she had to avoid confrontations that could quickly escalate. She would visit Sally tomorrow when Jake was at work and give her some friendly advice.

She almost jumped at the sound of something heavy hitting a wall in Sally's house, followed by a burst of shouting and another high-pitched scream.

Eva sighed. She really didn't want to get involved, but she also hated the idea of leaving the diminutive Sally at the mercy of her much larger husband.

Eva had met Jake on just one occasion, at a barbecue the couple had hosted. He'd come across as a real man's man, full of confidence and aware of his good looks. He'd flirted with Eva a couple of times that day, though she'd been careful not to reciprocate. Her appearance attracted unwanted attention wherever she went, and being married hadn't seemed a barrier to Jake. He also didn't seem the type to put up with anyone questioning his actions—male *or* female.

Another cry came from their house, and Eva recognized the sound of a woman in pain.

She had to act, but she couldn't simply rush in. This needed to be handled delicately, without any chance of blowback. She would try to defuse the situation, but if Jake pushed it, she'd need a get-out-of-jail-free card.

Eva went back to her car and locked her purse inside, then walked across the lawn to the Holman residence. She opened the camera on her phone, set it on top of the mailbox by the sidewalk, and zoomed in so that the front door filled the center of the screen. She pressed the Record button, then walked up the path and rang the doorbell.

The shouting stopped. She wondered if that simple act had been enough to end the altercation, but it wasn't to be. Jake threw the door open and glared at her, his face red and contorted with fury.

"What?" he yelled.

Eva pretended to flinch. "I want to make sure Sally's okay."

"How about you just fuck off and mind your own business?"

Jake tried to slam the door, but Eva threw out a leg so it hit the ball of her foot. The door swung back open, and she could see Sally standing in the middle of the living room, her hair a mess and a couple of red welts on her face.

Jake wheeled around and stood over Eva so they were a couple of inches apart.

Perfect.

"I want to see Sally," she said quietly as she leaned in and pressed her thumb into the pressure point above his elbow, "and I'm not gonna let a chickenshit like you get in my way." She knew the camera wouldn't be able to see her gripping him, and it brought about the reaction she was hoping for.

Jake howled with rage and pushed her. Eva stumbled backward for a couple of steps, then collapsed onto the ground. Jake followed her, and Eva hid a smile as he approached. She couldn't have choreographed it more perfectly if she'd tried.

He leaned over her, snorting like an enraged bull.

"That's the last time I'm going easy on you," he shouted, his pointed finger inches from Eva's face. She swung a foot at his hand and connected; in retaliation, he aimed a kick at her ribs. Eva blocked it with her arm and rolled away before springing to her feet. Her back to the camera again, she whispered a taunt.

"You kick like a pussy."

Jake was unable to contain himself. He lunged at Eva and swung his fist in an arc, but she saw it coming. She ducked slightly and the arm flew over her head; while Jake was off-balance, she delivered a vicious punch that connected with his jaw. Jake wobbled but managed to stay on his feet, which wasn't in the script. He kicked at her again, but she pirouetted into him and caught him on the temple with her elbow.

The fight was over.

As Jake lay still on the grass, Eva turned him over and checked his breathing. He was groggy, but alive. She put him into the recovery position, then collected her phone and stopped the recording as she walked back up to the house.

Sally was standing in the doorway with her hand over her mouth, tears flowing down her welted and bloodstained face. Eva recognized the signs of shock. She took Sally inside and sat her down, then went to make a hot drink.

She brought two cups of coffee into the living room and put one in Sally's shaking hands.

"I called the police and an ambulance," Eva said. She thought about tending to Sally's injuries but decided to leave that to the professionals. Her current state would make the case of self-defense more credible. She had a black eye and a cut eyelid, and her top lip was swollen and seeping blood. Nothing that wouldn't heal in time.

"He's going to kill me," Sally sobbed as she reached for a Kleenex from the box on the table.

"No, he isn't," Eva assured her. "You should tell the police what he did and then come and stay with me tonight. Tomorrow you can move on and get out of this relationship."

"I can't," Sally wailed. "He'll find me."

"Then you apply for a restraining order. He won't be able to come near you."

"He's a cop. That won't stop him."

"It will if he knows it'll cost him his job. He has no power to enter my home, so all you need to do is stay inside my place, keep your head down for a couple of days, and look for somewhere else to live."

"I can't do that," Sally insisted. "He's the only one working. That's what the argument was all about. He's angry that I haven't been able to find a job for the last three months. There's almost nothing left in the bank. I've got about ten bucks to my name."

"Don't worry about money. I can help you out until you're back on your feet."

Cash was something Eva had plenty of. Spread across bank accounts around the world, her personal fortune was close to a hundred million dollars, money she'd stolen from the people who'd murdered her brother and then tried to kill her, bad actors who no longer walked free—or walked at all.

Eva got to her feet when she heard the first of the sirens. Flashing red and blue lights tore through the curtains as the emergency vehicle pulled up outside.

"You stay here," Eva said, and walked into the garden. The ambulance crew got out and jogged over to Jake, who was still lying on the lawn.

"What happened here?" one asked as Eva went to join them.

"He was beating his wife and I interrupted them. He tried hitting me, but I got in a lucky punch. His wife is inside, and she needs attention, too."

The paramedics fussed around Jake for a few moments, then one of them took a bag into the house.

"He'll be fine," the other medic said. "Possible concussion, but he'll live."

Eva left him to do his job and went to see how Sally was getting on. She had run a brush through her hair but still looked a mess. The blood was being cleaned from her face, revealing dark bruising.

"How is she?" Eva asked.

"She doesn't need to go to the hospital. I'd suggest a couple of Advil and an early night."

A knock came at the open door, and two cops walked in and removed their caps.

"I'm Sergeant Makin, this is Constable Powell," one of them said to Eva. "I understand you're responsible for the man on the lawn."

"Actually, *he* was. I came to check on my friend and he went for me. I just protected myself."

Makin looked her up and down. "You took down a man that size?"

Eva shrugged. "I took self-defense classes a few years ago. Looks like they paid off."

A skeptical nod. He took out his notepad and asked for their names. Eva gave them, and Makin pointed at the couch. "Take a seat and start from the beginning."

Eva dropped into a chair instead. "There's not much to tell. I arrived home from eating out and heard screams and crashes coming from this house, so I came to see if Sally was okay. I rang the bell, Jake came out, and I asked to speak to her. He tried to slam the door in my face, but I stuck my foot in the way, then he came out and went for me. He pushed me to the ground and stood over me in a threatening manner. I kicked him, he kicked me, then I managed to get up. He swung and missed. I didn't. He kicked me, I hit him again, end of story."

Makin looked at Sally for corroboration.

"I don't know," she said. "By the time I got to the door, it was all over."

Makin nodded. "How did you get your injuries?"

One of the ambulance crew stuck his head around the doorframe. "We're taking him to The Alfred."

"What's his condition?" Makin asked.

"He's stable, no serious damage. He'll have one hell of a headache and we need to take a look at his jaw, but nothing long-term. He'll probably be out tomorrow."

Makin thanked him, then turned back to Sally. "Can you tell me who did this to you?"

Sally blew into a Kleenex, and Eva could see she was reluctant to tell the police what had happened. Eva got up and sat next to Sally, putting an arm around her shoulders.

"Just tell them exactly what happened. You don't have to put up with this. I told you, I'll make sure you're safe."

Sally took a couple of deep breaths, then it all came pouring out. She described how she'd met Jake eight years earlier and been swept off her feet, only for the relationship to turn sour a few months after they were married.

"At first it was just little things, like giving me the silent treatment if dinner wasn't ready when he got home, or the trash wasn't taken out every day, but things got worse over time. The shouting started after about a year. He would erupt for no reason. If I didn't get beer and chips in for his weekly poker game, or I suggested going out with my friends, he would start screaming at me. He goes out with his mates, but I have to stay home every night."

"And when did he start hitting you?" Makin asked, taking advantage of an empty armchair. "Was this the first time?"

"No, it started last year. Mostly he would just slap me or grip my arms really tight. He's a cop, and I guess he knows not to leave visible bruising."

"So what changed tonight?"

"I fought back." Sally sniffed. "He was ranting about me being out of work. He called me lazy and a waste of space. I've been to thirty job interviews in the past few months, but I'm always up against a hundred other people. He was telling me to take anything. Flipping burgers or working the checkout at Coles, but that's not what I want to do. I went to uni for a career, not to make minimum wage. Anyway, he grabbed my arms and was squeezing them real hard, so I kicked him. It must have set him off. He gave me a backhander and split my lip, and I told him I was going to get him fired. That's when he really laid into me. I . . . I can't remember the details."

Makin appeared sympathetic. "Where's he stationed?"

"Melbourne East."

"That's why I don't recognize him. I'm from Caulfield." Makin stood and smoothed out his trousers. "Have you got somewhere to stay tonight?"

"She can stay at my place," Eva said. "I live next door, number 523."

"Great." He handed Eva his card. "I'll need you both to make a full statement tomorrow. You can come to the station—or, if you prefer, I can send a couple of guys round."

"That would be better."

"Okay. They'll be able to put you in touch with local shelters that specialize in domestic violence."

The cops left, and once Sally had been treated for her injuries, the ambulance departed, too.

Eva told Sally to pack a bag, and tidied the living room while she did so. Twenty minutes later, they were sitting in Eva's kitchen, drinking the remains of a bottle of wine she'd opened a few days earlier.

"I shouldn't have told them anything," Sally said. "I should have said I fell."

"You did the right thing," Eva told her. "Do you want to face that for the rest of your life? What if he got drunk and decided to use his gun on you?"

"He wouldn't do that."

"They never do," Eva said sarcastically. "Why do you think there are so many refuge centers? He's not going to change just because I gave him a kicking. He'll be mad as hell and it'll be even worse from now on. You have to leave him."

"But where would I go? He's a cop. He'll find me."

"Not if he loses his job, and after tonight, he probably will."

"Then he'll ask his mates to find me," Sally insisted.

Eva got up and walked into another room. She returned a few minutes later with a paper bag the size of a hardcover book.

"There's ten thousand. Leave the city and only pay cash. Find a lawyer, file for divorce, and get a restraining order as soon as you can, so he can't follow you."

Sally sat stunned for a moment, then pushed the package across the table toward Eva. "I couldn't possibly take that! There's no way I can pay you back."

"Don't worry about that," Eva said, pushing it back. "It's rainy-day money. You can make it up to me when you get back on your feet."

Sally fingered the package. "Are you sure?"

"I'm positive. Tomorrow morning, we'll get what you need from the house and take a trip. Perth, or Darwin, somewhere miles from here."

"What if he comes back before I leave?"

"I'll be here with you," Eva said. "He won't touch you."

Sally went silent for a moment. "Was it true what you told the cop, about the self-defense classes?"

Eva considered telling her the truth, but only fleetingly. How could she explain to a virtual stranger that she was once a CIA-trained assassin, and now she was on the run from the ESO, the most powerful organization on the planet? In that respect, they were similar—both looking to escape their pasts.

"Yes, it's true," she lied. "I was in the same situation a few years ago. Only, the first time he hit me, I was outta there. He came after me because I was foolish enough to hang around the same neighborhood, but I'd already started the classes. Let's just say he never bothered me again." Eva didn't think Jake would travel the length of the country to find Sally, but she should prepare for the worst. "It's a good idea to learn how to protect yourself. If not from Jake, then the next one that comes along."

"I'll do that."

Sally yawned, and Eva felt the same way. She cleared away the wine glasses and showed her guest to the bedroom, then fetched some clean bedding.

"Sleep well," Eva said as she left the room. "Like they say, tomorrow's the first day of the rest of your life."

Eva chose a comforter from the closet and got settled on the couch, but as tired as she was, sleep wouldn't come easily. Makin seemed to have believed her story, and she had the video as backup if anyone wanted further proof, but that wasn't what concerned her.

The nagging feeling that she'd made the wrong decision simply wouldn't leave her.

CHAPTER 2

All faces turned to the boardroom door as Vincent May entered the room. He was fifty-seven but looked a decade younger, his hair still years away from the first sign of gray. He undid the button on his Dormeuil suit jacket and took his seat at the head of the long, polished table. It had room for twenty people, but there were only three others present—the top men in the Executive Security Office, the most powerful and secretive group in the world. Everyone had heard of the US Senate and House of Representatives, but they amounted to little more than puppets, with the ESO pulling the strings.

"Gentlemen," May said as he poured himself a glass of water from a crystal decanter, "I understand you have an update on the North Korean project."

"We do," Larry Carter, the representative for the military–industrial complex, said. "And it's not good news. The security services are refusing to provide the personnel unless the president sanctions the extraction and, as we all know, that's not going to happen."

May was disappointed, but not overly so. Getting the CIA, NSA and Homeland Security on board had been a long shot, at best. Once upon a time it would have taken a single phone call to get whatever they wanted, but that had all changed two years earlier when they'd crossed paths with Eva Driscoll. An encounter that had led to the president—not the one they'd planned to install—creating a task force to bring the ESO to justice. They'd lost their longtime leader Henry Langton, though that had been a blessing in disguise. He'd gone off the rails and had been taking the organization in a dangerous direction, making his death fortuitous, to say the least.

The result of the witch hunt was that the ESO had been forced to pare down their activities. Avenues of power had been cordoned off, access to governmental departments revoked. While May viewed it as a temporary setback, it did leave him without the power he needed to operate the organization efficiently.

Today was a prime example.

"The clock's ticking." Ben Scott, head of foreign policy, popped an antacid into his mouth. "Everything's set, we just need the right people to go in and get Hong. The longer we leave him dangling, the more anxious he'll get. If he brings attention to himself it could spell trouble."

"Why don't we use military contractors?" James Butler asked. "It's not as if we can't afford it."

Larry Carter provided the answer. "Because a large team of ex-soldiers would be spotted the moment they crossed the border. We need one person, perhaps two, with the right skills."

"Then find two guys who used to be in Special Forces," Butler, the chief finance officer, suggested. "Those people know how to blend in."

"They're trained to deal with the current threat, which is the Middle East," May said. "We need someone who knows the region and speaks the language. Someone who won't stick out."

"How about someone who's retired? An ex-spook?"

"And how long will that take?" Carter asked. "We'd have to find a list of suitable candidates, vet each one, then convince them to take on the mission. That's if we can find someone with the skills we need who didn't quit from burnout."

"There is one person we could use," May said, "though we'd have to be at our most persuasive."

"Who?"

May paused. If he shared his thoughts, they might think him delusional. If he didn't, they might lose an opportunity to get the upper hand over one of the most troublesome regimes on the planet. Better to put the name out there and let his peers decide.

"Eva Driscoll."

The room fell silent. May wouldn't have been surprised to see tumbleweed drift across the table.

Carter ruined the moment with an explosion of laughter. It melted away when he saw the look on May's face.

"You're serious? Eva Driscoll?"

"I'm with Larry," Butler said. "The woman hates us with a passion, and rightly so. How the hell do you expect to convince her to work for us?"

"Money," May told them.

Scott waved a contemptuous hand. "She's already got tens of millions. What else could we possibly offer her?"

"I'm talking about her own money," May said. "We have access to each of her bank accounts. If we were to divert the funds elsewhere, she'd have no option but to do as we ask."

"Am I the only one who remembers what she did to Alexander Mumford?" Carter asked.

Mumford had been a top executive in the ESO under Henry Langton. Driscoll had paid a visit to his home and castrated him, before choking him to death with his own private parts.

"Mumford was sloppy," May said. "The way Langton ran things, he was inviting trouble. There's no way Driscoll could identify any of us, let alone get close enough to do us any harm. Besides, we're not looking to hurt her; we'd be offering her work."

"I still don't like it," Carter complained. "Taking her money might be all the excuse she needs to come looking for us."

"We'll do it to get her attention, that's all. We can put the funds back immediately once we have her cooperation."

"She's not going to like that," Carter persisted. "Once she knows we've been tracking her for the last two years, she'll be pissed."

Ever since Driscoll had dealt with Henry Langton, May had kept tabs on her. His people had followed her to Melbourne and sent back weekly reports on her actions. Not that there had been many. She volunteered at an animal shelter twice a week, didn't have any close friends, and liked to dine out.

Some had suggested taking her out permanently, but May had always vetoed the idea. He'd had a feeling she would one day be useful, and that day had come.

"If we want Hong out, we've got no choice. Driscoll speaks the language and knows how to take care of herself. Plus, she's less likely to attract attention than a Rambo type. She's got everything in her favor. We'll be handling her through cutouts, so there'll be nothing to lead back to us."

The three men considered the proposal.

"I still don't like forcing her to work for us," Carter eventually said. "She might kill Hong just to spite us."

"Then we throw her a few million for her trouble," May suggested. "But I don't think that'll be necessary. As you said, she'll know we've been keeping an eye on her since the Langton debacle. If we can get that close to her without her knowledge, she'll think twice before crossing us, especially if we control her resources."

"I wish I had your confidence," Carter said. He leaned back in his chair and stared at the ceiling for a moment. "Okay, send her in, but I want it on the record that I think it's a bad idea."

"Noted," May said. He took out his phone and hit a preset number. When the call recipient picked up, he asked, "What's Driscoll's status?"

He listened for a few moments, then hung up. "Driscoll had a run-in with a neighbor last night. A cop. The guy was beating his wife and Driscoll stepped in. The wife stayed with her overnight. I can use that." He turned to James Butler. "Move her money and let me know when it's done. I'll give her a call and get things started. Larry, is the exfiltration plan in place?"

"They've been set and ready to go for a couple of days. They just need the word."

"They'll get it soon enough. Okay, let's get this done."

May rose and buttoned his jacket, ending the meeting. It was a little after five in the evening, New York time, which made it nine the next morning in Melbourne.

Still early enough to ruin Driscoll's entire day.

CHAPTER 3

"That smells wonderful."

Eva turned from the stove to see Sally standing in the kitchen doorway.

"Just standard bacon and eggs. Coffee?"

"I'd love some." Sally took a seat at the table. "I didn't thank you for what you did last night."

"Don't mention it. Just take my advice and move out. We don't get long on this planet, so you can't waste it hanging around with people who make you miserable."

"I know, but I can't help but think it might be my fault that he—"

"Stop right there." Eva turned off the gas and scraped the breakfast onto two plates, then took them over to the table. "If you stay, you're effectively telling him he can do what he likes and you'll put up with it." Eva fetched a fresh pot of coffee and they made a start on their food. "When you've finished breakfast, we'll go to your house and get your belongings before Jake gets home. In the meantime, we'll book our accommodation and buy the plane tickets."

"*Our* accommodation? Are you coming with me?"

"Just for a week or two," Eva said, though she wouldn't be returning to Melbourne any time soon. The cops would be by later, looking to interview her, and if they decided to take her to the station and finger-print her, the ESO were sure to pick up on it. That was the last thing she wanted or needed. It would be better to quit the city and start again under another name.

Once Sally was taken care of.

"Where are we going?" her neighbor asked.

"Darwin, Cairns, Perth . . . take your pick. Anywhere that isn't Melbourne."

"I have a sister in Perth," Sally said.

"Then that's out. It's the first place Jake will look. We need to go where you have no ties."

"But if I file for divorce, surely he'll get my address."

"By that time, you'll have a restraining order," Eva said. "And you'll be using a lawyer, so you'll use their address. Make sure it's a lawyer from another town, just in case."

Eva opened Google Maps and let Sally pick the destination. After a few minutes of indecision, she settled on Darwin.

Eva navigated to a flight-comparison website and found one that left at six that evening. Plenty of time for Sally to pick up what she wanted from her house and get to the airport. She selected two seats and paid extra for baggage.

When it came time to pay, she entered her credit card details and hit the Submit button. The page went gray, then refreshed with an unexpected message.

Transaction Declined

Eva looked at the card and tried to remember the last time she'd bought anything with it. She could only think of the meal the night before. Apart from that, she hadn't used it since she'd received the last statement and paid it in full.

She put the card back in her wallet and took out her debit card. She'd been to the bank three days earlier, and knew there should be more than twenty grand in the account. She entered the card details and froze at the result.

There was only one way her debit card would be declined, and that was if the account was empty. She quickly opened another browser window and logged into her bank account. The hundred-dollar balance came as a complete shock.

Someone had cleaned out her account. A cold shiver went through her as she thought about the other money she had spread around the world. Forty million in the Cayman Islands. Twenty million in Switzerland. The other accounts were much smaller, each containing a few million. If they'd all been emptied . . .

Eva logged into her Cayman account and found her worst fears confirmed. It showed that she had five hundred bucks left. With panic rising, she tried the Swiss bank, then the ones in England, South Korea, and Russia.

She was broke, and there was only one explanation. Following her altercation with Jake Holman, a record would have been created in the police database. The ESO must have come across it.

But that wouldn't explain the missing money. There was nothing to link the accounts to "Melanie Carr" because they had been opened using a different identity, one created specifically to hide the money. She never used that name for anything else.

Which meant the ESO had been watching her all along. She'd spent the last two years thinking she'd given them the slip, but it had all been a sham.

The phone rang, the timing too coincidental for comfort. She let it ring five times, then relented and picked up.

"Hello, Eva."

Her worst fears were confirmed. No one in Australia knew her real name, and none of her friends or ex-associates would have contacted her on an open line. They certainly wouldn't have used a device to disguise their voice.

Eva held up a finger to Sally and walked into the bedroom, closing the door.

"What have you done with my money?" she growled.

"Straight to the point as always," the male voice said. "Your money is safe. We'd like to offer you the opportunity to add to your already considerable pile."

"Why? So you can steal it again?"

"Not at all. That was just to get your attention."

"You have it," she said, gripping the phone tightly. "What do you want?"

"We have a job for you."

Despite the tense situation, Eva found herself laughing. "Are you kidding me? You steal everything I have and then ask me for a fucking favor? And let's not forget the time you tried to kill me, or has that slipped your mind?"

"No, that memory is still painfully fresh. However, we're not the same organization you dealt with before. Langton was a rogue who put his own interests first. You actually did us a favor by getting rid of him. We have a new vision for our country, one that—"

"Spare me the bullshit."

"As you wish. I'll get straight down to business. We need you to perform a delicate task for us."

"You mean you want me to kill someone? How about I start with you?"

"You could try," the voice admitted. "But as I said, we've evolved. No more meetings in gentlemen's clubs or anything as clichéd as that. What you did to Langton made us re-evaluate our security arrangements. So, thanks to your actions, you'll never discover who we are. As for the assignment, we want you to help someone escape."

"Then use the military. That's what they do best."

"This has to be handled . . . subtly. We need someone with your language skills who can blend in with the locals. A large force is out of the question."

Eva thought about the languages she knew, but it didn't help her narrow down the possible locations. Over the last dozen years she'd learned to speak the native tongues of the nations she was most likely to be deployed in. At least, she had until her role with the CIA was consigned to history. This ESO man could be talking about dozens of places in South America, Europe, Russia, and Asia.

She shook her head. *Why am I thinking like an operative?* There was no way she'd work for the people who had killed her brother.

"Well, good luck with that," she said.

The phone went silent for a moment, during which time she thought about how to escape their clutches once and for all. She had one remaining false identity, but she'd need more in the coming years. She could use the Melanie Carr documents to get her to Europe, then switch to the new one and travel the region before flying out to her new destination.

But where? Was there still a country that wasn't in bed with the ESO?

It was all academic. With less than a grand to her name, disappearing was going to be impossible.

"If you check your banks, the money is back in place," the voice said. "Consider it a sign of our sincerity. We'll also add another twenty million once the job is complete."

Eva returned to the kitchen, ignoring Sally's inquiring expression, and logged back into the Cayman account. The balance looked the same as it had weeks earlier.

They had her over a barrel. They could bankrupt her at will, and they clearly knew where she was. If she tried to grab her money and run, they'd be on to her before she could leave the country.

Eva needed a plan to get away from them for good, but that would take time to put together. Time was a luxury she didn't have, but perhaps she could buy some.

She would do their bidding. It would at least allow her a grace period to come up with something, even if the idea of working for her brother's killers was repulsive.

"Are you still there, Eva?" said the altered voice.

She walked back into the bedroom. "I want guarantees that you'll leave me alone after this is over," she said.

"Whatever you say. And, if you like, we can even ensure that Jake Holman never gets close to his wife ever again."

So they *did* have people watching her. "And you give me whatever I need to carry out the mission, no questions asked."

"You got it."

Eva sighed, then asked him what the job was.

"Not over the phone. There's a bar at the north end of Princes Bridge. Be outside at six this evening. Our man will find you."

The call ended, and Eva immediately began working out her post-op escape plan.

She would have to convert her money into something portable. Precious stones were the first thing that came to mind, but she would have to research that later. She would also need a new set of identities, but she'd already exhausted her list of forgers. And the ESO had found her, so those people might be compromised anyway. She would have to choose a country, seek out the criminal underbelly, and go from there.

But first, she'd need to help the people who'd once wanted her dead.

Eva returned to the kitchen, this time meeting Sally's stare.

"What's wrong?" Sally asked.

"An old acquaintance needs my help," Eva lied. "I'm afraid you'll have to go on without me. You go next door and grab whatever you need while I book your ticket."

Sally looked scared. "I'm not sure I can do this on my own."

"Of course you can. I promise, nothing's going to happen to you."

If the ESO can be trusted . . .

Sally left, and Eva completed the online purchase and printed out the boarding pass. She would help her neighbor start a new life, then do all she could to achieve the same for herself.

CHAPTER 4

The sun was still a few hours from setting when Eva reached the bar. The place looked busy as Eva glanced through the window, a happy knot of patrons enjoying a cold one after a day at the office.

She stood to one side of the window, pretending to play with her phone while using her peripheral vision to seek out threats. She wasn't comfortable being out in the open with the ESO's eyes on her, but they'd have killed her by now if they wanted to.

Three minutes after arriving, a man approached. He was in his forties and looked like he took care of his body. The dark slacks and open-necked shirt suited him. A backpack hung by one strap from his left shoulder, and he walked past Eva and simply said, "Follow me."

She tucked in behind him and they strolled across the bridge in silence. When they got to the far end, they crossed the street and he led her down a path and into a park. They walked around for ten minutes, neither of them saying a word, until he found an empty bench and they sat.

"You can call me Johnson," he said, and took the backpack off his shoulder. He dug inside and produced a manila envelope. "The man you're to bring out is Hong Soon-won."

He gave Eva the envelope and she took out the first item, a headshot of an Asian man in his late fifties to early sixties. "Out from where?" she asked, but the picture had already given her a good idea of what the answer would be.

"North Korea."

"It figures."

Johnson looked at her. "What? You thought we wanted you to escort him to prom?"

"What do you want him for?"

"Need to know," Johnson said.

Eva handed the file back to him. "Then go find another sucker." She got up and started walking away.

"Okay, sit down."

Eva returned to her seat. "I was told I would get everything I need to do the job, and that includes information. Don't piss me off again, or you can go get him yourself."

Johnson handed her the file once more. "I apologize."

Eva ignored the token contrition. "Who is Hong?"

"He's a high-ranking officer in the DPRK's nuclear program. Specifically, he's responsible for missile targeting. The program is compartmentalized so that no one person has access to everything. That way, if there's any sabotage—or, as in this case, someone defects—the damage is isolated and easily repaired. However, Hong has the dirt on a colleague overseeing the deployment section. He's gained control of the codes they use to access the launch sites for the mobile units. With that information, we could target the launchers accurately should we ever get close to a nuclear confrontation."

"So when Hong disappears, his superiors will clean up the mess in *his* department."

"Exactly. There's no way they'll know we have access to the other information."

It all sounded plausible so far. Still, she'd trust a rabid, snarling dog before she trusted the ESO.

"How long have I got to prepare?"

"We need you there in a week," Johnson told her. "We're sending you in as part of a tour group, and the earliest they have is next Friday. If you went in alone, they'd assign a chaperone to you; foreigners aren't allowed to walk around by themselves. This way, you won't draw any attention."

A week would give her time to brush up on her Korean. She hadn't used the language for a few years, but it wouldn't take her long to get back up to speed.

"If I'm with the tour group, how do I meet up with Hong?" she asked.

"He's made arrangements. The details are in there, but the short version is: you feign illness, miss the tour, then put on a soldier's uniform and walk out the back entrance of the hotel. Hong will meet you inside a department store. Directions are in the file."

"Then we make our way across the border."

"No. At your first meeting, you'll hand him a memory stick. It's also in the envelope."

"What's it for?" Eva asked.

"It contains code that will divert the missiles and force them to crash into the ocean if they are ever launched. Hong will take it, install the malware, then meet you the following night for the exfiltration."

"But the North Korean military will check everything Hong touched before he defected. They'll find the code in minutes."

"Yes, they will, and they'll think they managed to foil his plan. It's a diversion, to stop them broadening the investigation and finding out he has the launch-site codes."

Pretty slick, she had to admit.

"What about the exfil? Is anything in place, or do we wing it?"

"That's all prepared," Johnson told her. "You'll use Hong's car and make your way to a cove on the west coast. It's about a two-hour drive, and the coordinates are in the file. There, one of our men will be waiting with a rigid inflatable. He'll take you to the rendezvous point five miles off the coast, where a submersible will pick you up and take you to a ship that will be waiting in international waters."

It was clear they'd been working on this for some time, confident that they could convince her—or someone who had already died or failed—to take on the mission. The logistics of the exfil aside, she knew that a visa was needed for all guided tours, and they took weeks to process. This hadn't been thrown together in the last few hours.

"And if your man doesn't make it to the coast?" she asked. "What do we do then? He could be spotted by a patrol boat, or a patrol on the shore."

"First of all, there are no patrols along that shoreline. Secondly, he'll be approaching underwater. The Zodiac and outboard will be packed into a waterproof bag and flotation devices will ensure the correct buoyancy to keep it fifteen feet below the surface. He'll inflate the boat only when he reaches dry land."

"Okay, you're confident that he'll be there, I get that. I just want to know what plan B is."

"Plan B is to revert to plan A because it's going to work," Johnson said.

"And it was all going so well." She sighed. "You've got five days to come up with two alternative exfil options, or the deal's off."

Eva pulled more documents from the envelope. There was an itinerary that had her booked into the Koryo Hotel in Pyongyang for seven days, plus a list of the tourist sites she was supposed to visit during her stay. There was also a plane ticket from Melbourne for five days' time. That would take her to Los Angeles, where she would catch her connecting flights to Pyongyang via China. It would add a day to her journey, but it made more sense for a US citizen to fly from her own country.

"You'll receive a US passport in the name of Natalie Drake in the next few days," Johnson told her. "It'll have an authentic entry visa."

Apart from an alternate escape plan, they seemed to have everything covered.

It was a scary thought. They must have known for some time that they could convince her to work for them, and they'd pressed all the right buttons. Or, they'd thrown this together at the last minute, but still had enough power to get everything in place at short notice. The idea that they had so much influence sent a shiver through her body.

"I'll need a contact number, in case I think of anything else in the next few days," she told Johnson.

He took a cell phone from his pocket and handed it to her. "It's encrypted, and mine's the only number in the contacts list. If you try to use it to call anyone who doesn't have the software installed, they'll just hear static."

He got up and walked away, leaving Eva to her thoughts.

They weren't pleasant.

All she could picture was the ESO setting her up. Perhaps not for the ultimate fall—they could have picked her off at any time over the last couple of years—but as a scapegoat. Point being, she couldn't trust their story one hundred percent.

She gave Johnson a five-minute head start, then walked back toward the bridge. She saw a bar close by and went inside, ordered a glass of wine and found a dark booth that gave her a view of the door.

Eva took out her phone and opened the Shield application that let her communicate securely with a couple of old associates. One of them was Farooq Naser, the creator of the encrypted software. She fired off a message, warning him that the ESO had found her and that he was probably in their crosshairs, too. She added that they'd contacted her to do a job rather than simply kill her . . . just in case Farooq panicked and did something stupid.

His reply was swift.

You're not going to do it, are you?

Eva replied that she had no choice, and told him about how they'd emptied her bank accounts. She then got down to the reason for contacting him.

Find out everything you can about Hong Soon-won. He's part of the DPRK nuclear program.

This time, she had to wait a couple of minutes for him to get back to her.

There's not much at first glance. Don't get your hopes up. I'll do what I can.

Eva thanked him and put the phone away. If Hong turned out to be genuine, she would feel a little better about taking the job on. If not, she would have to establish what the ESO really had in mind.

CHAPTER 5

When Eva stepped into the arrivals hall at Pyongyang Sunan International Airport, she felt as if she were among the first visitors to use it. The place was spotless and eerily quiet—her fellow passengers were her only company. She followed the crowd down a set of stairs to the quarantine and immigration desks, where she joined one of the lines. The people ahead of her were handing over passports, phones, and luggage tickets. Eva got hers ready and waited her turn.

It had been touch-and-go as to whether she would even take the flight. Farooq had waited until the very last moment to come up with a file on Hong Soon-won, and it confirmed the ESO's story that he was part of the nuclear program. She'd also learned that he had no children, and that his wife had died two years earlier.

Hong was fifty-seven, which was a concern. If things got hairy, his age could become a factor. She just hoped he'd looked after himself over the years.

It took twenty minutes to reach the head of the line, where her documents and visa were checked. Once through, Eva made her way to the luggage carousel and picked up her solitary suitcase. She wheeled it to the customs checkpoint and joined another line.

This time, the wait was even longer, and during that time she saw a young man being led away. From what she could understand of the conversation, the officials had found a copy of the Bible in his suitcase. It was one of the items heavily frowned upon by the regime, along with camera lenses over 150mm, GPS devices, and satellite phones.

Eva couldn't understand how anyone could travel to the country without looking into the restrictions. It was the first thing she'd done once she'd got back to her house after her meeting with Johnson, as getting arrested by the DPRK police wasn't part of her plan. She needed to be squeaky-clean on arrival, or the whole mission would be blown.

The terrified twenty-something being led through an unmarked door clearly hadn't done his homework.

When it was her turn to be examined, she handed over her documents, phone, and luggage ticket. Her small suitcase was opened, and two middle-aged officers began removing her belongings. She waited calmly, knowing they'd find nothing untoward. Another member of the customs team told her to unlock her phone, and she entered the four-digit code and gave it to him. She couldn't see what he was looking at, but guessed it was her browsing history and pictures. Thankfully, she'd sanitized both before travelling, so there would be nothing to raise a flag.

Five minutes later, she repacked her case and followed the directions to where their two tour guides were waiting. Ten other members of the tour were already there, and she learned that they were waiting for three more. Fifteen minutes passed before the group was complete, and the two local tour guides listed all the rules that had to be followed to the letter. Eva already knew most of them from her preparation, but some came as a surprise. For one, they were warned about always taking pictures of entire statues, not just close-ups of the heads. Their phones and cameras would be checked on departure, and anyone flouting the rule would lose their equipment—and probably their liberty.

"Do not walk away from the tour," one of the guides ordered. "Not even two steps from the group. If you do, you will be arrested."

That last warning was used as a suffix for most of the rules: do not leave the hotel alone or you will be arrested; do not speak to anyone in the street or you will be arrested; do not say anything that is critical of the government of the Democratic People's Republic of Korea or you will be arrested.

The list went on for some time, with warnings not to disrespect the country by calling it North Korea—only the Democratic People's Republic of Korea was acceptable—and to avoid any sort of religious practice.

By the time they made the short journey to the tour bus, most of Eva's fellow travelers were scared even to breathe. They set off for the hotel, and on the way the guides stood in the aisle and reminded the passengers of the penalty for taking photographs of the poorer areas they might pass.

Eva kept her camera in her purse, as did most of the others. One or two held theirs ready in case they passed something worth capturing, but they didn't get the opportunity to use them until they hit the city. During that time, Eva had to put up with the advances of Duncan Sellers.

He'd attached himself to her the moment they'd arrived at the airport, introducing himself as a twenty-five-year-old vlogger destined to become the next YouTube sensation. Eva read that to mean he was out to make a name for himself on this trip, which suggested he was trouble. Unfortunately, Sellers was quite good-looking, and he knew it. He clearly thought he had a chance with her, even if she was a few years his senior, but she was determined to correct him on that score. She smiled politely when appropriate, but spent most of the time ignoring him and pretending to be engrossed in the passing landscape.

Traffic was heavier than Eva had expected. She'd imagined a few beat-up vehicles on the road, but most of the cars looked new. The roads were in a good state of repair, the skyline dominated by high-rise buildings matching what she'd seen in photographs before leaving Australia. There were few people on the streets, which didn't bode well for the mission. It would have been nice to have crowds to disappear into if her rendezvous with Hong were compromised.

She would have to ensure that didn't happen.

The bus pulled up outside the entrance to the Koryo Hotel, a twin-towered building that looked like a miniature, poor man's version of the Petronas Towers in Kuala Lumpur. They piled off the bus and gathered at the entrance, where the tour guides had more words of warning.

"Welcome to your gilded prison," one of them said. "This line of stone is your boundary. If you go beyond this line without a guide . . ."

". . . you will be arrested," Sellers finished for him.

The attempt at humor didn't go down well, and Eva wondered how long it would be before the vlogger disappeared from the tour.

They were taken through the glass revolving doors and into a foyer Eva could only describe as lavish. Marble everywhere, with a giant fresco of a waterfall dominating one end. She could have been in New York or Dubai.

She waited patiently for her turn to check in, then took the surprisingly small lift to the seventeenth floor.

Her suite was not quite what she had expected after the opulence of the foyer. The bathroom was straight out of the 1970s Soviet Union; the living area comprised an empty fridge and two semi-comfortable chairs. The bedroom contained a TV, a couple of single beds, and a phone. Not quite luxurious, but habitable. The only thing that riled her was the lingering aroma of stale cigarette smoke from the previous occupants.

She unpacked her suitcase and hung her clothes in the closet, then put her toiletries in the bathroom. That done, she turned on the TV in the bedroom to check out the wonders of North Korean broadcasting. She was surprised to find that as well as local channels, there were news programs from around the world. She picked the BBC World Service and left it on while she took a shower.

After fifteen minutes under the tepid drizzle, Eva gave up. She wrapped a towel around herself and picked out fresh jeans, a T-shirt, and a wool sweater from the closet, then got dressed in front of the television. She'd done a casual sweep for hidden cameras but hadn't found any, though she did see a couple of items that could have been microphones. Perhaps the Supreme Leader was satisfied with audio surveillance and didn't see the need to film every guest. It might, after all, give his men ideas about seeing more of the West.

After dressing, she sat on the bed and watched the news until it was time to meet up with the rest of the tour. She went downstairs a couple of minutes before four in the afternoon and saw that a few of her fellow travelers seemed to be in the grip of jet lag. Eva had managed a decent sleep on the plane trip over. Plus, after months in Australia, her body felt as if it was in the correct time zone.

The bus was waiting, and they climbed aboard, with the Tower of the Juche Idea their first call. It was only three miles away, across the Taedong River, so Eva wouldn't have to put up with Duncan Sellers for too long. She'd managed to get a seat next to a female college student from Kansas, but Sellers had dropped into the row behind her and was leaning on the back of her chair.

"Have you checked out the pool in the basement?" he asked her. "Be pretty cool to go skinny-dipping in there one night."

"Cool as in ten-years'-hard-labor cool?"

"*Pffft.* You believe that nonsense? They just say all that stuff so the tour guide doesn't get fined if you get lost."

Eva wondered how anyone so naive could have reached adulthood. Perhaps Charles Darwin's theory of natural selection didn't apply to vloggers.

"Still, if swimming isn't your thing, I've got a couple of movies on my laptop. You're welcome to come to my room later, have a few beers, hang out, you know . . ."

Eva looked at the girl sitting next to her, who mouthed three letters. *O-M-G.*

Eva couldn't have summed it up better. Time to put him out of his misery.

"I'm afraid my partner back home wouldn't like it if I went for a drink in someone's hotel room," she said.

Sellers smiled. "Then don't tell him."

Eva turned to face him. "Her," she said.

She faced forward again and saw her companion fighting hard to contain herself.

When Sellers sat back in his seat, dejected, Eva allowed herself a brief smile of her own. With the vlogger put in his place, she could now get down to the task of pretending to be interested in Pyongyang's architecture.

They pulled up at the monument and climbed out. The wind had picked up and it was bitterly cold, around twenty Fahrenheit. Eva was glad of the thick jacket she'd brought with her, and almost felt sorry for Sellers as he shivered in his puffy vest.

The two guides led them to the monument. Both of them faced it and bowed, then invited the others to do the same. Eva was aware that this was practically mandatory and complied, commenting on how magnificent it looked.

It wasn't exactly what she'd thought. The granite tower was 490 feet tall, with a 66-foot metal torch perched on top. They were told how it had been built from 25,550 blocks of stone, each one commemorating a day in the life of Kim Il-sung, the country's first leader. They called it a monument to the ideology of *Juche* introduced by Kim, but Eva figured Freud would have put a different slant on it.

They took the elevator to the top and looked out over Pyongyang. A couple of people who weren't comfortable with heights stayed back from the edge, but Eva wanted the best view possible. She took in the sights, particularly the area around the hotel.

After thirty minutes, they returned to the elevator. Darkness was falling by the time they reached street level, and Eva was thankful that the tour was done for the day.

She wanted nothing more than to grab a bite to eat and have an early night.

Tomorrow was going to be a long day.

~

Eva woke early the next morning. Sirens calling people to work invaded her dream, and military music soon floated up from the streets below.

At least I won't need a wakeup call tomorrow.

She went to the bathroom and ran a brush briefly through her hair, enough so she still looked a little haggard. She then took the napkin from her pants pocket. The previous night, at dinner, she'd poured a little ground pepper into it. She licked her finger and dipped it in the powder, then ran it across both eyelids. Her eyes began watering immediately.

Resisting the temptation to wash her eyes, Eva took the elevator down to the dining room for breakfast. She gave her room number and joined the short line for the buffet. There wasn't much to tempt her, so she settled for toast and orange juice.

"You look terrible."

Eva turned to see Cherie, the student she'd sat next to on the bus the previous day.

"Believe me, I feel worse than I look."

"Bummer. We're going to see so many cool sights today."

"I know," Eva said. "I really wanted to see the Palace of the Sun. I'll see how I feel after breakfast."

They sat together and chatted for a while, until Eva couldn't take the eye irritation any longer. She excused herself and got back to her room as fast as she could, heading straight for the bathroom. After a few minutes of rinsing her eyes with cold water she felt much better, but knew she would have to go through it all again.

Eva went to the bedroom to lie down and saw the large package on the bed. She'd been told to expect it, and she knew what the contents would be. She ripped open the brown paper and lifted out the khaki jacket. The soldier's uniform looked the right size, and she tried on the hat, which fit perfectly. Whatever her feelings about the ESO, she had to admit that they were meticulous. Whoever had guesstimated her size did a great job.

She lay on her bed for half an hour, then left her room and called the elevator. Thankfully it was empty, and she took the napkin from her pocket and put a pinch of pepper into each nostril. By the time she reached the lobby to meet up with the others, the sneezes were explosive. The guides were already there, and she approached the less sullen of them and held a Kleenex over her nose as she explained how bad she felt.

"I'll have to miss the tour today," Eva told him. "Hopefully I'll feel better tomorrow."

He offered to have a doctor sent to her room, but she graciously declined.

"I'm sure I'll be fine with some bed rest and a couple of Advil."

Eva went back to her room and stripped off, then got under the shower and washed away all traces of the pepper. When she got out her eyes were still red, but that would soon fade. She took a tube of moisturizer from her toiletry bag and twisted it in the middle, breaking the seal on the label. She unscrewed the bottom half to reveal hair dye.

An hour later, her chestnut hair was jet black. She'd cut it to shoulder length before traveling—as, according to her research, that was how most female soldiers wore their hair in North Korea.

Next, she applied her makeup, giving the impression of high cheekbones and an Asian look to her eyes. The last touch was a pair of brown contact lenses to disguise her emerald irises. When she'd finished, she was pleased with the result. Even up close, it would stand up to scrutiny.

Her rendezvous with Hong was to take place at midday, giving her thirty minutes to exit the hotel and reach the department store. She dressed in the uniform, which had the insignia of a colonel, then checked the jacket pockets and found the instructions she'd been told to expect. The small piece of paper had a sketch of the first floor of the hotel as well as directions to the store. She took a good look, then screwed it up into a little ball, wrapped it in toilet paper and flushed it down the toilet.

Her next task was to retrieve the flash drive. She took the charger for her camera from the suitcase and ripped out the cord, leaving only the plastic connector, which she put in her pocket.

Finally, Eva put the uniform cap on and studied her reflection in the mirror.

Showtime.

CHAPTER 6

Eva had conducted many operations for the CIA, a few of them abroad, but she'd never felt so conspicuous. There was no reason for anyone to stop a colonel in the Korean People's Army, but in a country where suspicion was rife, she had to be wary.

She took the elevator down to the lobby. When the doors opened, she strode purposefully to the right, towards the rear of the building. She found the door that had been marked on the note and walked through it into a service corridor. Two men in chef's uniforms were carrying plastic bags full of trash to a door at the far end, but they paid her little attention. She followed them out into the cold, grateful for the long overcoat that had been provided in the package.

Eva turned left and walked past the adjacent building, then took another left onto the main street. From there she walked to the corner and followed it to the right, onto Sosong Street, where she found herself outside the Yokjon department store.

Eva walked in as if she belonged there. She assumed military officers were allowed to shop in the store, otherwise Hong wouldn't have chosen it for the meeting. She took the escalator up to the second floor, where the electrical appliances were displayed. She was one of only five shoppers in sight, which made her feel as if all eyes were on her.

After a few minutes pretending to browse the widescreen televisions, Eva saw Hong. Besides having the telltale mole on his right cheek, he was the only other person wearing a military uniform. Like her, he was doing a good job of playing the curious shopper. She slowly made her way over to within a few feet of him and stood admiring a locally manufactured dishwasher.

"The cold hurts my bones every winter," Hong said.

It was the passphrase she'd been given by Johnson in Melbourne.

She replied in Korean with the words she'd burnt into her brain: "I hope to see many more winters in my lifetime."

Hong stepped closer to examine the kitchen appliance. "Do you have it?" he asked.

Outwardly, he seemed cool and calm, but Eva imagined the turmoil within. She knew the penalty for what he was about to do, and he must have considered the danger, too. She had to admire him for that. Of course, if his wife had still been alive, or he had children to think of, he probably wouldn't be here.

"Look behind the stand of the largest television," she told him. "I hid it there."

Hong continued to inspect the dishwasher. "Meet me at eleven tomorrow night outside this store. I'll pick you up."

He walked over to the televisions, and from the corner of her eye Eva saw him look around the back of the largest TV on display. When he walked away from it, he put something in his pocket.

The drop made, Eva walked out of the store and back to the rear entrance of the hotel. Five minutes later, she was in her room. She took off the uniform and put it in her suitcase, then locked it. After that, she took off her makeup, then jumped in the shower and washed out the hair dye.

With all signs of the disguise gone, she turned the television on and lay on the bed. There was little more she could do until the time came to meet with Hong and make their way to the country's west coast.

It promised to be a tense—and boring—thirty-four hours.

CHAPTER 7

The following morning, Eva woke with a sense of dread. It wasn't that she feared something going wrong at the pickup that night, but the thought of another fourteen hours in the room.

Her plan had been to skip the tour once more, but now the idea of getting out of the hotel felt a lot more appealing. She freshened up and went down for breakfast, where she saw Cherie.

"Feeling better?"

"Much," Eva said. "What did I miss yesterday?"

"The Palace of the Sun was magnificent, and so was the Arch of Triumph. It's a shame you couldn't be there. If you give me your email address, I'll send the pictures to you."

"Thanks. I'll do that."

After having skipped dinner the previous evening, Eva more than made up for it with two trips to the buffet. She'd be using a lot of nervous energy in the coming hours, and needed to keep her strength up.

After breakfast she joined the others in the foyer. Sellers had attached himself to another unfortunate woman travelling alone; like Eva, she seemed uninterested in his advances. At least he wouldn't spend the day drooling all over the back of Eva's seat.

Their guide announced an unexpected first stop. They would buy snacks for the journey at a store around the corner.

When Eva found herself outside the Yokjon store once more, she wondered if it was more than a coincidence, but the guide told them that it was one of the few stores that foreigners were allowed to visit.

She picked up some potato chips, a chocolate bar, and a bottle of orange juice, all the while checking to see if anyone was paying her particular attention, but the staff seemed uninterested in her presence.

She then had to go through the old Soviet method of paying for her goods. She took them to a counter and handed over some dollar bills, but was told to take her money and a list of items to another assistant at the other end of the store. She did as she was told and handed the money to a second staff member, then went back with her receipt to pick up her food.

"Such a stupid way of doing things," Cherie complained as they walked back to the hotel.

"It's the communist way." Eva shrugged. "Why have one person do a job when you can have three?"

The bus was waiting when they arrived, and Eva spent the day pretending to be fascinated by the monuments to the country's leaders. She had to admit that some of the architecture was impressive, but she couldn't help thinking the money could have been better spent.

By the time they reached the hotel that evening, Eva had had enough bowing to last a lifetime. All she wanted was to get dinner out of the way and prepare for the mission.

She spent a couple of hours in the room, then went to eat. It could be her last hot meal for some time, and she wasn't one to waste an opportunity. She filled up on pasta before returning to her room to don her disguise once more.

It took an hour to get ready, and during that time she kept worrying about how exposed she would be. Few people haunted the streets at the best of times; she might be the only one within a few blocks at eleven at night.

When she finished her transformation, Eva had an hour to wait. She spent half that time meditating, controlling her breathing as she sought to remove the tension from her body. It was a technique she had recently come across, and it worked well. She felt relaxed as she put her coat on.

The clock in the huge radio next to the bed told her she had ten minutes until the meet. She waited two, then left her room, having timed the journey the day before. The last thing she wanted to do was turn up early and be the only person on the street. Nothing was more likely to set off alarm bells.

As it turned out, she arrived a minute before eleven. As she feared, there was no one around. The pavements and streets were deserted in all directions, and the glow from the nearby streetlamp made her feel as if she were standing in a spotlight.

Rain started falling as seconds turned into minutes, and Eva felt more anxious with every breath. She was considering returning to the hotel when a pair of headlights appeared in the distance, heading her way. She eased back into the doorway as a military sedan passed by, none of the occupants looking her way. She watched the taillights disappear around a corner as silence returned to the streets.

She glanced at her watch. Hong was eleven minutes late, and it definitely wasn't due to traffic.

The meeting was blown, and Eva felt wound up like a clock spring. There could be many reasons for Hong not showing, but she could only imagine the negative ones.

She cursed herself for not having an out. She'd made contingency plans to get out of the country with Hong, but alone it would be a challenge. All she could do was stick to the plan and try to make the rendezvous with the Zodiac. That would mean stealing a vehicle and—

A car pulled up at the corner, then turned toward her. Eva instinctively reached for a weapon, but her pockets were empty.

She was defenseless.

Her body told her to run, but her head said that would be a bad choice.

Pretend you belong here.

She looked away from the car and stamped her feet as it pulled up. She glanced back and saw Hong in the driver's seat.

Relief flooded through her as she walked to the vehicle.

"You're late," she said as she opened the passenger door. That was when she saw the welts on Hong's face, and her eyes were drawn to the man in the back seat holding the pistol to the defector's head.

Eva slammed the door and ran, her only thought survival. She headed for the corner, hoping to get to the hotel's parking lot and steal a car before Hong's captor gave chase.

Hope evaporated seconds later as she turned onto Changgwang Street and saw five vehicles blocking the road. A dozen soldiers had their automatic weapons pointed her way, and more appeared behind her.

Eva had no choice but to freeze; running would get her killed.

A senior officer barked and gestured with his rifle for Eva to raise her hands, and she did as instructed. Three soldiers approached and threw her to the ground, then landed a few kicks before putting handcuffs on.

She was dragged to a truck and hauled into the back, where six soldiers climbed in beside her. They laid her in the aisle and sat either side of her, a couple of them adding to her misery by stomping on her as she lay helpless.

The truck set off, and Eva closed her eyes and soaked up the punishment. There was little point trying to take them all on. She'd find better opportunities to escape later, and that was exactly what she planned to do. But in order to do that, she had to make them think she was weak and vulnerable. All they knew about her was the false name she'd used to get into the country, though now they would probably assume that she was working for the US government.

That could be problematic. If they tried to instigate diplomatic negotiations for her release, she was sure to be disavowed. The administration would not easily admit to complicity in sabotaging the DPRK's nuclear program. Which meant nothing would stop the North Koreans from locking her up for life—or worse, putting her before a firing squad.

One of the soldiers stood and opened his fly, and his comrades cheered as he emptied his bladder all over her.

Eva was powerless to do anything about it, but she promised herself that someone would pay.

CHAPTER 8

Eva felt black and blue by the time she reached the prison. Her captors had given her another kicking during the journey, and blood oozed down her face where one of them had booted her in the head. If an opportunity to escape did present itself, she feared she'd be in no state to take advantage of it.

When the truck finally stopped, the tailgate lowered and the soldiers jumped down. Two of them grabbed her legs and dragged her out, and none of them bothered to prevent her crashing to the wet pavement. She was hauled to her feet and had a moment to take in her surroundings.

All she saw was gray. They were in a courtyard between the thirty-foot outer wall and the main building. They'd driven through two sets of gates, the outer one solid metal, the inner consisting of inch-thick bars.

She was dragged to a solid steel door, which opened with a buzz as they approached. As they went through, Eva saw no handle on the inside.

That wasn't going to be her escape route.

She was taken through two more sets of barred gates, neither of which had visible locks. All doors in the prison seemed to be controlled remotely, which didn't bode well. She would need help if she were to fashion a way out of the place—someone to control the exits for her.

Not going to happen, said a voice inside her head.

She didn't give up hope, though. She'd only been in the building for a few minutes. Once she got an idea of the layout and protocols, she'd come up with a way out.

Eva was pushed into a room with white-tiled walls and her handcuffs were removed. She rubbed her wrists to get some circulation back into her hands, but the guards pulled her arms apart and started stripping her. One of them shouted that she was insulting the DPRK by wearing the uniform, and Eva did her best to look cowed. Though she understood almost everything they said, she didn't dare let on.

They stripped her naked, leaving her to cover herself as best she could. The guards spent a few minutes making lewd comments about her body before one of them threw an orange jumpsuit at her. Eva put it on, and the cuffs went immediately back on, as tightly as before. She was taken into the corridor again and through another set of gates, then made to wait outside an office for five minutes.

When the door opened, Eva was pushed inside and forced to stand on a red spot on the floor, two yards from a plain wooden desk. Sitting behind it was a bald man, who looked like he hadn't been affected by the waves of famine that regularly swept the country. He didn't stand when she entered, and Eva wondered how he even managed to get out of the chair at the end of each working day. Behind him, the wall was dominated by a portrait of the country's similarly rotund leader. A metal sign on the desk gave the warden's name as Kwok.

"Is this the spy?" the man asked.

A guard confirmed that she was.

"What is your name?" Kwok asked in decent English.

"Natalie Drake," Eva said, using the name on the false passport the ESO had given her.

"I mean your real name, not the one on your passport."

"That is my real name," Eva said.

Kwok nodded to one of the guards, who delivered a vicious punch to her kidneys. Eva collapsed to the floor, clutching her side. Mostly it was for show, but it hurt nonetheless.

She was dragged back to her feet, and Kwok repeated the question.

"Melanie Carr," she said, using the name she'd adopted before moving to Australia.

Kwok seemed satisfied with that. For now.

"Why did you meet Hong Soon-won?"

"I was waiting for a lift. I thought he was my ride."

"A lie!"

Eva was knocked to the floor once more, this time from a punch to the side of her face that came from nowhere and caught her by surprise. She stayed down, trying to clear her head.

"Pick her up," Kwok growled.

Once more, Eva was pulled upright.

"Hong told us everything," Kwok said. "You are a spy."

"I want a lawyer," Eva said, the fear in her voice not entirely fake.

Kwok's face went from angry to curious, then he burst into laughter. He repeated Eva's request to the guards for the benefit of those who didn't speak English, and they joined in the merriment.

Finally, Kwok silenced them. "Spies do not get lawyers, or phone calls, or visitors. You will remain in my jail until the State Security Department sends someone to question you thoroughly."

With a wave of his hand, Eva was dismissed. The guards turned her around and pushed her out through the door, then took her through two more barred gates and finally through a solid metal door. When it opened, the smell was overpowering.

The guards seemed acclimatized to the sewer stench. They pushed her forward into a corridor fifty yards long with nothing but bars on either side. At least fifty people were crammed into the first cell she passed, which was barely big enough to allow half of them to sit or lie on the stone floor. If there were any toilet facilities, they were either broken or not being used.

The next three cells she passed looked the same, and the guards stopped at the fifth. They waited for the buzzing sound that signaled the lock being released, and the occupants stood back. After her handcuffs were removed, Eva was forced inside and the door was slammed back into place with dreadful finality.

The guards quickly retreated, perhaps not as inured to the smell as Eva had thought. It would certainly take some getting used to.

She faced her cellmates, a mixture of men and women plus a couple of kids who looked to be around twelve years old. A few were gaunt, as if they'd spent their entire lives a dozen meals behind everyone else. Some simply appeared emotionally beaten, their spirits broken.

The two men at the back displayed a different attitude.

Trouble.

They had seated themselves on the only thing that could be classed as furniture, a stone bunk that protruded from the back wall. It could easily fit half a dozen people, but only they were using it. The others stood or sat on the cold, concrete floor.

They looked fit, and she guessed they hadn't been there long. She also pegged them as brothers because they appeared so similar. Twins, perhaps.

Whatever their relationship, they seemed interested in Eva, which was the last thing she wanted. Her best chance of escape was to make her captors think she was no threat. If these two showed more than a passing interest in her, she had two choices, neither of which she liked. She could submit to them, the very thought of which repulsed her, or show her true colors and put them in their place.

Eva looked away from the two men and found a space against one of the walls. She leaned against it and stared down at her feet, hoping no one would take any further interest in her.

It wasn't to be.

The two heavies pushed people aside as they sauntered over to her. They seemed bulkier up close, but only stood a couple of inches taller than her. Both gave her lascivious looks as they discussed what they could do with their new plaything, and it struck Eva that they must be desperate. Here she was, her makeup streaked, her face dirty and bloody and her body stinking of stale piss, yet these two clowns were trying to decide who was going to have his way with her first.

Eva wasn't about to play that game.

One of them was already fondling himself through his prison uniform, and Eva smiled as she moved his hand out of the way, putting hers on his groin. He made appreciative noises and mocked his brother for being the ugly half of the family, while she gently massaged his manhood.

His taunts turned to screams as Eva wrapped her fingers around his scrotum and squeezed with every ounce of strength in her body. The high-pitched shout emanating from her victim sounded like a steam whistle, and she felt a satisfying pop as one of his testicles gave way.

Her victim's brother had been stunned into inaction, but when Eva let his sibling go, he screamed and reached for her with both hands. If he intended to grab her throat, he didn't get close. Eva easily blocked his hands and spun to the side, then put an arm around his neck and twisted him off balance. He landed heavily on his back, and before he could recover, Eva followed through with a couple of punches to the side of his neck.

She leaned over him and whispered in his ear in Korean: "If you tell anyone I did this to you, I'll kill you. If the guard asks, you had a fight with your brother. Make sure he tells the same story."

When he swung a fist at her head, Eva realized she'd underestimated him. Her assault should have knocked the fight out of him, but he was tougher than she'd expected. His blow glanced off the back of her skull, and she drove her head down into his face, her forehead connecting with his cheekbone as he turned away at the last moment. Eva grabbed his ears and slammed his head on the concrete floor, twice, then a third time, and put his arm across her knee and pushed the wrist down. His arm snapped at the elbow, and she left him in a screaming heap.

With the brothers out of action, Eva assumed their throne. She sat on the stone bunk and gestured for the children and a couple of elderly prisoners to join her.

It wasn't long before the guards came to investigate the noise. The two thugs were lying in the middle of the cell, with everyone else jammed up against the bars.

The gate buzzed open and one of the guards entered, while the other stood outside with his rifle raised in case it was an escape ploy.

"Who did this?"

No one said a word, but the guard noticed Eva sitting on the bunk. He strode over to her.

"Who did this?" he asked again.

She pretended not to understand and got a slap across the face for her impudence.

"He did it," the bully with the broken arm moaned. "We were fighting."

The guard looked at him, then back to Eva. He spat a profanity at her, then stormed out of the cell.

The brothers clearly would not be receiving any treatment . . . not that she cared. Her only thought was of escape.

She sat for two hours until the guards returned once more. The thug with the broken arm asked to see a doctor, but his plea was ignored. Instead, the guards told Eva to get up. She followed them out of the cell and let them put the cuffs on again.

Once through the barred gate, Eva was pushed down a corridor and through an unmarked door. Inside the room, the antiseptic hospital smell was a welcome relief from the stench of the cell, but she tensed up when she saw the gurney and an assortment of medical instruments.

She weighed the chances of taking out her two escorts and the doctor, who had his back to her while he prepared something on a bench, but it wasn't necessary. When he turned around, he had a needle in his hand, but he wasn't about to inject her with an unknown substance. She'd had blood drawn enough times to know what was coming.

The doctor asked for her name and compared it with a sheet on a clipboard, then nodded to the guards. They unbuttoned the front of Eva's jumpsuit and pulled it down over her shoulders; the medic put a tourniquet on her bicep and took two vials of blood.

Her clothes were pulled back into place, and Eva was escorted back to the cell.

She didn't have to wait long. A few minutes later, she heard her name again. This time the guards took her to a room even more ominous than the doctor's office.

It contained only a worktable and, in the middle of the room, a chair fastened to the floor with leather straps on the armrests and legs. She'd seen similar setups in the past; the news was never good for the person in the seat.

Despite the handcuffs, Eva had to act. She kicked out at the guard to her right, raking her foot down his shin. With her bare feet, it didn't have the effect she was hoping for, and before she could turn on the other one, a rifle butt slammed into her head.

~

When Eva recovered consciousness, she tried to raise a hand to her head, but it wouldn't move. She opened her eyes and saw why. She was strapped in tight and they'd stripped her naked.

She recognized it as part of the process to break her, but that wasn't going to happen.

Standing before her was the first civilian she'd seen in the building. He was dressed entirely in black, and a cigarette hung from his mouth.

He took off his hat and placed it on the worktable, then took a drag and dropped the butt on the floor. As he ground it out with his foot, he looked at Eva with interest.

Despite her nakedness, he didn't seem to be enjoying the scenery. He looked more like a chess master weighing up his next move.

"Let's start with names," he said, a lifetime of smoking making his voice harsh. His English was excellent, more British than American, and with only a slight accent. "I'm Dong. What's yours?"

Apt name, she thought. "Melanie Carr."

Dong lit another smoke. "I mean your real name. We sent word to the Americans that we caught their spy, but they claim they don't know you."

He betrayed no anger in his voice, which told Eva he was trouble. The calm ones saw torture simply as a means to an end. It wasn't personal, only a process intended to obtain information. He would inflict as much pain as necessary to get what he wanted and think nothing of it.

"I don't work for the Americans," she said.

Dong raised an eyebrow. "You don't? Then who?"

Eva had spent time working on her story. Now she'd see how it played out.

"A private enterprise."

He chewed the phrase over. "An interesting idea, but I can't imagine Bloomingdale's having much use for missile launch-site information."

"I don't know who they are, just that they would pay me well to get Hong out of the country."

"And to install a virus on our servers, let's not forget that."

Eva dipped her head in an admission of guilt.

"So, tell me what you know," Dong said.

"I met a guy called Johnson and he gave me instructions. That's it."

She didn't hesitate to give up her contact. He'd undoubtedly used a false name and his description would match that of a million people.

Dong looked at her with curiosity, as if deciding whether she was telling the truth. He shucked off his coat and threw it on the bench.

"Sorry, but I don't believe you."

He looked at a few of the tools on the table, picking them up and inspecting them before moving on to the next one.

Eva recognized the ploy, designed to instill fear. He was doing a pretty good job of it.

Dong picked up something so small she could barely see it. "It's amazing how much pain you can produce with such a tiny implement," he said.

As he drew closer, Eva saw that it was a pin. A simple, metal push-pin like those used to stick papers to corkboards.

She knew exactly where he would use it and tried to curl her fingers into fists, but the straps made it impossible.

Dong hadn't exaggerated; the pain was excruciating. He put the pin under the nail of her right forefinger and pushed it in a couple of millimeters.

Eva screamed in an attempt to force her body to ignore the pain, but it didn't work. She screamed again, this time involuntarily, when Dong pushed the pin in a little more and started wiggling it around.

"I have lots more of these," he said. "Is there anything else you would like to tell me about Johnson, or should I get the rest?"

"That's all I know," she sobbed, some of the tears real. Her only hope was to appear human in his eyes and pray she could trigger something in his conscience, even though she'd already recognized the psychopath in him.

"How unfortunate."

Dong returned to the table and appeared to discard the pin approach. He ran his hand over the assembled tools and settled on a plastic bag.

Panic flooded her, but she concentrated on her breathing. She could hold her breath for more than a minute and twenty seconds, but this and waterboarding had been her worst fears realized during training.

Eva wriggled as best she could when Dong put the bag over her head, and took a deep breath just before he held the open end tight against her neck. She counted to forty, then began thrashing about as if she was starved of oxygen, hoping he would release his grip and allow her respite while he questioned her further.

He didn't.

One minute ten.

One-twenty.

One-thirty.

Eva sucked in but inhaled nothing but carbon dioxide. The thrashing became real as every molecule in her body screamed for oxygen. Darkness began to cloud the edges of her sight, and it felt as if her head were in a vise, slowly being tightened . . .

Dong let go of her neck and air flooded into the bag. Eva gulped it in, but as she exhaled, he closed the supply once more.

Eva experienced full-blown terror for the first time in her life. She opened her lungs as far as she could, but the bag was now tight over her mouth and nose.

Nothing flashed before her eyes; her brain was too busy receiving signals from every part of her body demanding air. The vise was back, constricting her head and neck like an invisible python.

She didn't hear the banging on the door, but it got Dong's attention. He removed the bag from Eva's head and threw it at the table.

"What?" he shouted.

The door opened. A soldier entered and bowed, then proffered a sheet of paper.

Dong snatched it from his hands and dismissed the soldier, who was eager to leave the room.

Eva was still gulping air. She'd been close to blackout, and didn't expect the resulting headache to pass any time soon. She knew if Dong tried the same trick again, she would cave and tell him everything. The ESO, the exfil plan, even her bank account numbers.

"It seems fate has other ideas for you," Dong said to her as he read the letter. "You're being transferred, and they need you in good health." He folded the paper in half. "Pity. I would have liked to learn more about this 'private enterprise.' Perhaps when they've finished with you at the next facility, we'll be given more time to coax it out of you."

Without another word he strode to the door and banged on it loudly. It opened, and he instructed the men outside to prepare her for departure.

Eva had no idea what had prompted the halt in proceedings, but she thanked all the gods she could think of for the respite.

One thing was sure: she would rather die than face another session like that.

CHAPTER 9

The guards removed Eva's restraints and handed back the orange jump-suit. Her heart was still racing from the bag incident and her finger hurt like a bitch. Her hands shook as she dressed, then she was cuffed once more and led out into the corridor. Instead of going back to the cell, the guards marched her in the opposite direction.

A group of soldiers was waiting near the entrance to the building, guarding two other prisoners. One of them was Hong. It was the first time she'd seen him since the failed rendezvous, and his facial injuries looked a lot worse now than they had then. They'd really gone to town on his face, and his left hand was wrapped in a crude bandage. It seemed he'd had a much tougher time of it than she had.

Hong saw her and turned away. Eva didn't know if it was because he blamed her for his predicament or was an effort to warn her not to talk to him. Either way, she said nothing; no point in inviting even more trouble.

They waited for a few minutes as their paperwork was checked; then, to Eva's surprise, the guards handed her and her fellow prisoners each a thick coat. Her handcuffs were removed to allow her to put it on, then locked on once more.

The main door buzzed open, letting in a jet of freezing air. Eva was led outside, where a truck was waiting with its engine running. The three prisoners were helped inside and made to sit on a bench. Soldiers sat either side of Eva, and Hong took the spot opposite. He kept his head down, still refusing to make eye contact, and Eva decided to let it go. If she tried to spark up a conversation, it would only anger their escorts.

The doors closed, but the temperature in the truck only climbed a couple of degrees. She was grateful for the coat, though she was still mystified as to why they'd provided it. The regime wasn't exactly renowned for its kindness, so there must be some reason for making her more comfortable. Perhaps they wanted her in good health so they could record her confession and use it as propaganda. Whatever the motive, she expected to find out soon..

As it turned out, the ride lasted for at least five hours, though without a watch it was hard to be sure. They stopped once for a bathroom break, and Eva saw that they were on a mountain road. Nothing but snow and trees in all directions, starkly beautiful but hard to appreciate in her current situation. As it was, she emptied her bladder as fast as she could. Not easy with half a dozen armed men watching.

When they reached their destination, Eva was helped out of the vehicle. She began planning her escape immediately.

The two-story building had a chain-link perimeter fence set fifty yards from its walls. Beyond the fence, trees had been cut back to leave another fifty yards of open space, the whole compound nestling in a valley, with steep hills completely surrounding it. She could see footprints in the snow outside the fence, suggesting regular patrols. One of her first tasks would be to try to discover how regular they were. The gate had a small wooden guardhouse on either side, and she was glad to note that the watchtowers appeared unused. One had its entire platform missing, while another had no roof and the ladder was broken off ten feet above the ground.

As she waited for the others to get out of the truck, Eva saw a white van appear around the side of the building. She noticed the apparatus stuck on the top, and knew it was a refrigeration unit. What it was doing at a prison, she didn't know. After so long without anything to eat, she hoped it was delivering food.

The three prisoners were led inside, through a wooden door three inches thick. There were no fancy remote locks here, only keys and deadbolts. Eva felt more confident already.

They were taken through another door and made to wait by a sliding window while their transfer papers were checked and the clerk inside assigned each of them to a cell. The soldiers left and prison guards took over, each strapped with a sidearm. They also carried nightsticks and small canisters that she assumed contained pepper spray.

Eva heard her name mentioned, followed by a cell number, and one of the guards took her through two more doors to an accommodation block. It stretched for hundreds of yards, with solid steel doors set six feet apart into both walls. As she walked past them, she could see names written in chalk on small blackboards next to the doors.

When they arrived at her cell, the guard unlocked it and pushed the door open, then removed Eva's handcuffs. She had an opportunity to take out her lone escort, but decided against it. She needed to know more about the layout and the guards' routines first.

She stepped into the small room, and the surprises kept coming. There was a real bed, complete with a mattress, and the toilet in the corner had a waist-high wall to offer some privacy to the room's sole occupant. There was even a small stainless-steel sink attached to the wall. The best was saved for last: a pair of army boots on the floor next to the bed.

The door slammed shut behind her, and Eva lay on her bunk and put the blanket over her feet to warm them.

The room had no windows, only a grille in the door with a sliding metal shutter. Below that was a rectangular slot, also with a retractable door. Probably for passing food into the cell.

The very thought had her salivating, and her stomach rumbled in sympathy, but she was made to wait two hours before the slot in the door opened and a tray slid inside. Eva took it and sat back on her bunk, expecting a bowl of rice, but she was pleased to see some protein on the plate, too. She couldn't make out what kind of meat it was, but she pretended it was beef and wolfed it down.

Replete, she lay down and put her hands behind her head, thankful for the decent treatment. But somehow it felt off.

While preparing for the mission, she'd done as much research as possible into the goings-on in North Korea. Mostly she'd found advice about how to behave without incurring the wrath of the authorities. That line of inquiry had led her to look into some of the human rights abuses carried out over the last few decades in the pariah state.

She'd found no shortage of testimonies. She'd read accounts of those who'd managed to escape from North Korea, either to China or the south, and all were at odds with what she was experiencing.

One political prisoner camp called Kwanliso 15 in Yodok had average winter temperatures of minus five degrees Fahrenheit, and provided no blankets for the prisoners. There was one toilet for every two hundred inmates, and public executions in front of other detainees were commonplace. Those who had committed serious anti-regime crimes were never released, while criticizing government policy or illegally crossing the border entailed sentences of between six months and ten years of hard labor. Beatings and torture were an everyday part of life in these places.

Compared to Kwanliso 15, her current accommodation was a five-star hotel. And Eva suspected she wasn't the only one being treated respectfully. *Why?* she wondered. Was it a setup, designed to fool the likes of Amnesty International? She'd seen reports from that organization, which had been highly critical of the regime. Perhaps they were going to be invited here to see the new DPRK prison system in action.

Whatever the reason, she didn't plan on staying long.

CHAPTER 10

The sound of a key turning in the lock woke Eva from a light sleep. She hadn't realized she'd nodded off, and she sat up quickly in case the pleasant conduct had been a ruse to get her to lower her guard. She was ready for them to launch an attack, but none came. Instead, she received staccato orders in English to leave the cell and put her hands behind her back.

Eva was taken through the door that separated the accommodation wing from the rest of the building, then up a set of stairs to an office that had the name Cheng Dae-sung etched on the door. Inside, she found a matching brass nameplate on an oak desk.

The man behind the name had the coldest eyes Eva had ever seen. They were almost black, devoid of any emotion. It was hard to pin an age to him, but she guessed he was in his early fifties. She could imagine him being the warden of the previous prison, but not this one.

Cheng picked up a sheet of paper and read from it, then looked up at Eva. "Melanie . . . Carr?"

Eva nodded.

"Not . . . real name." It was a statement, not a question.

Eva said nothing, and Cheng looked back down at the paper. Something seemed to please him, as the merest hint of a smile fleetingly appeared on his face.

"These are the best blood results I've seen in a long time," he said in his own language, as if thinking out loud. He raised his arms as if lifting imaginary weights. "You . . . work?" he said in English.

Eva guessed he meant "work out." "A little," she said.

He seemed happy with that. "You do medical. Then talk."

Cheng told the guards to take her to the medical wing, and they steered Eva out of the office and back down the stairs. The area they took her to contrasted starkly with the rest of the building. The moment they opened the door marked with the red cross, she entered another world. The walls, floors, and ceiling were white, and the corridor smelled like the hospitals of her youth. Two cleaners stopped mopping so that Eva and her escorts could pass, then continued to clean the floor. She saw three doors on the left-hand side, and beyond that a small window. She was curious to know what was behind it, but she wasn't given the chance to find out. The guards stopped at the first door and opened it. Eva entered and found herself in a shower that contained soap, a clean towel, and a pressed prison uniform on a shelf.

"Five minute," the guard said, holding up his hand and spreading his fingers.

He removed her restraints and closed the door. Eva wasted no time. She hadn't expected to see a shower again for a long while, so she was determined to make the most of it. She turned the water on to the hottest setting, letting it warm up while she undressed. She stepped under the stream and discovered that the DPRK's "hot" was not quite up to international standards. Still, the tepid water washed the stench and bloodstains from her body. Before she knew it, the door was pushed open with an order to dress.

The prison guards stood and watched as she dried herself and put on the new uniform, then took her to the next room.

The door was opened by a man wearing a surgical gown. He stood aside so that Eva could enter, then closed the door. One of the guards remained with her while the other waited outside.

"Name," the doctor said sternly.

"Melanie Carr."

Satisfied that he had the right patient, he instructed the guard to remove her restraints, then told Eva to strip and lie on the gurney. She checked the area for any instruments of torture but saw nothing to raise any concern, only an ultrasound machine and a device for monitoring her vitals.

Eva stepped out of her jumpsuit and lay on her back, ready to move if she spotted anything suspicious in the doctor's hands, but he simply squirted some gel onto a probe and ran it none too gently over her abdomen. He ordered her to turn onto one side, then the other, and after twenty minutes he was done.

Eva was given a Kleenex to wipe away the residue, then ordered to provide another blood sample. After that, electrodes were attached to various parts of her upper body and she was told to get on a treadmill in the corner of the room. A mask over her nose and mouth checked her breathing rate. The machine was set for a gentle jog, and she might have enjoyed the cardio workout if she hadn't still been naked.

She was finally allowed to dress and led to a door at the far end of the corridor. As she passed the small window, no bigger than an old television screen, she saw that the room beyond held an operating room. Not just that, but surgery was in progress. Something made her plant her feet to watch the proceedings, and she witnessed the surgeon reaching inside the body of a man in his twenties. The guards tugged at her, but she resisted long enough to see the doctor pull out what looked like the man's heart.

"It'll be your turn soon enough." One of them grinned and hit her on the leg with his night stick.

Eva pretended not to understand, but she let them take her through the door and back into the main building.

She hadn't seen this wing before. It looked much like the rest of the building, except halfway down the hallway was a room with large waist-high windows. Behind the glass, at least twenty children were sitting on the floor, some playing games, others reading, a couple enjoying a nap. Their ages ranged from a few months to fifteen years, and it broke Eva's heart to think they would be punished for the sins of their parents.

Guilt by association was a stick with which to subjugate the population. If a person were convicted of a crime, the family was often punished, too. Husbands, wives, children, parents—all were deemed to be guilty. Eva had read accounts of children being forced to watch their parents being executed in prison, usually at the whim of the warden. The children were then re-indoctrinated before being released years later, though some were also executed or sentenced to a lifetime of hard labor.

Eva couldn't understand how anyone could inflict such pain—physical or emotional—on anyone so young. She had no kids herself, but she didn't need to be a mother to know it was wrong to hurt the innocent. She could take the life of a man who deserved it without remorse, but it took a special kind of psychopath to harm a child.

The room was soon behind her, but the image of one little girl—sitting on her own with only a knitted doll for company—remained. She was still thinking about the child when one of the guards handed her an overcoat that had been hanging on a peg, then opened a door to the outside world. Eva followed him out into the cold and saw an exercise yard, complete with weight station and pull-up bar.

For thirty minutes, she pushed herself, glad to get her heart rate up without the aid of a psycho with a plastic bag. By the time she'd finished, she wanted another shower but didn't dare ask, lest the nice-guy act come to a swift end.

On the way back to her cell, they went through another hallway identical to her own, with cells on either side. She noted the names scribbled next to each door.

One of them was Hong Soon-won.

Eva memorized the route from his cell to hers. She'd already decided to take Hong with her when she made her escape, even though it would mean trawling the prison to find him. He'd risked his life to get the launcher details to the United States. The least she could do was get him out of the country. For his sake, not because the ESO wanted his secrets.

Knowing where they held Hong made her job much simpler.

She was back in her cell a couple of minutes later, having passed through two doors and a barred gate, all opened by her escorts using keys. As she lay on her bunk, she wondered at the primitive lock-up. Security at the other prison had been high-tech digital compared to this analogue version, and would have been a nightmare to escape from. Getting out of here would be much simpler. Maybe the people in charge thought escape less likely due to the inmates' relatively pleasant conditions. Or maybe it was the sheer isolation of the facility. But to Eva, a prison was a prison, and she treasured her freedom too much to hang around.

She tried to formulate a plan, but something the guard had said kept jumping in to disrupt her thoughts.

It'll be your turn soon enough.

What had he meant? She would be dead soon? Eva had noticed that the body on the operating table hadn't been intubated; she'd seen no anesthetist in attendance, which suggested the patient had already passed away. Perhaps the doctor had simply been performing an autopsy.

But even that didn't seem right. Why waste such resources on a prisoner when they were normally buried in unmarked graves?

She expected it to take a couple of days to plan her escape, and hoped she could find the answers to these questions during that time.

CHAPTER 11

If anyone asked him what the hardest part of running a prison was, Cheng Dae-sung would have said the boredom. As it was the DPRK, no one ever asked. Anything. You simply did as you were told or ended up in a place like this.

Not that Cheng would have minded. The conditions here were better than he'd known growing up in his family's two-bedroom home. They were certainly far superior to those in the other prisons he'd run.

Not that he planned to do anything to warrant a trip to one of the country's many camps. Compared to most in the DPRK, Cheng had an easy life. The pay was good, the food better, and on his infrequent trips to the capital, he shopped in the exclusive stores reserved for the country's elite. In fact, being so far from Pyongyang was the only downside, apart from the boredom.

Cheng had taken steps to address the latter by installing a window in the operating room. At first, he'd insisted on being inside the room to observe the operations, until a batch of organs failed due to contamination. Always one to apportion blame, he'd had the surgeon replaced and installed the window so that he could continue to indulge his interest.

As a young man, Cheng had studied medicine in the hope of becoming a doctor, but even in a country where the criteria were less than stringent, he'd failed to make the grade. Nor had his family's connections been enough to convince the qualification board to show him leniency. His practical work had been adequate, but academically he'd never had a hope.

With that career avenue turned into a cul-de-sac, Cheng had accepted his uncle's help in securing a commission in the army. He'd only taken the position after being assured a cushy post, but even then the pace of his advancement had been underwhelming. It had taken three years to go from junior lieutenant to lieutenant, one rung up the ladder. His idea of leadership had been shouting and impromptu beatings, and the brass had soon seen enough.

After he was drummed out of the army, his family had enough clout left to get him a position within the prison system. His lack of empathy made it the ideal vocation, and he found himself in his element. Instead of being reprimanded for striking the prisoners, he was actually encouraged to mete out ad hoc punishments.

His ascension through the ranks had been swift and brutal. Anyone who got in his way—colleague or prisoner—suffered his wrath.

Early in his career, Cheng had learned that a cowed prison population was much easier to maintain than one harboring any thoughts of rebellion. Troublemakers were dealt with the moment they were identified, usually through executions in the prison yard—the other inmates forced to watch the punishment for disobeying his rules.

It wasn't long before he had an unrivalled record when it came to escape attempts. In two years, not one prisoner had tried to flee his prison at Yodok, gaining him notoriety among his peers. In an industry renowned for its cruelty, Cheng excelled.

Until he was transferred to Kwanliso 33. His superiors saw it as a reward for his work, but to Cheng it was worse than a slap-in-the-face demotion. He was given strict instructions not to harm any of the prisoners in any way, which he found both strange and disturbing. He couldn't imagine running an effective facility in which prisoners were treated as human beings. It also meant that he had to rein in his violent impulses.

When he found out the reason for the bizarre orders, Cheng suddenly understood. Those sent to his prison had to be kept in the best of health for good reason, but it still pained him to keep himself and his staff in check. The idea of giving them decent meals and comfortable cells didn't sit well with him.

That was, until the reason for their visit finally arrived. Although he couldn't mistreat them during their stay, he could at least enjoy their final moments.

Today was the turn of a religious prisoner by the name of Ho. He'd been at Manpo prison for five days, a little less than the one-week average. His crime had been having a copy of the Christian bible in his home, a serious offense. More than half the people interned in the DPRK were religious or political prisoners, although Ho's wife and son had been incarcerated at Kwanliso 18 in Bukchang. The results of their medical tests had precluded a spell under his care.

Cheng was standing outside the operating room when Ho arrived with his escorts. The man looked serene, completely unaware of the fate that awaited him.

Ho was ushered through the first door and ordered to strip. When he was naked, a spray erupted from the ceiling and walls, covering his body. He was instructed to dry and don the blue gown hanging on the second door; then the door opened and he walked from the outer chamber into the operating room.

Through the observation window, Cheng watched the prisoner lie on the table and flinch upon contact with the cold surface. The surgeon asked his name and Ho replied, then asked what he was doing there. Nobody had told him anything about requiring surgery, he said.

"Your latest scan revealed a large cyst on your liver," the doc told him, a lie he'd delivered countless times. "We're going to do a biopsy to determine if it's malignant. It won't hurt."

"How large a cyst?" Ho wanted to know, his respiration rate elevating as a cannula entered the back of his hand.

"Three centimeters in diameter," the surgeon said as he pushed a syringe into the cannula and injected a small amount of clear liquid. "They are not uncommon, and usually benign."

The succinylcholine went to work immediately. It inhibited neuromuscular transmission, leaving Ho paralyzed within a minute of administration. As cardiac muscle fibers have intrinsic automaticity, the heart was not affected. It continued to beat strongly as Ho was lifted by two of the men in the room and the third removed the plastic-covered mat he'd been lying on. Underneath was a standard mortuary table that sloped gently from the sides into the middle, where a drain collected blood and other body fluids that were likely to escape during the operation.

The surgeon stood over Ho's head and held a small kidney dish a foot above his eyes. When he dropped it, there was no reaction as it hit the bridge of the prisoner's nose and bounced away.

The patient was ready, and with the dose he'd received, he'd be compliant for another nine minutes. Not that he would last that long. The diaphragm was one of the muscles affected, which meant that Ho was slowly suffocating to death.

Time to get to work.

Cheng watched the surgeon perform the Y-shaped incision, starting at the shoulder joints and meeting at the mid-chest, then down to the pubic region. Cheng knew the pain would be excruciating for the prisoner, but the psychological effect of Ho seeing his own body being sliced apart in the ceiling mirror justified the cost of having it installed.

There were many ways the operation could have been performed. The patient could have been given a general anesthetic, or killed with a severing of a major artery, but no such treatment would have given Cheng any pleasure. The prisoners here enjoyed too easy a life as it was; this was his only way to make them pay for their crimes and still ensure a proper harvest.

As per Cheng's instructions, the first organs to be removed were the kidneys. This was done while Ho was still alive and able to feel every cut. By the time they had been placed into an icebox, his body, badly starved of oxygen, had given up. The heart that had been pounding like the pistons on a steam liner fell still, and Ho's suffering came to an end. From outside the operating room, Cheng couldn't discern the precise moment of passing, but he was satisfied that the prisoner had received his proper punishment.

Cheng stayed until the pancreas, heart, and eyes were loaded into transportation coolers stored in the floor-to-ceiling refrigerator, then walked back to his office.

Ho was gone, his body to be taken to the crematorium and disposed of, much like thousands of others before him. Unlike inmates in other camps, though, the people who died here provided a much-needed boost for the economy.

Until a decade earlier, China had been harvesting its own organs, mainly from its many Falun Gong prisoners. The Taoist-Buddhist sect had become the subject of a crackdown in 1999 by the Communist government, and with tens of millions of followers, new prisoners hadn't been hard to come by. Organs were forcibly removed on demand, and even though official figures suggested only ten thousand transplants were performed in China each year, the actual number was twenty times higher.

When the scandal was made public, the Chinese government denied any wrongdoing. But when mud is thrown, some inevitably sticks. The practice was halted, but demand remained as high as ever. Private clinics had sprung up all over the country to perform the operations, and with organs now rarer than rocking-horse shit, both clinics and patients quickly became desperate for a new supply line.

Step forward the DPRK. With an economy in dire straits and an expendable population of more than twenty-five million, it was an opportunity not to be missed. Those unfortunate enough to be arrested and found to be in good health were sent to Kwanliso 33, just outside the small town of Manpo on the Chinese border. Further tests revealed whether they would make suitable donors. Those who wouldn't went to other camps to complete their sentences, while those who remained under Cheng's control provided the Chinese with the goods they required and the DPRK with a large amount of foreign currency. Cheng was no economist, but even looking at only his own records, he estimated that his camp was responsible for nearly 1.5 percent of the country's GDP of $28 billion a year. That four hundred million dollars might hardly seem worth the effort in most countries, but with international sanctions crippling the DPRK, it became a vital source of income.

Security had been kept light to fool the American satellites that constantly flew overhead. Officially—and ironically—the prison was designated as a meat-processing center. The guards were forced to treat the inmates with a certain level of dignity, though all prisoners were warned that if they misbehaved in any way they would be sent back to their previous facility to die. With the alternative being daily beatings, torture, and death from malnutrition, Cheng's prisoners chose to keep their heads down and behave themselves.

Originally, Kwanliso 33 had been a prison that held more than five thousand souls in overcrowded cells. These days, the prisoners resided in private cells, thus ensuring that fights would not damage their valuable bodies.

Back in his office, he looked through the list of prisoners to be harvested that day. He found four more scheduled to donate to the country's coffers, but it was a message written by his secretary that caught his attention.

A request had come through for a rush order. That usually meant someone important in China had suffered acute organ damage, probably a car accident or something of that nature. It wasn't unknown for such urgent demands for organs to hit his desk, and he had protocols in place to deal with it. The secretary would already have passed a copy of the request to the resident director of medicine to find a suitable match, and the donor's name would come to Cheng within the hour.

When the medical director knocked and entered his office, he handed Cheng a small piece of paper. It wasn't so much a list as a prisoner profile.

There was only one match, and it presented a problem.

A delegation was due to arrive the following day to interrogate the American woman. If Cheng fulfilled the customer request for her organs, he would learn nothing from her. However, to turn down the Chinese would be a mistake. If they ever discovered that Cheng had the matching donor and didn't keep his end of the bargain, his head would roll.

A rare smile lit up his face as he came up with an idea to please both parties and add some much-needed spice to his tedious existence.

Cheng picked up his phone and called the State Security Department.

CHAPTER 12

This wasn't how his life was meant to end.

Hong Soon-won had few regrets in life, but thinking he could get away with betraying his country was definitely one of them. He'd once rued the fact that his wife was unable to bear children, but looking back, perhaps that had been a blessing. If she'd managed to provide him with a son or daughter he would never have taken such a treasonous risk, for fear of leaving them to face his same fate.

At least his wife couldn't be punished for his transgression. Cancer had taken her two years earlier, and in her final days he'd been grateful for her passing. She'd spent the last three weeks at home in agony, and even with his connections he hadn't been able to secure enough of the morphine she required. What he had managed to get his hands on had been used sparingly, only administered when her screams ripped his heart apart. There were rumors that he could get methadone—known as Amidon in the DPRK—on the black market, but he knew that if anyone discovered him inquiring about forbidden goods, his own life would end as well.

So he'd watched her deteriorate before his eyes, refusing to eat, unable to move without grimacing in pain, until the cancer that had spread from her cervix to the rest of her body had become too much for either of them to bear. Hong had seen his wife suffer long enough and done what any loving husband would. He gave her a swift end. While she was asleep, he'd injected her with the last of the morphine, then put a pillow over her face and pressed it in place for ten endless minutes. She'd fought briefly to push the pillow away, but in her weakened state she'd been powerless to stop him. Hong had cried throughout the ordeal, though he knew she would have viewed it as an act of kindness.

If only he could wish for such a dignified end.

Hong was well aware of the fate that awaited him. As a *chungjang*, or lieutenant general, he'd often met with his peers to discuss the latest news. Three years earlier, he'd first learned about the sinister reason behind the reactivation of Kwanliso 33.

Originally a political-prisoner camp, it had been closed a decade earlier on economic grounds, but now it was back in full swing. He'd asked how the funds had been found to reopen it, and that's when he learned the prison would be self-sufficient. One colleague had joked that the conditions inside the camp were better than what he had at home, though few who were sent there ever enjoyed it for long.

Hong rolled onto his back and immediately regretted it. The wounds inflicted by the torturer's whip were still raw, even though they'd been treated upon arrival. The cuts and bruises on his face and the two missing fingernails on his left hand were other reminders of the punishment he'd undergone before arriving here. Still, he took solace in knowing that they hadn't got the truth from him. He'd eventually admitted to trying to install the virus onto the computer network and had given up the foreign agent who had provided it, but he hadn't revealed the real purpose behind his treasonous act.

Not that it mattered now. His silence might have saved the life of the man he'd blackmailed into giving him the launch-site codes, but he would never deliver them to the Americans.

In a country where the life expectancy for men was the late sixties, he'd known for some time that he didn't have long left. At fifty-seven, he was entering his twilight years, destined to spend his last decade or so on the planet alone, serving the corrupt regime that had done so much damage to his country. The super-elite enjoyed all the luxuries, from good food and high-end cars to international Internet access, while the rest of the population couldn't afford basic medicine to offer decent end-of-life care for their loved ones.

His wife's death had changed him forever. He'd spent his entire life believing the lies the party had spewed forth every day, never questioning, only obeying. It was only once he'd seen how little his wife's life meant to the ruling class that he began to see through the deception. It wasn't a party for the people, it was one for the few, and Hong wasn't in that number.

One night, he'd gone to bed a loyal-if-reluctant servant to the ruling party and woken up with only one thought on his mind. He'd nurtured it for days, weeks, until he had a risky yet workable plan.

At his wife's funeral, Hong had discovered that a cousin, Jang Hang-su, worked for the State Security Department. He'd also learned through observation that the man was fond of his alcohol. One night, Hong had surprised his relative by turning up at his apartment armed with two bottles of Johnny Walker Red Label, and though Jang had been suspicious at first, he'd let his guard down once the whisky started flowing. Hong had asked him about life in the SSD and begged his cousin to regale him with tales of his exploits. Jang had been all too happy to oblige; after a few drinks, Hong had steered the conversation towards Leng's current role: monitoring diplomats overseas.

As the evening wore on, Hong asked Jang how he kept himself busy when he wasn't ensuring the embassy staff weren't planning to defect. It turned out to be a lot, little of which his superiors would have approved of. Hong had recorded it all. When he confronted a sober Jang the following day, he told him that he had given copies to several friends who would pass them to the police in the event of Hong's death or disappearance.

Hong Soon-won now had a way of communicating with the West.

After that, it was a simple matter of exerting the leverage he had with his colleague to get the missile codes, then finding a way to hide his tracks. The computer virus had been the Americans' idea, and it had seemed a good one at the time.

Instead, it had led to his downfall.

He hadn't known that every terminal was monitored for the installation of new software. Within seconds of inserting the flash drive into his computer, two guards had appeared at his side and dragged him from his seat. A third had arrived and sat in his chair to run diagnostics. It had taken less than a minute to find the flash drive, disable the hostile software, and send Hong to a local detention facility for interrogation.

It was a beating he'd never forget.

Not for the few days he had left on the planet.

CHAPTER 13

No matter how hard she tried, Eva couldn't stop thinking about the children.

Before leaving Melbourne, she'd read plenty of testimonies from prison escapees. Harrowing as they'd been, there was always a certain disconnect in second-hand accounts of atrocities. Much as people couldn't begin to imagine the horror of the Nazi concentration camps of the 1940s, Eva had found it hard to comprehend similar cruelty occurring eighty years later.

It was different when you could put faces to the names. The couple of dozen children she'd seen in the prison's nursery felt real, whereas the many tens of thousands who had perished in the internment and re-education camps remained statistics. For some reason, the human mind could process the loss of a roomful of people, but increase the dead to hundreds of thousands, or even millions, and the scale was beyond computation.

The saddest part was that Amnesty International and other human rights organizations had been bringing the inhuman treatment of North Korean prisoners to the world's attention for many years, yet nothing had been done about it. The DPRK denied any wrongdoing, and the atrocity continued unabated.

Eva was roused from her troubled thoughts by a key rattling in the door lock. She sat up on her bunk as two guards entered her cell. They gestured for her to assume the position so that they could apply the handcuffs, then took her down the corridor toward the medical wing she'd visited the previous day. But instead of passing through the door bearing the red cross, they took her out of the building and marched her through the snow to a building that oozed despair.

A chill swept over her as one of the guards struggled with the huge padlock on the door. He eventually got it open, and the door creaked as he pushed it inward. The air inside smelled stale, as if the room had been unused for years. Eva thought it might have been an old storeroom, but she soon saw its purpose when she was pushed inside.

This had once been the interrogation center. In the middle of the large room, a sturdy oak chair had been bolted to the floor, complete with leather straps for arms and ankles.

Eva had seconds to make a decision. She'd really wanted a couple of weeks to get to know the layout of the facility and the strength of the guards, but she wasn't sure she could survive another bout of torture if it meant wearing a plastic bag. The interrogator from the previous prison was sure to have mentioned that it had been effective, and the mere thought of it spurred her into action.

One of the guards held her bicep tightly while the other removed her handcuffs. As soon as her hands were free, she spun on the one holding her arm and caught him in the temple with the sharp point of her elbow. As he fell, she kicked the other in the chest and followed him as he staggered backward. She slammed his head into the wall and punched him in the throat, then whipped out his pistol and cracked him over the head with the butt.

She turned and faced the other guard, who was struggling to his knees.

"How many guards at the camp?" she asked in Korean, the gun pointing at his head.

She glanced around and saw that the room had been left as it must have been the last time the door had been locked. Rusty torture implements lay under a blanket of dust on the metal table. They would still serve their purpose.

"Fifty," the guard said, his hand hovering near his weapon.

Eva wanted this part to go quietly. Any shooting, and the rest of the guards would show up. "Get up, and take your gun out slowly."

He eased himself to his feet and thought for a couple of seconds, then used his thumb and forefinger to take the pistol from its holster. He dropped it, and Eva took a few steps to her right, toward the table.

"Take your coat off, turn around, and put your hands on your head."

When he complied, she picked a knife up from the table and closed the gap silently. She rammed the blade into the base of his skull and cut back and forth, slicing his spinal column. He was dead before he hit the ground.

Eva picked up his discarded weapon and checked him for spare ammunition. She found one more magazine, then turned to the other guard, dazed but conscious.

"How many guards?" she asked again, in case the first had been lying. She got the same answer and learned that only half would be on duty, the rest sleeping in the barracks at the rear of the complex.

She ordered him to his feet and told him to strip the other guard. While he did, Eva opened the door and checked outside. No one appeared to have heard the commotion, so she closed it and watched the guard pull the overcoat, pants and shirt off his dead colleague. Once he was stripped, Eva shed her prison garb and dressed in the khaki uniform. As estimated, the fallen guard's height matched hers—the reason he'd died first.

She told the remaining soldier to lose the nightstick and hand over his pepper spray, which went into her coat pocket. She checked outside once more and saw no sign of life. The main building stood some twenty yards away; she wouldn't be exposed for long.

Eva pulled the woolen hat down onto her head and made sure her hair was tucked inside, then gave the guard his orders.

"We're going to walk quickly to the front entrance. You unlock the main door and walk in first. If you try to raise the alarm, I'll shoot you in the lower back. That's a slow and painful death."

The man nodded meekly, and Eva opened the door and ushered him outside. They walked in step, Eva trying to project normalcy despite the tense situation. When they got to the door, she let the guard use his keys to open it. He went in first. Eva followed, then waited while he started to lock it behind them.

"Leave it open," she whispered. "Just pretend to lock it."

The guard followed her instructions, then walked to the next gate.

"Is there any way in without going past the front office window?" Eva asked.

There wasn't. She asked about other ways out of the camp, but that came back negative, too.

She had no choice but to press ahead.

As she braced herself for the gauntlet, an idea came to her.

"When you get to the window, tell the man inside that your colleague wants to come in the office. I'll be standing beside the door. Understand?"

He shook his head. "No one is allowed in there, only the clerk and Cheng."

"Who's Cheng?" Eva asked, aware that seconds were ticking away.

"He runs the prison," the guard said, glancing back at the exit. "He was supposed to . . . speak to you back there."

Right. The one with the dead eyes. Even the guard seemed to shiver when he said the warden's name. If Cheng had been planning to interrogate her, he would be making his way to the outer building soon.

"How many people in the office?" she asked.

"Just one. He sleeps in there, too. He has a room at the back."

That room housed something important, if the clerk never left and no one but the warden was allowed entry. She buried the thought for later. Right now, she had to find a way past it and into the bowels of the building without alerting anyone.

"You go to the window and distract him," she said.

"How?"

"I don't know. Just ask him for something that will make him get out of the chair and turn around for a few seconds."

He looked worried, but there wasn't time for anything else. She showed him the weapon to remind him what would happen if he failed, then watched him unlock the barred gate and walk through.

Eva stuck to the wall so the clerk couldn't see her clearly. The guard arrived at the window and received a gruff greeting. She heard him say that Cheng wanted her file in order to check something; a second later, he looked at Eva and made a face that said "Go!"

Eva didn't hesitate. She walked quickly past the window while the clerk faced the other direction, keeping her head down and to one side. Once clear, she planted herself against the wall and motioned with the gun for the guard to follow her. He paused for a moment, and she feared he was preparing to betray her, but instead he accepted a sheet of paper from the clerk and came her way.

She stood aside so he could unlock the next door in her path, and when she walked through it, she stopped short. The next door was open, and someone was coming through it.

~

Cheng Dae-sung was in an unusually buoyant mood. He'd called the State Security Department and asked if he could perform the interrogation on the Carr woman, explaining that her organs had been requested for immediate dispatch. He'd been given the go-ahead, on the condition that her overall health wasn't compromised. Rush orders were usually reserved for the Chinese elite, or those close to them. To fulfil them meant influential people would be grateful: it was good business practice to have powerful people on your side.

It had been some time since Cheng had performed a proper grilling, not since his days at Yodok. Back then, his job had been to extract confessions, more often than not from innocent people—but this one was definitely guilty. She'd been caught red-handed, wearing the uniform of the Korean People's Army at a rendezvous with the traitor Hong. All Cheng needed from her was a confession that she was working for the United States government, which shouldn't be too hard to come by. He'd even been given a tip from her previous interrogator and looked forward to seeing how the suffocation technique affected her the second time around. But only after he'd tried more conventional methods. First, he thought, would be her left hand; she wouldn't need that to sign the confession. After that, the soles of her feet. If she started talking before he used the bag, that would be her choice. Cheng would see the interrogation through to the end, no matter how much information she offered.

After that, it would be a short trip to the operating room, where she would make her most valuable contribution.

The guard accompanying him unlocked the security door and held it open for Cheng, who stopped dead.

It was *her*. The Carr woman. Wearing a guard's uniform and carrying a pistol.

"Stop her!" he shouted as he pushed his escort through the door and pulled it closed. Through the small grille set at head height he watched her dispatch both guards in seconds.

She's coming for me.

It had to be. She had no other reason to fight her way *into* the prison. If she wanted to escape, she would have been racing for the exit.

Cheng was no coward, but she was armed and he wasn't.

83

Shouting as he ran, he ordered all guards to report to him immediately. One of his subordinates stuck his head out of a doorway to see what the commotion was all about, and Cheng relieved him of his weapon and told him to hold off the woman who would be coming through the security door any second now.

The guard took out his nightstick, unaware that he was vastly outgunned. He learned the hard way moments later.

Cheng missed the kill. He was too busy retreating to the safety of his office, which had a reinforced door designed to protect him in the highly unlikely event of a prison riot. He was now glad he'd taken the precaution. He sprinted up the stairs, and as he ran past his secretary's office he barked an order to sound the alarm and have everyone guard the administrative block, then he dived into his office and locked himself in.

When Cheng picked up the phone, he was relieved to hear the dial tone. She hadn't cut communications, and it would be her downfall. He began dialing the State Security Department to inform them that the prisoner had escaped, but he stopped halfway through entering the digits.

Melanie Carr was one woman with a gun against fifty of his men. Minus the ones she'd already killed. How would it look if he called in reinforcements when she was clearly outnumbered?

The alarm shrieked into life, a constant high-pitched bell that clawed at his ears. He looked out of the bulletproof window and saw a few of his men gathering in the lobby below. They seemed unsure what the emergency was, so Cheng cracked open his door and summoned one of them up to his office.

"The American woman has escaped and is heading this way. She is armed. Stop her at all costs, but try for a headshot. If her organs are damaged, you and the man responsible will join her in the operating room."

The guard swallowed hard, then nodded and ran to pass on the message. Cheng slammed the door shut and locked it once more.

~

When the guard came through the door, Eva barely registered him. Her eyes were on Cheng in the background. He'd been on his way to inflict pain on what he'd thought would be a captive audience, and she was happy to disappoint him. In fact, she would have liked five minutes with the roles reversed.

It wasn't going to happen any time soon.

Cheng slammed the hallway door shut and Eva turned her attention to the guard, who was fumbling for his pistol.

She put an end to his efforts with a bullet to the heart, then dispatched the one who had brought her this far. She snapped up his keys and the other guard's weapon, then opened the door Cheng had disappeared behind.

As she stepped into the next corridor, Eva heard the alarm sound, and her heart skipped a couple of beats. They would be on her in seconds, and all she had was a pair of pistols and the spare ammo she'd taken from the fallen men.

She was torn between finding Hong and bolting for the exit when the alarm cut out. The ancient PA system took over, ordering all available staff to the administration block to deal with an armed, escaped prisoner.

Cheng must have guessed I'm coming for him.

The governor's ego had bought her—and the defector—a little time. Remembering a previous journey through the prison, she bypassed the admin block and took the circuitous route past the children's playroom to the corridor where Hong was being held. She peeked through the grille and saw two soldiers heading away from her at speed; once they passed out of sight, she unlocked the door and ran to Hong's cell.

Eva slid the grille to one side and saw him lying on his bed in the fetal position. After three attempts, she found the correct key and unlocked the door. Hong's only reaction was to curl into a tighter ball.

"Can you walk?" she asked when she closed the door behind her.

The defector's head snapped up. "You? How . . . ?"

"Can you walk?" Eva asked again, more firmly.

Hong sat up gingerly. "I think so."

"That's not good enough. I'm getting out of here. You're either coming or staying. Make up your mind."

He sprang to his feet.

Nothing like a little tough love to focus the mind.

Eva handed him one of the pistols, along with two spare magazines. Favoring his injured hand, he pulled out the mag and checked for a round in the chamber.

Good. No need to teach him how to use it.

Eva was first out the door. She checked up and down the corridor before pulling Hong out after her. They jogged to the security door that Eva had left open and saw that the next section of the prison was clear, too. Cheng's decision to concentrate his men in the admin block was proving a godsend.

They made it to the final corridor without resistance. Eva told Hong to take a coat from one of the dead guards while she went to deal with the one in the front office. When she approached the glass, he was on the phone. She heard him relaying the incident, probably to his superiors, and she had no idea where the closest reinforcements were stationed. They could be here in an hour or in the next two minutes. Eva ended the call by putting two rounds through the glass and into his head, then urged Hong to follow her to the exit.

This was where she expected things to get dicey, and she wasn't disappointed. The moment she threw the door open and stepped out into the cold, two guards opened up with AK-47s from the guardhouses next to the main gate. She threw herself to the ground and replied with the

Type 68 pistol. At less than forty-five yards, she had no trouble hitting her targets. The moment the second guard fell, she dug herself out of the snow and checked on Hong. He hadn't been hit, so she pulled him to his feet and ran over to the corpses, stripping them of their weapons and ammunition.

The wire gate was secured simply, with a long steel bolt. Eva pulled it aside and ran, Hong's footsteps ringing in her ears.

It wasn't all she heard.

The chatter of Chinese-made AK-47s reached her as the snow at her feet danced like geysers, and the growls of approaching dogs made her blood freeze.

Eva turned to see the hounds sprinting toward her, and she prioritized them over the guards with the automatic rifles. The two German shepherds seemed to fly across the ground like heat-seeking missiles. She hated the thought of killing them but had no choice. Eva fired a couple of three-round bursts at the animals; no time to feel sorry as they crumpled to the ground. Their handlers were still in the game, though, and Hong was already engaging them. His discipline with the rifle wasn't the best, and he used up a whole magazine on one of the targets.

Eva was more economical, needing only a few rounds to neutralize the other.

"Head for the woods!"

Hong did as he was told, and they ran for the relative safety of the trees. The snow wasn't so thick on the ground here, and they made better time.

"Where are we going?" Hong panted after a few minutes.

It was a good question. Eva had no idea where they were, let alone where they were heading.

"Away from here," she said, not letting up the pace. "First, we need to find out where we are. Then we can think about getting to the border."

"We're near . . . Manpo," Hong said, fighting to get the frigid air into his lungs. "The Chinese border . . . is . . . a couple miles north."

"How do you know?"

"I've . . . heard . . . about the camp," he panted.

The details could wait. For now, she needed to concentrate on putting distance between themselves and the prison. She also needed to know which direction was north. She'd seen the sun in the sky a couple of times during her exercise period the previous day, its transition across the sky giving her a fair idea of where north lay in relation to the exercise yard. She brought up a mental map of the prison and determined that they were currently heading west.

"This way," she said, as shouts rose in the distance. Cheng must have realized that she wasn't coming for him and sent his men out in pursuit.

She also caught the howls of more dogs.

CHAPTER 14

"How easy is it to get across the border here?" Eva asked Hong. "Is it heavily guarded?"

"There are . . . a few checkpoints . . . but only at the bridges. The Yalu River . . . not far."

They'd only been exposed to the elements for a few minutes, and already Hong was suffering. Asking him to swim across to China was definitely out, as was walking across a bridge and asking for free passage.

"How deep is the river?"

Hong shook his head. "Don't . . . kn-know. But wide."

"Then we'll have to try to find a boat to get us across."

They couldn't cross that river until they got to it, though, and ahead of them the ground rose sharply. She'd noticed the mountains surrounding the camp when she'd first arrived, but had no idea what lay beyond the first peak. Hopefully it would be downhill all the way to the Yalu once they crested it.

It was slow going. Even on her own it would have been a strength-sapping climb, but she had to keep stopping and backtracking to keep Hong up to the task. The snow lessened the higher they climbed, but the ground beneath was frozen solid, making progress slow and dicey. She had to sling her rifle over her shoulder and use her hands to pull herself upward, which soon took a toll on her fingers. They were bloody and numb within minutes, and Hong wasn't faring any better.

"Take a minute," Eva said the next time he caught up. She thrust her hands into her armpits to get the circulation working again. From below, the sound of dogs drew noticeably closer. It was a trade-off: letting them get closer so her fingers warmed sufficiently to use the AK-47. As the first hound came into view, she put the rifle to her shoulder and let the dog get to within fifty yards before she felled it with her second shot. Gunfire erupted from behind the dog—pistols, useless at this range.

More barking split the frigid air, but much farther away now. Eva hoped they'd learned a lesson and would keep the other hounds leashed.

"Come on," Eva said, grabbing Hong's collar. She dragged him to his feet and shoved him ahead of her. If he slipped, she could stop him from sliding down the hill, which was showing no signs of leveling out.

She watched Hong push himself from tree to tree and followed his example, and five minutes later she saw a break in the trees ahead. Eva scrambled to the top, eager to know what lay below. It was good news and bad. The river lay half a mile ahead, a straight run downhill, but Hong had been correct about its width. It spanned at least two hundred yards and looked to be frozen over. Beyond it, she could see the outskirts of a town.

"That's Ji'an," Hong said as he came up beside her. "China."

"Then that's where we're going."

Eva set off at a tentative pace, listening for Hong as she navigated the slippery slope down. As she had on the way up, she bounced from one tree to the next, nearly freefalling where the foliage grew sparsely on this side of the mountain. She lost her footing a couple of times, ending up on her backside, but eventually made it to level ground. Hong slithered the last ten yards on his back and Eva helped him to his feet.

"You okay?"

"Okay," he confirmed.

"Good. We haven't got long. Once we're across, we can rest."

She set a pace he could keep up with, constantly scanning left and right for danger. They had no cover to hide behind, so if they encountered trouble, they would simply have to shoot their way through.

When they reached the river, Eva saw that boating was out of the question. The ice she'd seen from the hilltop wasn't the thin sheen she'd hoped for, but she couldn't be sure it would support their weight, either.

"What now?" Hong asked.

Eva tested the ice with her foot. It felt solid enough . . . but it always was solid close to the bank. No doubt it would thin out as they reached the middle. She looked around and found a stone about the size of her fist. She threw it as high and far as she could, and it hit about a third of the way across, bounced a couple of times, then settled in the thin covering of snow.

"Will it hold?" Hong asked.

"We've got no choice. I'll go first, you stay five yards behind me."

Eva stepped out onto the ice and stamped down hard. It showed no sign of giving, so she walked another ten yards and tried again. Still firm. She ventured farther out, checking now and again to make sure Hong was doing as she'd instructed. He was, but shouts from the hillside above made him quicken his pace.

"Five yards!" Eva warned him, though she herself was keen to get across now that the enemy was closing in. If the North Koreans got within range while they were still on the frozen river, it would be game over.

Eva pushed on, testing each step before putting her full weight on it. She passed the stone she'd thrown to test the surface, putting them in uncharted territory.

She was a few yards short of the middle when her luck ran out. She put her foot down gingerly, but that was all it took. The ice spiderwebbed instantly, and the cracks zigzagged in all directions, including the spot where she stood.

Eva plummeted into the freezing water. She threw out her arms to stop herself going under, but the ice at the edge of the hole gave way and the weight of her heavy coat and the AK-47 dragged her down. Her body's cold shock response desperately wanted her to gasp for air and flail for solid ice, but doing so would have killed her. Instead, Eva tried to relax—not an easy thing with the surface receding above her. Her lungs were already at bursting point, and tiny white stars invaded her vision. Seconds later, her feet hit the bottom. Eva dropped the weapon, shucked off the coat, and kicked to the surface as every inch of her body screamed for oxygen.

When her head breached, she gulped in air, then fought her way to the side, looking for firm ice. Her first couple of attempts simply made the hole larger. Hong threw himself flat on thicker ice and held out the stock of his rifle for her to grab hold of. She got two hands on it and pulled, but the old man's fingers weren't prepared. The gun slipped from his grasp and Eva went under again, letting the gun sink as she fought to reach the edge of the hole again. Eventually she managed to find ice that held her weight. She took a few seconds to compose herself, then kicked her feet until her body was perpendicular to the surface. She kept kicking as if she was doing the front crawl, until her chest and hips were clear of the water, then dragged herself onto the fragile ice.

"Stay back," she said when Hong advanced toward her. "Stay on your st-st-stomach and pull your . . . self al-along."

He nodded.

She looked for thicker-looking ice in the direction of the far shore. *Impossible to tell.*

"Follow me," Eva said. She found even inching along on her belly difficult as her body started shutting down non-essential muscles. Hypothermia was heading her way, which meant she had to get warm before it completely overwhelmed her.

After thirty yards on her stomach, Eva used her elbow to test the ice once more. It was much stronger here, closer to the far bank; a glance behind her showed tiny figures rushing down the hill towards the river. She had no choice but to trust that the remaining ice would hold them.

"Get up. Run!"

Eva reached the far bank in half a minute, and Hong wasn't far behind her. He took off his coat and wrapped it around her shoulders.

"Thanks," Eva said, but it wouldn't do much good unless she could get to a warm building and ditch the wet prison uniform. They also needed to find cover before the men following them got into range. Thankfully, a tree line began a dozen yards away. Eva led Hong into it.

"We need tr-transport," she said.

"First you need clothes. I go . . . find some. You wait."

"No."

Much as the thought of nice warm clothes appealed to her, she wasn't letting Hong out of her sight. He might run into trouble, and she had no idea how welcoming the locals would be; she had read that most of the people who fled North Korea to China were repatriated if caught. Besides, if she stayed where she was, she would succumb to the cold. Better to keep moving and get a little warmth into her body.

"I'll . . . come with you." She shuddered, her teeth chattering, but she led the way once more.

The tree line ended abruptly at a road, across from which seemed to be an industrial area: low brick buildings topped with corrugated-iron roofs and adorned with signs written in Chinese. She had no idea of the time, but the sun was high overhead. That made it about midday, which meant that many of the buildings should be open. Mixed blessing. They needed to avoid meeting anyone, if possible.

"We should . . . avoid this place," she said. "Too many . . . people. Find . . . find a . . . house. Or car."

They skirted the area, sticking to the trees as they looked for any site that offered warmth and isolation.

As they scanned the town, they didn't see the car cruise up behind them.

CHAPTER 15

Eva realized too late that the cold must have dulled her senses, because the car was level with her before she even registered it. Her hand instinctively went for her waistband to retrieve the pistol.

Gone—probably when she'd fallen through the ice.

"Are they . . . police?" she whispered to Hong.

The vehicle wasn't displaying police insignia, but she had no idea how the local authorities rolled. Perhaps unmarked cars were the norm.

"No. Private security."

That was a temporary relief, but when the car stopped and the driver got out, his hand came to rest on his sidearm. He was large, but in a bad-diet way. A second man appeared from the passenger side, the polar opposite. They looked like Laurel and Hardy, except the large one had a stringy goatee rather than a mustache.

"Looks like we're being invaded," the driver said in Chinese to the Laurel-like thin man, earning a smile from him.

"Should we surrender now?" his companion asked with a laugh.

Hardy drew his gun and aimed it casually at Eva. "I have a better idea."

She understood every word, and knew they were in trouble. If these guys turned them in to the police for a reward, she and Hong would be back in the DPRK by the end of the day, and dead by morning.

Normally she would have fought her way out of this situation, but right now she couldn't trust her chilled body to obey her commands. The temperature would continue to drop as night approached, piling more misery on her already freezing frame, and Hong didn't look like he was holding up much better. With the gun trained on her, their predicament seemed hopeless.

"I'm going first this time," Laurel said.

"Yeah . . . with the old man!"

Hardy thought his joke was hilarious, but Eva wasn't amused. She'd got their intentions wrong. They weren't planning to hand them over to the police. At least, not straight away. The lecherous look in Hardy's eye told her exactly what he had in mind.

She couldn't believe her luck.

When Hardy gestured with the gun at the car, Eva gladly walked toward it and got in the back, though she maintained a submissive look as she did so. She sat in the middle of the seat, exaggerating her body's shivering, while Hong and Laurel got in either side of her. She'd picked the spot to draw the maximum body warmth from the men, though her companion wouldn't be much of a conductor.

Hardy got behind the wheel, and the moment they set off Laurel had his hand on Eva's thigh. It made her flesh crawl, but she put up with it. In the close confines of the vehicle she couldn't guarantee taking them both down without the car crashing.

The journey didn't last long. Within minutes they parked outside an apartment block. It looked dilapidated but at least held the promise of a warm shower and heat of some sort.

Hardy had put his gun away and now led Eva by the arm. He took her through the building's outer door and down a concrete corridor that smelled of rotting vegetation and the faintest hint of urine. Eva pretended to be scared and planted her feet—not to launch an attack, but because anyone in her situation would be fearful of such a place. She let Hardy slap her about the head and acted cowed, hoping to put him at ease.

They climbed two flights of stairs and walked halfway down a hallway dimly lit by a single working light bulb. Hardy stopped at a door with a number above a peephole, and put a key in the lock.

The interior didn't smell much better than the rest of the building, but at least he'd had the sense to leave some form of heating on. She saw an ancient radiator in the small living room and made for it, crouching down to get the maximum benefit.

The door slammed, and the men pushed Hong onto a wooden chair next to a Formica-covered table.

"I'm serious," Laurel told his partner. "It's my turn first."

"You went first last time." Hardy was already removing his jacket as he eyed his prize.

"Bullshit! You always go first!"

Eva kept her hands on the radiator, glad to get some heat back into her body. She could already feel her fingers starting to respond, and it wouldn't be long before she had the strength to take the two men on.

Unfortunately, Hardy didn't seem the patient type. He grabbed her by the hand and tried to pull her to her feet.

"Please," she said in Chinese. "If you let me get warm first, I'll do anything you ask."

Hardy took hold of her with both hands and dragged her away from the radiator. "I like them cold and feisty."

She had no choice but to do as he said, and he seemed to get a good look at her face for the first time. Up until now she'd kept her head bowed to avoid this moment.

"Hey!" he said to Laurel. "This one's white!" He squeezed Eva's jaw with his meaty hand. "You American?" he asked in English.

Eva shook her head as best she could, now acting more frozen and disabled than she felt.

"English? Italian?"

Eva played dumb. The longer he questioned her, the more responsive her body felt. She kept her hands behind her back, squeezing them to make sure they were in working order. The only thing holding her back now was the damp uniform, and that was easily solved.

She met his eyes meekly, shook her coat off, then slowly undid the buttons on her shirt. She let it hang open, revealing her cleavage, while she unzipped her pants. She let them fall to the floor, then removed the shirt and stood with her hands by her sides.

"I'm definitely going first," Laurel said, stepping between Hardy and Eva. He took her by the arm and started walking her toward a door, but Hardy wasn't giving up his turn so easily. He got hold of Laurel's collar and pulled him backward, then stuck out a leg and tripped the thinner man onto his ass. Laurel ended up on his back, spitting expletives Hardy's way as the larger man barked a cruel laugh.

"You might as well stay there and pleasure yourself. I'm going to take my time."

Hardy had his back to Eva now, his holster within easy reach. Piece of cake. She went for the gun, but her fingers weren't as responsive as she'd hoped. When she tried to unsnap the leather strap holding the pistol in place, her first attempt failed, and when she tried again Hardy slapped her hand away. He turned surprisingly quickly for a large man and swung his arm in an arc, catching Eva on the side of the head and knocking her sideways. She collapsed over the arm of a threadbare sofa and tumbled onto the floor, but swiftly scrambled back to her feet.

Hardy came at her quickly, hands reaching for her throat. Eva easily deflected his arms and brought her knee up into his midriff. He doubled over, wheezing and coughing, and Eva landed a blow to the base of his skull, dropping him to the floor, hard.

Eva turned to deal with Laurel. He climbed to his feet, already drawing his weapon, well out of her reach. She charged him, but Hong was ahead of her. He threw himself at Laurel and hit him like a linebacker from the side, pinning the Chinese man's arms to his side. The pistol clattered to the floor as Laurel hit his head on the corner of the glass coffee table. He was out cold, but Hardy was back for more.

He rushed Eva again, and it proved to be a fatal mistake. In his position, Eva would have used the pistol he had in his holster, and taken an injuring shot, but Hardy was fueled by rage and humiliation and sought to deliver a more visceral punishment. If he meant to demonstrate his power, he instead got a lesson in physics. Eva swiveled at the hips as Hardy reached her, and used his momentum to send him crashing to the floor next to Laurel. Only now did he remember the weapon still at his hip, but Eva was too quick. She landed a knee in his chest, pinning him, and picked up a jagged shard of table glass from the floor near his head. A second later, it was buried in Hardy's eye socket, his struggles ending as his brain's death spread to the rest of his body.

Laurel was still breathing, but unconscious. That suited Eva fine. She relieved him of his weapon and took Hardy's, too, which she handed to Hong. She also searched them for cell phones and found one in Laurel's pocket. She hit the Home button and swiped the screen, but it asked for a password.

"Keep an eye on him," she said, putting the phone on the table. "I'm going to take a quick shower and dress. Then it's your turn."

"Shouldn't we leave?" Hong asked.

"I think we'll be fine. My guess is that shouting and banging from this apartment isn't anything unusual, and I doubt they're expecting visitors. If anyone knocks on the door, just ignore it. I need to warm up before we move on."

She found the bathroom and was disappointed to see that it only had a bath, not a shower. It was still better than nothing, so she turned on the hot faucet and waited for the water to heat up. After a minute it was still running cold, so she wrapped a towel around herself and went in search of a boiler. There was one in the kitchen, but no matter which dials she turned or buttons she pressed, nothing seemed to kick it into gear. Whatever was feeding the radiator, it wasn't the boiler.

"No bath tonight," she murmured as she went into the only bedroom, looking through the closet for something to wear. It turned out that they were in Hardy's apartment—the clothing five sizes too large for her. Eva returned to the living room and looked at Laurel. He was a much better fit.

It took a couple of minutes to strip the unconscious man and dress in his clothes, then Eva told Hong to make some tea or coffee while she prepared Laurel for interrogation. She found a roll of duct tape under the sink and used it to bind his hands, then his ankles. She finished off by stuffing one of Hardy's socks into his mouth and securing it in place with the tape.

"Rise and shine," she said, and splashed cold water onto Laurel's face. He jerked awake and tried to bring his hands up, and that's when his eyes widened with fear. Crouching in front of him was Eva, a knife from the kitchen drawer in her hand. He tried saying something, but the words were lost behind the gag in his mouth.

"I'm going to ask you a couple of questions and I want quick, honest answers, okay?"

Sweat was already forming on Laurel's brow, and she could see his limbs start to shake. He nodded vigorously.

"Good. What's the code to open the phone?" she asked, then removed the tape over his mouth.

Laurel stammered four numbers. Eva entered the digits into the cell.

"Well done. You answered honestly. Now, tell me what time you're due back to work."

"Tomorrow morning. Eight o'clock."

"Perfect."

Eva replaced the tape over his mouth and thrust the knife into his throat. If she let him live, he would eventually free himself and raise the alarm. Since she planned on stealing the car, she couldn't let that happen. The fact that he'd been so eager to rape her made the decision easier.

Using Hardy's phone, Eva dialed a number she'd committed to memory. It was answered on the third ring.

CHAPTER 16

"Johnson, it's me."

The line fell silent for a few seconds, and Eva assumed he was running a trace. She would have done the same.

"What happened?" he asked at last.

"Long story, but I've got the package. We crossed the border but need an exfil."

"Can you get to Shenyang?" he asked.

Eva asked where it was, and Johnson told her that it was a five-to-six-hour drive northwest.

He was *running a trace.*

"I can make that. Where do we meet?"

"I'll make arrangements. I won't ask how you got that phone, but ditch it and get a burner, then call me back in two hours."

The phone went dead, and Eva put it in her pocket. "We need to clean this place up," she told Hong. "Wipe everything you touched."

"What about the bodies?"

"Don't worry about them. We just need time to get out of the country, and if our prints are found at the murder scene, they'll be looking for us at all the airports."

Eva got to work herself, using a dishcloth to get rid of any signs she'd been there. After a few minutes, she was happy that she'd erased all traces. She thought about staging the scene to make it look like the two men had killed each other, but given the blood pooling near their corpses, it would be impossible. She only hoped the wheels of justice turned slowly in these parts, and that any perpetrator DNA the police found would take time to process.

When Hong was done, Eva put her old clothes into a plastic bag and shoved it under her arm, then took the weapons from the dead men. She also checked their pockets and took all the money they had. Her final act was to remove the dressing on Hong's left hand and check his wounds. Two of his fingernails were missing, and it looked like an infection had set in. She would need to clean it soon, but a quick search of the apartment revealed nothing that would help.

"We'll get some antibiotics on the way," she told him, and used a clean set of underwear from a drawer as a makeshift bandage.

She closed the door behind them, then led Hong outside to their captors' car. The first thing she did when she got behind the wheel was to crank the heater up to the highest setting. While waiting for it to kick in, Eva drove a couple of miles from the apartment, then pulled over in a parking lot and used the phone to plan their route.

"I never thanked you for coming to get me," Hong said. "Not many people would do that."

"You're welcome."

Eva didn't add that one of the main reasons she'd gone back for him was to get the ESO off her back. If she'd turned up empty-handed, or called to say she'd made it out alone, they would take a dim view. At the very least, they'd take her money for good, leaving her no resources with which to disappear. The worst-case scenario didn't bear thinking about.

Besides, Hong had earned it. He'd known what to expect if caught helping the West, but he'd gone through with it anyway.

"I was prepared to die," he said quietly, "but not in Kwanliso 33."

"What's the difference?" Eva asked. "Camp 33, Camp 15, you're still dead. At least in Camp 33 they treated you decently. It was certainly a lot better than I was expecting."

"And that didn't strike you as odd?"

"It did," Eva agreed.

"Then let me explain. There are many prisons in my country. Some house political prisoners, others thieves and murderers. The conditions inside are atrocious, apart from Kwanliso 33. It was reopened a few years ago for one purpose: to harvest organs to sell to the Chinese."

Eva looked up from the phone. "You're kidding."

"I wish I was. The facilities are comfortable because extreme cold and malnutrition can cause damage to vital organs, even after just a few days. All prisoners are given medicals after they are arrested, and those who make good donors are sent to Kwanliso 33."

"But . . . why?"

"Money," Hong said. "Hard currency. The DPRK is on its knees, and sanctions are crippling the economy even further. This was seen as a way to bring in much-needed revenue."

Hong's words meant that the man Eva had seen in the operating room hadn't been undergoing an autopsy after all.

"There are children at the camp," she said.

"I know. It isn't just adults that need new livers and hearts."

They fell silent. The thought of children being murdered for their body parts left Eva speechless.

She'd spent ten years of her own life killing people in cold blood, but she'd done so in the belief that she was protecting the United States. All of her targets had been threats to national security. Or so she'd thought. It turned out that most of the people she'd killed had only been threats to the bank accounts of the ESO.

But it was still a far cry from mutilating babies for profit.

When young, Eva had suffered nightmares after watching an old werewolf movie. Over time, her mother had managed to convince her that monsters weren't real, but years later Eva had discovered that they did exist, and they were everywhere. They were the Stalins, the Hitlers, the Pol Pots . . . real people who used their power to bring death to millions. Those monsters were consigned to history, but many more of them walked the earth today. The only difference was that they didn't kill on such a massive scale.

People were murdered every day. More than a thousand daily, at conservative estimates, and while some were carried out in the name of jealousy or revenge, love or greed, many slayings simply satisfied evil desires. It was those people who Eva considered monsters: when given positions of power, they fed to their hearts' content.

No one with a conscience could run a facility like Camp 33. To help facilitate the slaughter of innocents, one had to be a true sociopath. She thought of cold-eyed Cheng, then of all the guards and medics, and everyone in the DPRK government who knew about the grisly deal with the Chinese. And that was only the tip of the iceberg. There were those on the Chinese side who knew where the organs were coming from. It could be a private enterprise, but it was more likely state-sanctioned.

Whatever the arrangement, it wouldn't matter to those interned in Kwanliso 33.

Her memory called up the small girl, sitting alone and holding the knitted doll. All alone in a den full of monsters, with no one to save her.

"We should go," Hong said, shattering the picture in Eva's mind.

He was right. She had to get to the rendezvous and hand Hong over to the ESO, then get out of China.

Eva took one last look at the route, then turned Hardy's phone off. She would buy another one on the way with the money she'd taken from the men she'd just killed.

Darkness would fall soon, which was a small blessing. The car would be harder to identify at night, though she didn't expect it to be reported stolen until the bodies were discovered, and she hoped that wouldn't be for another twenty-four hours at least.

"How long have you known about Camp 33?" Eva asked as they joined the highway.

"A year . . . maybe more."

She was about to ask why he hadn't done anything about it but stopped herself. It would be unfair to blame Hong for not acting. In the United States there would have been many ways to voice his concerns, but to do so in the DPRK would be a death sentence. To shut down the operation on his own would have been impossible, and even suggesting it to a colleague could have landed him in prison for the rest of his life.

"How did you find out about it?"

"I make it my business to know as much as I can. In my country, little has intrinsic value, but knowledge is priceless. The more you know—especially about others—the better your chance of living to an old age. It makes sense to know who is harboring thoughts against the regime, for example. Those are the people you either disassociate yourself with, or report to the State Security Department. Failure to do one or the other tends to prove fatal.

"As for Kwanliso 33, I found out about it by chance. During an inspection of our facility, a member of the SSD was talking to his colleague about the camp. They thought their conversation was private, but I overheard. One said the organs they sell to China are worth hundreds of millions of dollars each year, and it was a slap in the face of the useless Americans trying to crush our economy."

That kind of money meant a lot of organs. Eva didn't know how much a kidney went for on the black market, but she expected around ten grand a pop. Figure the same for the other body parts, and the math suggested a thousand organs for every ten million bucks. If they could get four or five organs per unwitting donor, it added up to a lot of dead bodies for someone else's profit.

Much like the ESO.

"Has anyone ever escaped from a prison camp before?"

"Lots of times," Hong said. "But they are always caught. The conditions make people weak. They never get far."

"What happens to the people running the prison?"

Hong looked puzzled. "I don't know. Why?"

"I was just wondering if they'd up the security."

The picture of the child with the doll had been hovering, and Eva knew what she had to do to banish it.

"That only matters if you plan to go back, and I don't think you are that foolish."

"Maybe I am," Eva said. "What are the alternatives? Forget about the place and move on with our lives, or report it to Amnesty International and hope they get an invitation to inspect the camp. Either way, people in Kwanliso 33 will keep dying."

"They'll die anyway. In that camp, another camp. Few people sentenced for crimes in my country are ever released."

"Not if I go back in and rescue them," Eva said.

Hong winced as he considered her words. "You'd be wasting your time, and almost surely your life. Even if you could do it, what would you achieve? A few hundred people would be free, some of them murderers and rapists. The prison would be restocked and the organ trade would continue. Unless you planned to do this on a weekly basis."

Hong had a point. Storming the prison and freeing the inmates would be a temporary setback for the organ-sellers, nothing more. A risky venture with little reward.

For the girl with the knitted toy, though, it would be everything. She'd done nothing to deserve a death sentence. None of the children had.

Although Eva had killed many over the years, none had come back to haunt her. She could see their faces if she thought hard about it, picture them in their final moments, but they never crashed her dreams or popped into her head while she was awake.

The little girl would. She was already beginning to consume Eva, and walking away now would leave the child stuck in her head forever.

By the time they reached a town two hours down the road, Eva had made up her mind. She pulled into a gas station and filled the tank, then drove to a department store to purchase a cheap cell phone. She considered sending Hong in, but his DPRK coat over prison-issue orange would have set off alarm bells.

It proved more difficult than she imagined. Having picked out a model that had the most basic screen and Internet access, she went to the counter and handed over a handful of yuan. The cashier scanned the barcode on the box, then asked Eva for her ID.

"I don't want to register it."

"You have to," the cashier told her. "It's the law."

"But I lost everything in a robbery. They took my wallet and passport. I need this to call my family and let them know what happened to me."

The cashier was unmoved. "Borrow a phone." Then he shrugged, the problem hers, not his.

Eva considered offering him a bribe, but thought better of it. If he took offense and made a scene, the police could become involved, and she didn't want to have to explain why she was wearing men's clothes.

She left the store, more than disappointed. But she desperately needed a new cell, and as with every city in the world, there would be a place to get one. She would simply have to drive around until she found one of the seedier parts of town.

On her way back to the car, she stopped at a pharmacy and bought some items to clean and treat Hong's wounds.

It took an hour of driving to find the place she was looking for. In an area where more stores were boarded up than open, she spotted one that specialized in electronics. She saw a few unboxed phones in the window, and the prices looked reasonable. Before going in, Eva went to a store three doors down and bought a pair of women's slacks and a sweater. She would have liked to have bought a heavy coat, too, but she had to preserve what little money she had. The important thing was getting out of the dead man's clothes.

Eva went back to the electronics store, and a few minutes later she emerged with two new burners that cost the list price plus an extra twenty for anonymity.

Eva got back in the car and told Hong to change into the men's clothing she'd discarded while she set one of the phones up ready to use. She entered Johnson's number, then hesitated, her thumb over the Call button. If she were going to follow through with the plan she'd been working on for the last few hours, she would require the ESO's help, but it was the last thing she wanted to ask for. The idea of being indebted to them made her skin crawl. But since she had no contacts in the region, she would need more than her own skills to pull this off.

Eva sighed and hit the Call button.

CHAPTER 17

"You're booked in the Shangri-La," Johnson said as soon as Eva identified herself. "What time will you be there?"

"About four hours," Eva said. She could be there in three, but planned on a short stopover on the way.

"Good. What condition is the package in?"

"It's fine. I need some help. Resources, logistics."

"Why? Is there a problem?"

"No," Eva said. "I'm going back in. They were holding me in a place where the inmates are killed for their organs. I'm going to shut it down."

"Denied. Take the package to the hotel. There'll be someone waiting. He'll recognize you and mention Melbourne. Hand off the package to him and wait in your room for further instructions."

Eva had expected resistance, but Johnson was only a cutout, a way to share her progress with the ESO. The only thing she could do was get him to speak to his superiors. "If you want the package, you'll do as I say. Pass on my request to the organ grinder: I'm done talking to his monkey. I'll call back in two hours. If they don't agree, the package will be destroyed."

Eva ended the call.

"What do you mean when you say the package will be destroyed?" Hong asked. "I know you were talking about me."

"I was calling his bluff," Eva told him. "I need them to help me, and you're the only leverage I've got. Don't worry, I'll hand you over to them."

But not necessarily today.

~

Vincent May clicked off the conference call and looked around the room. As the head of the ESO, he sat at the head of the table; three other members of the group were in attendance.

"What do you think?" Ben Scott asked. As the ESO's chief of foreign policy, he'd brought Hong's desire to defect to the ESO's attention in the first place—and argued strenuously in favor of it.

The United States government, however, had seen the plan as too risky at a time when relations with the DPRK were improving. Pyongyang seemed willing to come to the table and discuss denuclearization in return for the lifting of sanctions and US investment in the country.

Scott was not alone in his willingness to risk disturbing the recent rapprochement. Larry Carter, the military–industrial complex's representative on the board, favored keeping the rival countries at odds. The corporations that built the weapons of war demanded conflict at any cost; little profit ever came from peace.

"I think she's crazy to want to go back in, is what I think," Scott scoffed.

"She's anything but crazy," May said. "That's why we chose her."

"What I'd like to know is how she escaped," finance guru James Butler said.

They had been informed that Pyongyang had reported capturing a female American spy a couple of days earlier, and since Driscoll had missed the rendezvous at the coast, it hadn't been a big leap to work out what had happened.

"That's irrelevant," May said. He turned to Scott. "If Pyongyang is selling organs, it would be to the Chinese. Could one of our people be behind it?"

"Could be. We've got a couple hundred spread throughout Asia, about thirty of them in China. I'll look into it."

"If it is one of ours, we can't possibly help her."

May looked at Butler in his five-thousand-dollar suit. He was all about money, bigger picture be damned. "If she does strike, I'm sure it'll only be a temporary setback. We need to think how we can turn this to our advantage."

"You have an idea?" Scott asked.

"Perhaps. James, what market share did renewable energy gain in the last five years?"

"Around 73 percent," the finance man said. "Projected to be 780 billion this year, up from about 450 billion in 2014."

The ESO had made a great deal from solar and wind energy, but it was still a pittance compared to income from fossil fuels. The businesses they controlled had invested heavily in carbon-reaping infrastructure and exploration; to cut loose in favor of wind and solar power would hit the bank balance hard. Of course, they would eventually wind down investment in coal, oil, and gas, but fossil fuels would remain the ESO's bread and butter for decades to come. In the meantime, renewables were gaining ground, and May would do anything he could do to maintain the gap.

One of the biggest threats to their carbon-fuel business came from Chin Long Cheung. He owned the largest green-energy corporation in the world, and—guided by his personal vision—it was growing at an uncomfortable rate, at least as far as the ESO was concerned. He wasn't exactly a threat to the ESO's empire, but he qualified as a major thorn in their side.

"Ben, build a dossier on Chin Long Cheung. I want a list of every business interest, particularly anything medical. If he hasn't got any, invent one, and make it realistic."

"What do you have in mind?"

"If I know anything about this woman, she won't be happy just hitting the facility. Let's give her the man behind it."

"I see where you're going," Larry Carter said. "Let her believe Cheung is the man buying the organs and she'll take him out for us. Nice idea, but we have another opportunity here. Why not just let Driscoll hand Hong to our man, promise to help her in her mission, then pull the rug out from under her? Let the DPRK know what her intentions are and they can arrange a welcoming committee."

"I know you want her out of the picture," May said. "You've made that clear. However, there will be other opportunities. Right now, she's the perfect choice to rid us of Cheung. When Driscoll calls back, tell her she can have what she needs."

"Everything?" Scott asked. "What if she wants troops?"

"If we had access to troops in the first place, we wouldn't have needed Driscoll. No, she'll have to find her own people. Whatever else she needs, make sure she gets it. And if she makes it out again, give her Cheung's file."

~

Eva parked near a shopping mall and told Hong to wait in the car. She walked inside the building, where it took ten minutes to find what she was looking for. Back at the car, she called Johnson once more.

"What did they say?" she asked when he picked up.

"They agreed to help you."

"Good. When I meet your man I'll have a list of items," she said. "I'll need everything in two days."

"I'll pass that on," Johnson said. "What's your ETA?"

"Two hours."

Eva clicked off. Despite what she'd just heard, she didn't trust the ESO to stick to their word. If they planned to renege, they would have a reception committee at the hotel, ready to snatch Hong from her. She wasn't about to let that happen.

Eva took the gun she'd taken from the dead Chinese man out of her pocket and removed the magazine. She inspected it and slid it back in place.

"Check the weapon I gave you," she told Hong.

The moment he took it from his pocket, Eva snatched it from his grasp and pointed it at his head.

"Sorry to have to do this, but I don't trust the people who sent me to help you."

Hong looked from the weapon to Eva and back again, and she could see he was weighing his options.

"Don't even think about it," she said. "You have no idea what I'm capable of. Sit on your hands."

Hong did as he was told. "Are you going to kill me?"

Eva didn't see fear in his eyes. A hint of sorrow, perhaps, but he didn't have the look of a man afraid to die.

"No."

That seemed to relax him a little.

"I need to go in and see them on my own. If you come with me, I don't think they'll honor the deal."

"What do you want me to do?"

"Tell me that I can trust you," Eva said.

"You can. I owe you my life."

Eva considered herself a good reader of people, and didn't detect any deceit in Hong. In a plastic bag she had duct tape that she'd bought in a hardware store, ready to truss him up. Her plan had been to put him in the trunk and dump the car in a remote location until she'd completed her mission, but if Hong was willing to play along, that wouldn't be necessary.

Eva spun the gun around and handed it back to Hong. "Here's what I want you to do. I'll rent you an apartment, and I want you to stay there for seven days."

"Then what?"

"That's it. I'll leave you the other phone, and when the week is up, you can call my contact and he'll pick you up."

Hong looked slightly surprised, but he nodded and put the gun back in his coat pocket.

"Remember, one week," Eva said. "I'm going to install software on your phone that will alert me if you use it before then. If you use another phone to contact the US authorities, or you leave the apartment early, I could be left stranded. You know what that means."

"I understand. I won't do anything to risk your life."

Eva believed him.

She readied the second phone and navigated to the website created by her friend Farooq Naser. When the page loaded, she entered her password and waited for the software to automatically install. A minute later, the Shield app appeared on the home screen.

Shield was Farooq's brainchild—a messaging service that used encryption even the US government couldn't come close to breaking. Eva used it whenever she wanted to communicate with friends and associates from her past. Like her, Farooq, Sonny Baines, Rees Colback, and Tom Gray had tried to disappear from the ESO's radar, but now that she was compromised, she knew the others would be, too. At least with Shield, the ESO wouldn't know about her immediate plans.

For a fleeting moment she wondered if perhaps she was the only one they'd tracked down, meaning her friends were safe. She dumped the thought into her 'Unlikely' folder. She'd spent ten years in the CIA honing her skills, so if she could be traced, the others would be in their sights, too.

Need you to find me a place to stay in Shenyang, China. Seven days, checking in within the hour, preferably with food available in the building. Must be prepaid and no ID required. The guest will be one male. I'll explain later.

Eva sent the message to Farooq.

"Why did you agree to come to my country if you don't trust the people you work for?" Hong asked.

"It's complicated." It wasn't, but Eva didn't have the time or inclination to explain her relationship with the ESO.

Her phone chimed, and she saw that Farooq had replied.

You scared the shit out of me! When I saw a message from you I thought you were going to say they'd found me again! I'll book a place now and get back to you.

Eva could have replied to say that he was right, that the ESO probably did know where he was, but there was little point. Farooq was a genius when it came to ones and zeros, but when it came to tradecraft, he was as helpless as a toddler in a bullfight. No need to alarm him unnecessarily.

When Farooq replied, he had good news. He'd found an apartment close to the river. While it didn't have room service, there was a restaurant on the first floor, meaning Hong would never have to leave the building. Farooq had paid for the week and put a thousand dollars on deposit to pay his restaurant bills.

Eva entered the address into the map application on the phone and it plotted a route. All that remained was to ditch the other phone—the one she'd used to call Johnson. She didn't want him tracking her to the apartment, and he would most certainly have a trace running on the cell.

She uninstalled the Shield app and, after entering Johnson's number into the contacts, gave the phone to Hong. She put the other cell on silent and turned the vibration off, then left the vehicle and walked back into the mall. She purchased a bag of prawn-flavored chips from a store and started eating them as she walked around, gazing in shop windows. When the bag was half empty, Eva slipped the phone inside and dropped the bag in the trash.

Back at the car, she once again reminded Hong that when he got to the apartment he was not to venture out of the building.

"People will be looking for you, so stay in your room and only eat in the restaurant on the first floor."

"I will. And . . . thank you. Not for saving me, but for what you are about to do. Not many people would risk so much to save strangers. It is a truly selfless act."

Eva didn't share his sentiments. While she wanted to save the prisoners from their awful fate, her overriding aim was to ensure the girl with the rag doll didn't drive her crazy.

Eva had been trained to remain detached, with each life taken seen as nothing more than a task completed. Whether her lack of empathy for her victims was a natural trait or something the CIA had pounded into her, it was hard to tell. Up until recently she'd had no issues, but now she saw a worrying pattern developing. First Sally Holman in Melbourne; now an unknown child. They needed her help, and she couldn't refuse.

Perhaps it stemmed from her inability to take on the ESO. She was one person up against an immense, unseen foe. She'd done it before and taken down the top people, but the organization had morphed into something new. Henry Langton had been arrogant, so sure of his own invincibility that it had led to his downfall. The new ESO wouldn't make narcissistic mistakes, and fighting them would be like shooting at fog. Was she making up for this impotence by helping innocent victims?

She'd read a biography a year earlier, and one quote had stood out:

Real living is living for others.

Perhaps Bruce Lee's words had penetrated deeper than she'd first imagined.

One day, she would visit a shrink and maybe her questions would be answered, but for now, she had work to do.

They reached Shenyang forty minutes later, and the app on her phone guided Eva to the apartment building.

"If they ask for ID, tell them you were just robbed and you're waiting for relatives to bring you cash and the embassy to issue a new passport. It shouldn't be an issue, but if they refuse to let you in, come back out and we'll make other arrangements. The room's prepaid and there's a thousand dollars in credit for the restaurant, so eat well. And remember—"

He nodded patiently. "Don't leave the room or call anyone. Don't worry, I want you to succeed."

Eva wished him luck, and Hong got out. She waited for ten minutes, by which time she was sure he'd been granted access to the apartment, then set off for the Shangri-La.

CHAPTER 18

Eva drove slowly past the entrance to the Shangri-La hotel, a thirty-story slab of glass-fronted luxury. She saw a few people lingering near the well-lit entrance, but they didn't seem the snatch-squad type. Perhaps whoever was waiting for her was in the lobby, or even the hotel room that had been booked for her.

She drove on for a couple of blocks until she came to a parking lot, where she wiped the car of fingerprints and got out. She'd considered abandoning it, but the men she'd killed in Ji'an would be found one day, and the search for the car would begin. She couldn't possibly remove all traces of herself from the vehicle and she didn't want it leading back to her. At least, not until she'd left the country. Better to have the ESO get rid of it once and for all.

She locked the car and pocketed the keys, then walked back to the hotel, wishing she'd splurged on a warm coat when she'd had the chance. The sidewalk was clear of snow, but it was still bitterly cold, the kind that seeps into the bones. Despite the freezing temperature, she stopped at each shop to check the opening times. Many of them stayed open until ten in the evening, which gave her about an hour to get what she wanted.

As she approached the entrance to the Shangri-La, she saw no one taking an interest in her, so she walked through the front doors and into sheer opulence.

The lobby was impressive in terms of both size and style. Eva's heavy boots squeaked on the highly polished stone floor, and she felt self-conscious in her twenty-dollar outfit.

A Chinese national wearing a tailored suit approached her, and she prepared to explain that she was meeting someone, but he simply put out his hand and said, "Welcome, Miss Driscoll. I'm Wong. Sorry the weather isn't as pleasant as Melbourne, but hopefully your stay here will be a memorable one."

He sounded like he'd spent his entire life in the United States. She shook his hand, and Wong looked past her toward the entrance.

"Where is your companion?"

"Safe. You'll see him once I've completed my mission."

Wong's friendly expression slipped off his face. "That wasn't the deal."

"It is now." She stepped closer and lowered her voice. "I don't plan to go back into North Korea knowing you can pull the plug any time you feel like it. Hong's got enough water to last a couple of days—three, tops. When that runs out, he's got about three to four days before his blood pressure drops so low it'll kill him, and the data he's carrying in his head will be gone. I suggest we get moving."

Driscoll had questioned Hong on the journey north, and he'd assured her that he had the information the ESO required committed to memory.

"My superiors won't like this," said Wong.

"I don't care. My only concern is getting out alive. That means we do this on my terms. I suggest you call them now and let them know how things stand."

Wong took out his phone, but Eva stopped him.

"I need a new cell," she said.

"I'll get you one."

"So that you can install software on it to listen to my calls? I don't think so. Give me three thousand yuan and I'll get my own."

Wong looked even more pissed, but Eva had all the leverage, unless he thought he could waterboard her in the hotel lobby. He dug in the inside pocket of his suit jacket and pulled out a thick wad of notes. He counted off a few bills and handed them over.

"Call your boss," she said, and tossed him the keys to the stolen car. "Tell him to get rid of the vehicle. It's a blue Dongfeng in a parking lot two blocks east of here. I'll be back in fifteen minutes."

Eva left the hotel and walked through the shopping district. She entered the first clothing store she came across and bought the thickest jacket she could find, then strolled the streets until she came to a phone store. She knew now that without ID she couldn't buy one herself, but there were ways around that. She went inside and identified the model she wanted, then left the store and waited for a suitable patsy to come along.

He was in his fifties, and dressed like he was in dire need of a cash injection. Eva placed herself in front of him, and he stopped in his tracks.

"Want to make a quick hundred dollars US?" she asked.

The man's eyes lit up at the prospect. "What do I have to do?"

"You got your ID on you?"

The man nodded.

"Go in there, buy me a Huawei P10, and register it in your name."

Eva handed the man 2,500 yuan. He took it eagerly and went into the store.

She checked the streets to see if anyone was watching the transaction, but she saw no one who looked even slightly curious. If someone picked the man off the street and got his name, they could easily go into the store and get the number of the phone he'd purchased, and Eva couldn't have anyone knowing that information.

He came out after around ten minutes and gave her a bag containing the new cell. Eva unboxed it to check everything was there before giving him his reward.

She hung around as the man walked off, watching in case anyone tailed him, but she appeared to have gotten away with it. She turned on the data and navigated to Farooq's website. She downloaded Shield once more, then went back to the hotel, where Wong was sitting in the lobby, nursing a coffee.

"What did they say?" she asked him.

"They were disappointed by your lack of faith. However, the deal stands. They will provide everything you need, except personnel. You must find your own people to do this. They can't have anything leading back to them."

That was a manageable problem. She didn't need a huge attack force, only a couple of men she could trust.

Two names came to mind.

"They also added that what you're planning isn't going to solve the problem."

"I know," Eva said. "This is just the start. While I'm gone, I want you to find out who's buying the organs."

"I'll pass that along."

A couple sat down at the next table, but Eva needed to speak with Wong in private.

"Let's go upstairs," Eva said. "I'd rather not talk here."

She walked to the bank of elevators and Wong fell into step. On the eighteenth floor, they walked down the hallway to her room.

Whatever her misgivings about the ESO, they knew how to live.

The suite was huge. It looked like one of those multimillion-dollar pads that overlooked Central Park in New York.

Good thing I'm not footing the bill.

She hung up her coat, then picked up a writing pad and pen from the desk, and took a seat at an oak table. Wong joined her, and she pushed the pad across to him.

"I'm going to need weapons, ammunition, clothing, night-vision gear, a way across the river for three people, and a way back for three hundred. We'll need transportation for all of them once we reach China, something stocked with enough food and water to take them to Mongolia, where you'll have a plane ready to fly them to South Korea."

Wong jotted it all down. "Anything else?"

"Not right now. I'm going to take a quick walk outside. Call that in and let me know what weapons you can get hold of. I want the best."

Eva put on her coat, took the hotel room's key card, and left. She rode the elevator down to the lobby and walked out into the freezing cold. She guessed the room had been bugged for all outgoing communications, and even though Farooq insisted Shield was the most secure messaging application on the planet, she didn't want to make it easy for the ESO or China.

She typed a message and sent it to two recipients.

CHAPTER 19

"We're almost out of Hop Zombie," the bartender said as she placed the cash drawer on the table.

"I'll order a new shipment, first thing." Simon "Sonny" Baines popped the cap on his second bottle of lager of the night, then made a note on a pad underneath a list of items the kitchen was running short of.

He checked the printout from the register. A decent night's take, but Sonny wasn't in it for the money. He had squirreled away plenty to keep him comfortable for the rest of his life, but he wasn't the type to sit idle.

The restaurant was his way of keeping busy, and it also gave him a chance to show off his culinary skills, something he'd been working on for a couple of years. Ever since the death of his best friend Len Smart, Sonny had been a changed man. He'd been tempted at first to seek solace in the bottle—and for a few days after the funeral, he had—but he'd awakened one morning knowing it wasn't the long-term solution. That same day, he'd packed his few possessions in a bag and booked a ticket to New Zealand.

The first few weeks had been spent exploring the beautiful country, and the decision to stay had been an easy one. The application for a resident visa was straightforward, mainly thanks to his bank balance. A small portion of his holdings, exchanged into six million New Zealand dollars, had been more than enough to satisfy the authorities.

The day the paperwork was completed, Sonny put a deposit down on a restaurant that was up for sale. He renamed it the Wayward Lamb, spent a small fortune refurbishing it, and a month later was in business.

His head chef Franco had suggested a soft opening, inviting local bigwigs to a free meal. It had been a fantastic idea. Newspaper editors and radio show producers were among those asked to attend, and the evening had gone better than Sonny could have hoped, the meals cooked to perfection and served on time. Every guest left only positive comments.

That had been eighteen months ago, and his staff had grown from five to nine. Sonny had started off behind the burners, creating the dishes and working with Franco to perfect them, but these days he let his head chef run the show. The three-man team working their magic behind the scenes had everything under control in the kitchen, while, out front, Sonny waited tables and ensured the guests had the best possible experience.

A day still didn't go by, though, without Sonny thinking about Len, Tom Gray, and the life he'd left behind.

At his core, Sonny was a soldier. Always had been, always would be. His newfound love of running a restaurant would never, even on the busiest night, be a substitute for the intensity of battle. Sure, it got hot in the kitchen sometimes, but not five-men-taking-on-the-Russian-army hot.

He missed the camaraderie, the rush of the firefight, and the smell of the aftermath that told him he'd made it through another battle alive. He still made a twice-per-week pilgrimage to the local shooting club, where he could practice with pistols and semi-automatic rifles up to a range of three hundred yards. While it made for decent reps, it felt far from thrilling.

The most excitement he got these days was wondering if the cheese soufflé would rise.

The last two members of staff said goodnight, and Sonny locked the door behind them. He considered having another beer for the road, but it was already past one in the morning, and he had to be up early to order the food for the lunchtime sitting. The crab-stuffed zucchini flower was selling better than he'd imagined, and the hake dish had become particularly popular.

Sonny put the nights' takings in the safe. On his way to the exit, he stopped at one of the full-length mirrors and checked his profile. In recent weeks he'd been neglecting his exercise and eating too much of his own product. That would have to change. He was carrying at least an inch more than normal around the waist, and if left unchallenged it would become three or four. A solid month of morning runs and the pool three times a week would sort that out. His new paunch apart, he still didn't look bad for a man in his early forties.

Sonny flicked a couple of short blond hairs back into place, then locked up and walked to his car. After six months of renting, never sure if he'd have to abandon his new home and go on the run again, he'd finally felt comfortable enough to purchase a vehicle outright. He climbed into the Range Rover and set off for home.

His place was a rental on the outskirts of Auckland. The house boasted two bedrooms, one of which Sonny used as an office, but he'd chosen the space mainly for its expansive kitchen. This was where he spent his one day off a week, trying to conjure up something new to add to the menu.

Sonny parked in the driveway and walked up to the front door, but before he could turn the knob, his phone beeped. At this time of night, he expected it to be one of the staff calling about something they'd forgotten to mention before closing.

He wasn't prepared for the Shield notification.

The blood seemed to pump through his veins at double speed, just as it always had seconds before a firefight. It had to be bad news. None of the people with access to the app would use it for a friendly chat.

Sonny unlocked the home screen, clicked on the notification, and read the message.

It wasn't the warning to run that he'd been dreading, which was a relief. After all the time, money, and effort he'd put into getting the Wayward Lamb up and running—not to mention successful—it would have pained him to abandon it.

To hand it over for a few days while he played Action Man was an entirely different matter; one that put a huge smile on his face.

Eva Driscoll's message didn't offer many details.

Need you for a private mission. Three of us against 50+ in hostile territory. Access to any equipment you want. You in?

Hostile territory could be one of a hundred places on the planet, but Sonny didn't care. It could have been a direct assault on the Kremlin and he would have signed up.

He crafted a short reply.

I'm in. Where do we meet?

There really wasn't much to consider. Clearly, the operation would be difficult. Sonny didn't care. Two years earlier, he'd seen his best friend gunned down in battle, and that was the way Sonny wanted to go. Not in his sleep in a dreary retirement home, or spending his last days being taken for walks in a wheelchair. If Sonny was going to his grave, it would be with an automatic rifle in his hands and a big, shit-eating grin on his face.

He unlocked the door and went inside his apartment. The first thing he did was inform Franco that he had the run of the place for the next two weeks at least, and that he should come to Sonny's place in exactly fourteen days for a catch-up on events.

Eva got back to him soon after. She asked how long it would take to get to Shenyang, China. After looking up flights, he responded.

28 hours, give or take.

That gave him time to clear immigration in China and get to any rendezvous Eva had in mind.

Her reply came almost instantly.

Meet me at the Shangri-La Hotel, room 1803.

Still no mention of the target, but Sonny didn't care. In a week he would either be back in the kitchen, preparing herb-crusted lamb with pea and mint puree, or lying dead, riddled with bullet holes or shrapnel. If it was to be the latter, it didn't much matter where he fell.

Sonny booked his flight, then packed a bag with enough clothes for five days. On top of his underwear he put an item that had been left to him by Len Smart.

With eight hours until his flight, he had one last beer while he wrote a letter leaving his car and the restaurant to Franco in the event of his death, and the contents of his bank accounts to the SAS Regimental Association in the UK.

That done, he set the alarm for 6 a.m. and got his head down.

~

Rees Colback was in the middle of a surreal dream when the notification from his phone woke him with a start. He'd set the notification tone of Shield to a blaring *awooga, awooga* siren to ensure it got his attention, and it worked. His hand shot sideways to grab the phone, and that was when he remembered where he was.

"You have to turn your phone down," the nurse whispered harshly as she appeared at his bedside. "Some of the other patients are sleeping."

"Sorry," Rees said. "I thought I'd put it on silent."

He had indeed, but the Shield notification was set to override such settings.

Rees waited with his hand out, and the nurse reluctantly handed him the phone from the nightstand next to his bed.

"Try to think of the others," she warned him.

Rees watched her return to her station, then concentrated on the phone. His hands were already sweating, and the pain in his leg was the worst it had been since the crash.

It had been a moment of sheer stupidity that had left him in a hospital bed for the last four days. Stupidity on behalf of the driver of the other vehicle, that is. The jackass had gotten behind the wheel after drinking eight bottles of beer, and pulled out of the parking lot just as Rees was passing. The resulting collision at thirty miles an hour left both of them in hospital—Rees with a shattered leg and the other driver with broken ribs and a punctured lung.

As far as Rees was concerned, she'd been lucky. Injury-wise, at least. A nurse had told him that the police had been with her when she arrived, and once she'd been stabilized, they'd charged her with reckless driving, causing bodily harm, and DUI, offenses that could see her put behind bars for a few years.

Knowing that he faced further operations to remove the metal pins, followed by months of rehabilitation, her punishment gave Rees little comfort.

He took a deep breath. If this message was Eva telling him the ESO had found him and that he should run, he was in deep shit. There was no way he could leave the hospital, never mind Canada.

His pulse quickened by the second, his heart hammering in his chest.

Unable to bear it any longer, Rees swiped his phone open and clicked on Shield.

Need you for a private mission. Three of us against 50+ in hostile territory. Access to any equipment you want. You in?

All heads in the room turned to him as he burst out laughing. It began as a chuckle at the absurdly poor timing of the request, but as relief swept over him, he found the whole situation hysterical. He didn't know if it was the painkillers in his system or the sheer exhilaration of knowing he wouldn't die that day, but he laughed like he'd never laughed before. The nurse came back in a huff, admonishing him for disturbing the others on the ward, and Rees eventually reined himself in.

Still giggling to himself, he composed a response.

Broke my leg earlier this week, out of action for a year.

He hit Send and, as he did, the humor of the moment vanished, too.

Eva had saved his life, and now she was going to risk hers on some kind of mission that defied sanity. It must have been something close to her heart to make her take on such overwhelming odds. Part of him wished he could be there to repay her.

He opened the app again and typed an addendum.

Best of luck. Stay safe. Let me know when it's over.

CHAPTER 20

It was Sonny's first visit to China, and the most populous country in the world lived up to his expectations. He'd spent time in Hong Kong when it was still a British colony, and Shenyang felt much the same—the streets teeming with people, and traffic a noisy constant. He'd expected a few more authentic Chinese-style buildings, but instead the city bristled with modern creations. On his way from the airport, he saw more skyscrapers than he could count.

Among them was the Shangri-La Hotel.

Sonny was stunned by the opulence as he strolled through the entrance. He'd seen places like this in Dubai and New York but hadn't imagined such things existed in China's lesser cities. He felt as if cash were draining from his pocket with every step he took.

As he walked toward the reception desk, he heard a familiar voice from the left.

"Sonny!"

Eva hadn't changed a bit. Well, the hair was different, but he'd seen her with three styles and colors since their first meeting more than two years ago. That apart, she looked exactly as he remembered.

Stunning.

For Sonny, though, looks were not the most memorable thing about Eva Driscoll. She possessed skills that many Special Forces soldiers would be proud of. More importantly, Sonny had always felt that her heart was in the right place. She would take on anyone to see justice done and the helpless protected, which reminded him of his dear friends Len Smart and Tom Gray. Both had proven time and again that loyalty was paramount. Eva Driscoll was cast from the same mold.

He walked over and offered a smile and his hand. To his surprise, she pulled him in close and hugged him.

"Thanks for coming," she said.

"Wouldn't miss it for the world." He eased himself off her. "So, which government do you need help overthrowing?"

"Nothing like that," Eva said as she led him to the elevators. "I'll tell you when we get to the room."

They rode to the eighteenth floor and walked down the corridor. When they reached 1803, Sonny stopped but Eva kept walking.

"We're going to meet the man who's organizing everything for us. There's still a lot of planning to do."

She knocked on the next door, and a youngish, Chinese-looking man opened it, beckoning them in.

"This is Wong," Eva said. "Wong, Sonny."

The men shook hands. "The restaurant is doing well, I hope," said Wong.

Sonny was caught by surprise. "How—"

"He's ESO," Eva said, taking a seat. "If you ever wondered if they knew where you were, there's your answer."

Sonny was stunned. He thought he'd shaken the ESO for good, but the last eighteen months had evidently been a sham. If they knew about his business, they probably had his home address and the ID he used in New Zealand, too.

More concerning, Eva seemed strangely relaxed in the ESO man's presence.

"You're working for these people?"

Eva shrugged. "It's complicated."

"Try me."

She sighed. "They blackmailed me into doing a job for them. I had to go into North Korea and help someone defect. I did that, and now I want to go back in to save some others. The ESO's agreed to help me."

"Just like that? You asked and they said yes?"

"Not quite," Eva said. "I hid their defector. He's got about five days before he dies from lack of water. Two can play the blackmail game."

Way ahead of the curve, as always.

"I'm guessing that five days is our maximum operating window," he said. "What's the mission?"

"We're going to raid a North Korean prison near the border and free the inmates. The facility's being used to harvest organs for sale here in China, and we're going to close it down. In the meantime, Wong's going to work on finding out who the organs are being sold to."

"And we take them down, too?" Sonny asked.

"Exactly."

"Okay . . . but excuse me if I'm not immediately sold on the idea. How good is the intel on the prison?"

"I was there," Eva said. "I've seen it for myself. Hong—the defector—and I were captured the day we were supposed to sneak out of the country. We were taken to a jail and given a medical, then transferred to this camp near Manpo. I was only there for a couple of days, but I saw enough. I'm guessing the prison holds about two hundred, but at least twenty are children."

"They're killing kids for their organs?"

"I'm afraid so."

Sonny didn't have children of his own, and he never would. In the past, he'd been too absorbed in his work to consider settling down and having a family. That, and his propensity for playing the field. The future held no better prospects for him. The ESO threat would be hanging over him for the rest of his life, and to father a child now would be reckless and selfish.

That didn't mean he would stand back and do nothing when children were in danger, however.

"Like I said, count me in."

It brought a smile to Eva's face. "I knew you'd say that."

Sonny wondered if she was looking at him that way simply because of the decision he'd made, or if there was something more to it. Did she see him now the same way he regarded her?

It had been a couple of years since her lover Carl Huff had died. He'd been killed alongside Len Smart, both taken by the same RPG round. Had Eva gotten over him? Was she ready to move on? Could she be seeing Sonny as more than a hired gun? Was—

"It's just me and you," Eva said, snapping Sonny out of his daze. "I tried to get Rees but he's incapacitated. Our other mutual friend is not contactable."

Nor would he ever be, Sonny knew. Tom Gray had been deadly serious when he'd said he wanted to disappear for good. He hadn't given even Sonny, his friend of twenty years, a forwarding address or contact information. Protecting his young daughter had become his sole goal in whatever life remained ahead.

"I'm still happy to go in if you are," Sonny said. "Shall we get started?"

Eva picked up a manila envelope and removed the contents. The top sheets were satellite photographs of the camp.

"These were taken this morning," she said.

Sonny looked at the first and found it much more detailed than he'd expected. Most satellite pictures shown on the news channels and websites were wide-angle shots, covering an area a couple of miles across, but this one showed the footsteps in the snow made by an armed guard and his canine companion.

"You said we'd be facing fifty-plus. Do we have a more accurate figure now?"

"I'm afraid not," Eva said. "That was based on the enemy strength when I was there. They could have doubled or tripled the numbers by now."

"Or they might assume that, as no other inmates have your skillset, there's no need to bump up security," Wong suggested.

Eva made it clear that she didn't think much of his input. "Either way, we assume a hundred and take it from there." She looked through the photos until she found one with markings on it. "Hong and I used this path to get out," she said. "It's a steep climb and won't be easy for a lot of the prisoners. Not all of them will be fit enough for a long hike, and as I mentioned before, we'll have children among them. We have to find a route that gets us to the border quickly, but that's accessible for everyone."

"That would have to be along this valley," Sonny said, drawing a line with his finger. "What's the planned insertion and exfil point?"

"Neither are confirmed. I was waiting for you."

"Okay. Then how about we follow the valley north, sticking to this stream. When we get to the road, we head west along this mud flat and cross at this island."

"I had the same idea," Eva said. "Good to see we're on the same page."

"Great minds and all that. Thing is, how do we get two hundred civilians across?"

"Hong and I crossed about a mile downriver. It was frozen, but the ice is thin at the halfway point. I fell through, but the water was only about eight feet deep and not fast-flowing."

"Still too risky for kids and the elderly," Sonny mused. "A boat is out of the question, too."

"I was considering a pulley system," Eva said. "We sink a pole on this bank, on the Chinese side, hidden among the trees. We make our way over the top of the ice pulling an inflatable, towing a rope behind us, and at the far bank we leave another pole. We can hide the end of the rope until we need it."

"You mean once we've got all the prisoners back to this point, we sink the other pole, get them to hang on to the rope, and we pull them across?"

"Exactly. Just like on an old-fashioned laundry line. We could attach a strap to the rope every six feet, something they can put their wrists through. That way, they walk across the ice, and if anyone falls through, we just pull them out."

"I like it," Sonny said. He turned to Wong. "Any chance we could get a fleet of helicopters to land on the Korean side and pick everyone up?"

"Out of the question."

Sonny turned back to Eva. "Then we go with your plan. Make sure the cord is white so it doesn't show up on the ice. It'll be there for a couple of days, I'm guessing."

"Correct. I want to check out the security measures they've put in place since I left. Wong, please start getting together what we need for the crossing. We'll also need at least ten buses to take the prisoners inland once we reach the Chinese side. Make sure they're stocked with food and water and have toilet facilities for a long journey, because I want them all taken to Ulaanbaatar. They won't be safe in China, but from Mongolia they can fly to Seoul. It's about a thousand miles as the crow flies, so probably about fifteen hundred by road."

Wong noted it all down on his pad, then took out his phone.

"And just so you know, you won't be getting Hong back until I get confirmation that they've reached Ulaanbaatar. If you decide to hand them over to the Chinese or ditch them by the roadside, the deal's off and Hong dies."

The ESO man wasn't pleased with Eva's ultimatum, but Sonny liked her style. Once again, she had all the angles covered.

While Wong made his call, Eva and Sonny discussed the hardware they would take with them.

"Before we go in, we'll have to neutralize the perimeter guards," Eva said. "They had dogs last time, so we'll assume that hasn't changed."

"So I saw . . . Suppressed sniper rifle?" Sonny suggested. "It would have to use subsonic rounds, though, which means I'd need to be within two hundred yards of the target."

"That'll do for the guards, but the dogs are another story. Shoot the dog, the guard will know we're there. Shoot the guard first, the dog might get loose and that would raise the alarm."

"We could drug the dogs. Something slow-acting—say, twelve hours before it takes effect. The dogs fall ill between shifts and the guards have to do their rounds alone."

"I like it," said Eva. "Put a hunting catapult on the list, along with a couple of pounds of raw steak and the sedative. Any particular sniper rifle?"

"A VSS Vintorez, if they can find one. It's got a built-in suppressor and fires 9x39mm cartridges. Twice the weight of a normal nine-mil, but subsonic and great stopping power. Spetsnaz use them. Failing that, anything by Accuracy International. The L115A3, maybe." Sonny scribbled the names down for Wong. "I'm also adding night-vision glasses, suppressed Sig Sauer P226s, knives, and grenades—smoke, fragmentation, and stun. What's your preferred automatic rifle? I'm going for the Colt Canada L119—the C8 CQB with the ten-inch barrel."

"I'll have the same," Eva said. "And add M203s."

"They won't fit on the CQB; the barrel's too short. Let's get us both a C8 SFW with the sixteen-inch barrel for the initial assault, and we can switch to the ten-inch CQBs when we get inside.

"Now, clothing . . . Arctic ghillie suits, obviously. We're gonna be lying in the snow for a couple of days, so I'll put down waterproofs, insulated boots and gloves, hats, and thermal underwear."

They spent the next fifteen minutes adding items to the ever-growing list, including comms units, dry rations, chocolate bars, and bags to crap into. They were only limited by what they could carry to the observation post, so Sonny was generous with the ammunition. He specified two twenty-round magazines for the sniper rifle, twelve thirty-round mags each for the C8s, and two dozen grenades for room-clearing.

"Can we get our hands on anything heavier?" Sonny asked Wong, who had finished his phone conversation.

"Such as?"

"An RPG-7 with four grenades, plus a shitload of C-4 and detonators. With timers, if possible."

"What do we need that for?" asked Eva.

"Breaching the building," Sonny said. "I'd rather not knock and wait for an answer. Also, I'm guessing you don't want them to be back in business any time soon, so we'll need enough C-4 to level the place."

"The explosives won't be a problem, but you'd be better off with the Chinese PF-89," Wong said. "It's disposable, but each unit weighs the same as an RPG-7 round. Easier to get hold of at short notice, too."

"Fine," said Eva. "We'll take two each."

"Looks like we have our shopping list," Sonny said. "When do we move out?"

"I'll need twenty hours to get everything on your list," Wong said. He looked at his watch and saw that it was almost midnight. "I'll have it all delivered to the crossing point this time tomorrow."

"Great." Sonny smiled and rubbed his hands together. "What's the beer like in this town?"

CHAPTER 21

It was countryside almost all the way to the border. From the moment they left Shenyang, the green hills seemed to envelop them, the tranquil scenery providing precisely the distraction that Eva and Sonny needed.

The previous evening hadn't gone as she'd expected. The idea was to have a couple of beers, a meal, and hit the sack.

Like most plans, it didn't survive first contact. The moment Sonny turned up at her hotel room door, all of her good intentions went to shit. Two beers became four, then six, and as the night wore on, she'd been unable to pull herself away from him.

Sonny was an excellent soldier, she knew that. She'd seen him in action twice, and both times he had been the consummate professional.

Well, if she excused the few seconds after Carl and Len had been blown to bits with an RPG round . . . Sonny had been a man in a trance, walking toward the enemy position like a robot with a death wish, but he'd come through unscathed.

That part of him aside, she'd never really gotten to know him. The last two times she'd worked with him, he'd been immature when they weren't in battle mode—often to the point that she would have gladly put a round through his thick skull—but last night she'd seen a completely different side of him. It was as if the child in him had grown up after Len's passing. He'd been a true gentleman throughout the evening, and seemed genuinely upset that his plans to make it in the restaurant business undetected had been shot down by the ESO.

They'd chatted about dreams they'd never be allowed to realize, about lives they'd never be able to live. She couldn't have imagined that they would have so much in common, and before she knew it, four in the morning had snuck up on them. She'd hated to end the evening, but she was there to work, not play.

Sonny had looked a little hungover this morning, but he'd shaken it off as the day wore on. He now had his head stuck in a Kindle—something else that surprised her.

"I didn't have you pegged as the reading type," she said.

"I wasn't," Sonny replied without looking up, "but Len left this to me in his will and I couldn't go against his last wishes. It's turned out to be one of the best things I've done."

"Yeah? Which books have you chosen?"

"None. The Kindle was already loaded, so I'm going through them one by one. This one's called *Morte Point* by Robert Parker. It's shaping up to be an absolute belter."

"Glad to hear it. Just make sure you're done by the time we get there. I need you one hundred percent focused."

"I will be. Finished and focused. How long until we arrive?"

"An hour," Wong said from the driver's seat. "Everything should be waiting for you."

That was one of the things Eva didn't like about the mission. Once they got to the border, there was no turning back. Nor could they afford to sit and wait for replacements if anything was missing or unusable. They would have to go in with what they had, and Eva hated starting a mission off on the wrong foot.

She needn't have worried. When they arrived at the banks of the Yalu, a truck was waiting, parked a hundred yards from the river, the closest building a factory half a mile away.

Sonny and Eva were almost frozen by the time they made the short transition from car to truck. They were ushered aboard, and inside they found everything they'd asked for, laid out with military precision. Eva and Sonny gravitated toward the weapons.

"These look brand new," Sonny said.

"Never been fired," Wong confirmed. "Straight out of the box."

They were indeed in immaculate condition, but Eva would have liked the opportunity to get a few rounds off before she crossed into enemy territory.

"Any chance we can test these out?" Sonny asked, thinking the same thing.

"The Vintorez, yes," Wong said. "It's suppressed, so that would be safe. The others, I'm afraid not. We can't draw attention to ourselves."

Sonny looked at Eva. "I don't like this. A few years ago, Len and I went to the Philippines to help Tom, and the weapons we were supplied turned out to be compromised. We nearly didn't make it out."

"I know what you mean," Eva agreed, "but these guys need us to succeed if they're to get their man. We'll have to trust them."

Even suggesting they put their faith in the integrity of the ESO brought bile to her throat, but they had no other choice. If the weapons failed to work, they would have to improvise. At least they'd have the sniper rifle to keep the bad guys at bay if they had to make a hasty retreat.

"You go and zero in the rifle while I check everything else," Eva told Sonny.

He grabbed a few rounds and inserted them into an empty magazine. As he disappeared out the back of the truck, Eva looked over the clothing that had been provided. They had everything down to the thermal socks and hiking boots, which looked like they'd been worn in. That would save her a blister or two; hopefully she wouldn't contract athlete's foot in the process.

As she began dressing, she heard a faint *clack . . . clack* coming from outside.

Moments later, Sonny reappeared.

"The rifle's all set," he said, tossing a couple of empty shell casings into the truck. He set the gun aside and began stripping the other weapons, making sure each was well-oiled and that they all had their firing pins. When everything was put back together, he dressed in his own set of winter gear.

"Nice fit," he noted as he did up the ghillie suit. Like Eva, he was now dressed completely in white.

They began packing backpacks with supplies. There would be no hot food or drink for them until the mission was over, only two days' worth of dry rations, water, and energy drinks. Sonny put a bundle of plastic explosive into his pack, followed by two sheets of white canvas, then began loading the magazines. Once it was full, he gave the other half of the gear to Eva. The final items were the disposable PF-89 tube-launched rockets. They each strapped two to the top of their packs, then jiggled them up and down to ensure nothing rattled.

"I guess we're set," Eva said, putting the night-vision goggles on. "Where's the crossing point?"

Wong told one of the men in the back of the truck to lead the way. Eva and Sonny followed him out into the cold and across the snow-covered ground to a clump of trees. In the middle, a pulley system had been set up between two sturdy oaks.

"They didn't need to sink a pole on this bank," said Wong. "My men assure me that these trees are more than strong enough."

Eva was no engineer, but the setup looked sturdy to her. "What about the other bank?"

"The equipment is already there and set up," Wong's helper said. "We took it over in three loads to make sure we didn't fall through the ice, but it's thick enough all the way across. You should have no trouble crossing. All you have to do when you want to come back is hook the rope in place."

That saved her and Sonny a job, but she wasn't about to take the man's word regarding the stability of the ice.

"We'll take the inflatable across anyway," she said. "It'll be useful for getting the younger ones over."

They were escorted down to the riverbank, where a camouflaged rubber dinghy sat next to the white rope. Eva threw her backpack aboard and Sonny did likewise. After a final comms check, they were ready to go.

There was no fond farewell, only a warning from Eva to Wong. "Be here when we get back, or I'll come and find you."

She picked up one side of the craft, Sonny took the other, and they started walking.

The ice felt robust at the shore, but when they neared the middle she felt the occasional crack beneath her feet.

"You get on and I'll pull it," she said.

"Thanks, but the age of chivalry isn't dead. Besides, you've fallen in once already. Hop on."

Eva climbed aboard and Sonny went to the front of the boat. He took hold of a mooring line and played it out about fifteen feet, then got down on his belly and started to crawl forward. It was slow going, but with his weight evenly distributed there was less likelihood of him crashing through the ice.

After fifteen minutes of constant testing, he judged the ice thick enough to continue upright. He stood up and pulled the boat up to his feet, and Eva got out and they carried it to the far shore just as more snow began to fall.

It took twenty minutes to cross the frozen river. Ahead of them lay a rugged, two-mile hike. They'd decided to stick to the hills on the way in, rather than leave tracks along their escape route, and it would be three miles on the way back.

Sonny pulled the inflatable ashore and hid it in some bushes that stood ten yards back from the bank. There he found the other end of the rope and the embedded pole that they would attach it to on the return journey. He tested it, and it seemed firmly anchored.

"Let's go," Eva said, as she took directions from her phone's map application.

Sonny slung the CQB over his shoulder and readied the C8 SFW with its underslung grenade launcher. The sniper rifle hung from a clip on his pack. "Lead on."

They took their time crossing the three hills that stood between them and Camp 33. The light snowfall had turned into a blizzard that would both help and hamper them. It made the going slow, but quickly began filling their tracks. It would also cover the rope that lay across the river, possibly even the rubber craft.

At four in the morning they reached the crest of the hill overlooking the target. The camp lay four hundred yards away, barely visible in the swirling snowstorm. That would work in their favor while they set up their observation post. Eva began the descent, and once she was twenty yards below the summit, she came across a small depression in the ground. It wasn't huge, but it would give them a clear sight of the compound while offering protection from prying eyes.

Eva instructed Sonny to start building their hide.

He took out one of the white tarps he'd brought along and laid it in the hole, weighing the center down with his backpack, then fought the howling wind to get the corners secured. Once their flooring was in place, it was another battle to create the roof from the other sheet. The wind threatened to whip it from Sonny's hands, but he eventually got the rear two corners tied down. At the front, he drove small branches from a tree into the ground and secured the sheet to the tops of them.

Eva had been foraging, and she returned with a few rocks to place around the edge of the roof to ensure their cover didn't fly off if the wind intensified.

The hide was almost complete. The only way in or out was through the twelve-inch gaps at the front and the left-hand side. Sonny gathered nearby snow to fashion a makeshift wall that would help protect them from the elements, leaving a gap of a few inches at the front so that they could begin their recce.

There wasn't much to observe. Only two guards were patrolling outside the perimeter fence, each one accompanied by a German shepherd. When one disappeared around the far corner, the other came into view roughly five minutes later. Neither looked particularly enamored with their duties.

Over the next three hours, Sonny and Eva noted the attributes of both dogs so that they would be able to recognize them later. If they were to succeed in putting all the dogs out of action, they had to know how many were in the camp and what kind of shifts they pulled.

At 8 a.m. on the dot, two more uniformed guards arrived at the front gate. They waited impatiently for the guards on patrol to get back, then switched places and began their stint while the others hurried inside, out of the bitter cold.

Eva wrote the time of the shift change and gave the dogs names. The first two were recorded as Donner and Blitzen; these two would be known as Dancer and Prancer. She jotted down the fact that Dancer had a near-white stripe behind his right shoulder, and Prancer's tail was entirely black.

"I don't expect we'll see much for the next few hours," Eva said. "You want to take first watch?"

"Sure. Get your head down, I'll wake you if anything happens."

CHAPTER 22

Eva tied a knot in the top of the bag and dug a hole in the snow, once again silently thanking Sonny for remembering to bring the roll of toilet paper along. It hadn't crossed her mind, but he was an old hand at this.

She walked back to the top of the hill and stuck her head over, checking the immediate area for hostiles. As for the last forty hours, it was clear. The guards' focus was on the camp, looking for people breaking out, not those trying to break in.

Eva crawled over the top and made her way slowly down to the hide, where Sonny was using the scope of the Vintorez sniper rifle to keep an eye on the goings-on below.

"Anything?" she asked, although she already knew the answer.

Nothing.

That was all that had happened in the two days they'd been there, with the exception of shift changes and two visits by the refrigerated truck.

It clearly hadn't taken long to get the organ-selling operation back up and running. Ship in some new guards and dogs, bury the dead ones, and get the money rolling in once more. Efficient, but a waste of time.

Eva was about to close them down for good.

She crawled back into the hide and lay next to Sonny.

"You all set?" she asked.

"Ready when you are."

There was nothing left to discuss. They'd gone over the attack again and again, refining their plan until it was as close to perfect as they could get it.

The first part had already gone as expected. During each of the guards' shifts, which were four hours long, Eva had crawled down the slope to the edge of the trees and used the hunting catapult to fire small chunks of prime beef laced with slow-acting poison at the fence. The dogs—eight in total—had come along one by one and gobbled up the morsels. The result was that, for the last three shifts, the guards had turned up for duty alone, and reinforcements were unlikely to arrive at this time of night.

She felt sorry for the animals. It wasn't their fight, but they had to be eliminated. She just hoped they hadn't suffered too much. A bullet to the head would have been nice and quick, but it would have meant tackling the animals up close, and eight fast-moving targets could have ruined her night.

The watch on Eva's wrist ticked past one in the morning, and the nearest guard was just about to disappear around the corner.

"Let's go."

They left the hide, threw on their backpacks and weapons, then slowly made their way down the slope, using their NVGs to light the way. They had to pause halfway down when a guard came into view, but once he'd gone, they continued the descent.

At the bottom of the hill they turned left, staying within the tree line, until they reached the point they'd agreed to launch from. They dropped onto their bellies and Sonny took out the Vintorez.

"Wait until he's level with the interrogation room," Eva reminded him.

When the guard fell, they wanted it to happen at the only spot along the fence that would hide his death from the guards manning the gate, and that was behind the outbuilding where Eva had been taken to be tortured.

When the target came into view, Sonny trained the weapon on the man's skull. The Cobra Demon night-vision adapter fitted to his scope lit up the scene perfectly. At this range, and with no wind to contend with, it would be harder to miss than hit.

As the man walked unwittingly into the kill zone, Sonny took a breath and let it out slowly.

CHAPTER 23

By the time the guard hit the ground, Eva and Sonny were on the move. The interrogation building lay directly between them and the gate, so there was little chance of anyone seeing them approach the fence. They sprinted over to the corpse, and Sonny relieved the dead man of his coat and hat. He stripped out of the white ghillie suit and put them on. Eva lay on the ground and Sonny covered her with snow, then waited for the next guard to appear.

This would be the make-or-break moment. If the second guard shouted out, it would attract the attention of others, and that wasn't part of the plan.

It took three minutes before Sonny saw the man round the corner of the fence. Sonny was standing side-on, looking down at the dead man. He gestured to the guard with a finger to his lips and pointed past the building within the fence. The other guard said nothing, but jogged over to Sonny, unslinging his rifle as he went. When he was two yards away, Sonny turned to face him and raised the Vintorez in one movement. The bullet slammed into the guard's chest and knocked him onto his back.

Eva leapt to her feet and threw off her ghillie suit. She stripped the other guard and, once in uniform like Sonny, readied her C8 SFW.

Both had webbing kits on under the coats, and they attached the stocks of the rifles to clips and let them hang from their chests. With the coats done up, the weapons couldn't be seen, but they could be brought into the fight in a second.

"Grab his arm," Sonny said.

Eva took the dead man by an elbow and followed Sonny's lead, dragging him toward the front gate, Sonny lugging his backpack in his other hand.

Twenty yards from the gate, Sonny shouted the Korean phrase Eva had taught him. It translated to 'Help us!' and it seemed to do the trick. Within seconds, the gates were pulled open and two men ran toward Sonny and Eva. When they got to within a few yards, Sonny dropped the dead man and reached for the rifle under his coat. It barked twice, and Eva was firing a second later. The two men dropped, and Sonny threw on his backpack and ran for the gate.

A man ran from the guard hut, firing from the hip, but his rounds were high and wide. Not so Eva's. She cut him down and sent another burst through the windows of the wooden hut. Sonny tossed a grenade through the open door as he passed.

"Fire in the hole!"

The explosion took care of anyone inside, but Sonny was already focused on the next stage of the operation. He took a knee and shucked off his backpack, then pulled one of the shoulder-fired rockets out and prepped it for action.

"Clear behind!"

He waited a second, then pressed the button that sent the warhead tearing towards the main entrance to the building twenty-five yards away. The thick oak door didn't stand a chance. Splinters shot past Sonny's head, but he didn't wait for the dust to clear. He slung his pack on once more. It was time for the CQB to dance.

Eva appeared at Sonny's side as they ran for the ruined entrance. He went in first and checked that the corridor was clear, then took the NVGs from the pack and tossed a pair to Eva.

Sonny felt alive. The last couple of years were a distant blur as he fell back into what he did best. His senses were so finely tuned that he detected the first threat before it presented itself. He directed Eva to the front desk window; she nodded and readied a grenade. A head fleetingly appeared behind the glass, too quick for Sonny to get a shot off, but Eva had it covered. She tossed the grenade through the gap between the window and the counter and took cover.

As soon as they heard the explosion, they were up and running for the metal gate that led to the accommodation blocks. Rather than fumbling with keys, they'd decided to blow all the doors. It also meant the guards couldn't lock them again, blocking their escape. Sonny had a small shaped charge prepared, and he stuck it to the lock and set the timer for five seconds, enough time to make a retreat.

The doors blew inwards. Sonny had used a little more C-4 than was necessary, but that was far better than using too little.

They ran through the gap and to the next door, which was made of solid wood and had a grille set at head height. Sonny repeated the process, attaching the explosive and setting the timer before getting out of the way of the blast.

The door swung open as the lock was destroyed, and AK-47s immediately opened up from the other side. Sonny was ready with a flash-bang grenade; he tossed it into the atrium and took cover behind the door. The resulting explosion gave them a few seconds to get in and eliminate the threat before the stunned guards had time to recover.

Four men lay dead by the time they'd cleared the area, but more would be on their way. It was time to gain the advantage. Eva pointed to an ordinary door with Korean writing on it, and Sonny knew this would be the way to the power generator. He put a few rounds into the lock and kicked the door open, then ran down the stairs and into the basement.

He saw a lot of sturdy-looking equipment that would probably be unfazed by his small charges, but Sonny was only interested in the weak link. He found the circuit board and set two small blocks of C-4: one on the board itself, and the other on the pipes leading out of the unit. He set the timers for ten seconds this time, to ensure he would be out of the confined space when they blew.

Sonny was back in the atrium by the time the lights went out. The sonic boom followed a split second later.

He and Eva both brought the NVGs down over their eyes, and the world turned neon green.

"This way," Eva said, leading Sonny to one of the three locked doors that fed off the central hub.

She'd told him that the other two doors led to the prison cells, but this one was clearly marked "STAFF ONLY." The rest of the guards would be concentrated here, in what must be the staff barracks block. At this time of night, most of them would usually be sleeping, but after their noisy entrance, some forty hostiles would now be alert and armed. If Eva and Sonny were to get the prisoners out safely, they had to eliminate that threat first.

Sonny handed Eva one of the PF-89 shoulder-fired rocket launchers, and she readied it while he placed another of his shaped charges on the metal door's lock. When she gave him the thumbs up, he set the timer and ran to the side.

The sound of the blast echoed around the chamber as the door flew inward, and Eva let fly with the rocket. It flashed through the doorway and exploded instantly, and by the time Sonny and Eva reached the mangled door, he could hear the screams from the dying.

It was utter carnage. Bloody limbs lay on the floor, and two men had been cut in half by the warhead. Others were shredded with shrapnel, and a few lay seconds away from death. Sonny counted at least twenty dead or dying, and figured they must have been behind the door, readying their counterattack.

As Sonny moved along the corridor, putting rounds into the heads of survivors, gunfire erupted at the other end of the corridor. Sonny and Eva threw themselves into doorways and fired back, but it wasn't a position they could maintain long. The Koreans would soon get men to both ends of the corridor, trapping them.

They had to push through.

Sonny pulled the pin from a stun grenade and lobbed it toward the enemy. "Flashbang! Ready to move!"

He closed his eyes in anticipation of the blast, even though the NVGs had a built-in cutoff that protected the user from a sudden burst of light. In the confines of the corridor, the sound was enough to hurt Sonny's ears, even thirty yards from the blast. It must have been a lot worse for those up close, and Sonny ran toward them before they could recover enough to get back into the fight. He stayed close to the right-hand wall, knowing Eva would be hugging the left. Both opened up from ten yards against opponents who were stunned and lacking the advantage of night vision. It was a massacre. Twelve more lay dead, giving Sonny a running total of almost forty. There was no telling how many remained, however. The Koreans could have brought in fifty, maybe a hundred more personnel following Eva's escape.

All they could do was clear the block and hope they didn't miss anyone.

They retreated back up the corridor and cleared every room, one at a time. Sonny kicked the doors in, Eva tossed in a stun grenade, and they went in on the B in 'Bang'. The first four rooms were clear, but the fifth—much larger—was occupied.

~

Cheng Dae-sung missed the initial confrontation outside the fence, but the explosion that demolished the main entrance shook him from his bed. At first, he thought it might have been a dream, but when he heard the next blast, followed by gunfire, he knew something was wrong.

A second escape in a week would be the end of him. After the debacle with the American woman, he'd barely managed to hold on to his position as prison warden—it had been touch and go whether he'd even keep his head attached to his body.

Cheng got up and threw on his pants and a shirt. He was struggling to get his shoes on when the lights went out following yet another explosion.

He froze. This was no escape attempt. None of his men had any heavy weapons or explosives, which meant someone was breaking *in*. Not only unprecedented, but also virtually impossible, since precious few people even knew of the camp's existence. Whoever it was, his men weren't equipped to deal with it. Their job was to prevent compliant prisoners from escaping, not repelling attacks by heavily armed foes.

Cheng scrambled for his phone. His hand brushed it off the nightstand, and he dropped to the floor to retrieve it. His hands were shaking as he tried to find the contact for the State Security Department. After what seemed like minutes, he finally brought up the number and hit the Call button.

Boom!

That one was much closer. It sounded like it was at the end of the—

BOOM!

The walls of his private room shook, and decades-old plaster fell from the ceiling. That one had been right outside his door, and now he could hear gunfire from what seemed mere feet away.

"SSD."

"This is Cheng Dae-sung at Kwanliso 33! We're being attacked!"

"Attacked? By who?"

"I don't know! Just send reinforcements immediately! Tanks, helicopters, everything you have!"

Another explosion, this one smaller, followed by even more gunfire. Cheng could barely stop his hands from shaking as he put the phone back to his ear. "Hello?"

"We need more information before we can—"

The rest of the sentence was lost as another blast shook the walls. The first had come from the right of his room, but this one detonated to the left.

"I can't hear you! Just send as many men as you can. They have explosives and heavy ordnance!"

Suddenly, the gunfire stopped. Someone was in the hallway, unopposed, and it sounded like they were going room to room.

They would find him at any moment, and he was unarmed.

Cheng thought about putting the wooden chair that was next to his desk under the doorknob, but that would be pointless. It would hold them for a minute at most, while confirming that someone was in the room. Better to hide and wait for them to leave.

His only options were the closet or under the bed. The latter seemed easier. Cheng threw himself to the floor and crawled under the metal frame of the bed, then grabbed the blanket and pulled it down so that the edge just touched the floor.

Not a moment too soon.

He heard the door being kicked open, then something bounced a couple of times on the carpeted floor.

Cheng Dae-sung had never heard a sound like it, and never would again. His eardrums were ruptured by the blast a couple of feet from his head, and the wool blanket blew off the bed. He didn't hear the pair of feet entering his room, nor could he see them. The six-million-candela flash of light had seared his retinas, and in daylight conditions it would have been at least fifteen seconds before he regained his sight.

The pitch darkness of his room was the last thing he saw.

~

It was Eva's turn to clear the room. Sonny tossed the M84 stun grenade in after she kicked the door open, and as soon as it went off, she spun inside the room, looking for targets. She found only one, lying under the bed and facing her.

Cheng.

His face was contorted in agony, and she could see powder burns covering half of his head. The grenade must have detonated close to him, and she could barely imagine how fucked he was right now.

Not that she cared. This monster had overseen the murders of hundreds, if not thousands of people. Okay, some had been real criminals—thieves, murderers, and rapists—but none deserved to die in such a terrible manner.

Especially the children.

As Eva thought of the innocent kids, any compunction she had at killing the helpless Cheng evaporated.

"What's the holdup?" Sonny asked from outside the room.

His words reminded her that she still had a mission to complete.

There was a special place in hell reserved for Cheng, and Eva helped him on his journey with a round to the gut. So what if he took his time getting there?

She joined Sonny out in the corridor.

"Problem?" he asked.

"Not anymore. Let's go."

They cleared the rest of the rooms in the hallway, finding a couple of non-combatants—likely the surgical team—who felt Eva's wrath.

Once the entire staff block was cleared, Eva and Sonny searched the dead guards for keys. Armed with a set each, they went back to the atrium and Sonny blew open the doors to the prison wings.

They took the first corridor together. Once they deemed it clear, they opened the first cells.

"Put all of your clothes on and stand outside the door," Eva said.

When the first inmates emerged, she gave them the keys and told them to release the other prisoners. As each left their cell, she reassured them that they were safe, but most seemed unsure of the situation, as if some sort of cruel trick were being played by their captors. Her strange-looking headgear didn't help matters. But there wasn't time to explain, so Eva simply told them to do as she said or they would be shot. Instructions they all understood and believed.

Sonny sized each prisoner up and put those who looked most capable of fighting to one side.

Once the block was empty, they went to the other corridor and repeated the process. This was where the children were housed, and some of them were too young to walk by themselves.

When the last cell had been emptied, Eva realized with a heavy heart that the little girl with the knitted doll wasn't among their number.

Eva lifted the NVGs from her eyes and wiped away a tear, then found a few volunteers to carry the younger children. She told everyone to follow her back to the atrium.

"Wait here," she said as they reached the doorway. She crept into the open space and scanned the upper and lower levels for danger, but the only armed men were ones she'd killed in the assault.

"You're going to follow my friend and pick up some weapons," she told the group Sonny had chosen.

A couple of minutes later, they returned from the staff block looking like a small militia.

"Listen up," Eva said, loudly enough that everyone could hear her. "We're going to walk to the Chinese border. It will take about an hour, but once we cross the Yalu River, you'll be safe. We're going to take you to Ulaanbaatar, and from there you'll fly to South Korea. Do you all understand?"

There were no shaking heads, only a few nods and lots of blank faces.

"Okay. If you've got a weapon, stay on the edge of the group. If we shoot at something, so do you. Let's go."

Eva led them toward the entrance, but when she came level with the clerk's window, she stopped.

"Wait."

She raised her weapon and fired a dozen shots at the lock on the office door, then kicked it in.

The room looked like a slaughterhouse. Whoever had been behind the glass when she'd tossed in the grenade was now plastered all over the walls and floor. She trudged through the gloop to a door at the back of the small room. It was locked, but gave way when she shot out the lock.

Inside, she found what she'd been looking for: more than a dozen filing cabinets containing hundreds of manila folders. She opened a file at random and saw that it was a prisoner record. It showed the person's name, personal details, and the crime they'd committed. The last page documented the date and time of the procedure and the organs that had been removed.

One entry on the page caught her eye, and it took a couple of seconds for the information to make any sense. Next to the time of the first incision came the time of death. It was a couple of minutes after the surgery had started.

The prisoners had been dissected while they were still alive.

She checked another file, and it showed the same thing; not a one-off, but standard operating practice.

Fighting the building rage, Eva grabbed a handful of folders, then tried the other cabinets. The first few contained more of the same, but then she struck gold. Invoices to a Chinese company, the majority of them for tens of thousands of dollars, all of them stamped as paid. A little more digging revealed a ledger with a running total for the year. Though it was still only January, the prison had accumulated a tidy sum.

Eva took the records back into the hallway and stuffed them inside Sonny's backpack.

"I'll be back in a minute."

She ran to the exit, scanned for threats, then sprinted over to her own pack, which she'd left next to the first kill of the night. It contained the shaped charges designed to put the facility out of action.

She took them back inside and told Sonny to get the column of former inmates moving. As he led the march to freedom, she ran back into the bowels of the prison and began setting the explosives. One block of C-4 went between the huge water inlet pipe and the wall, another on the outer shell of the power generator. She set the timers for twenty minutes and hurried back upstairs. The devices contained ten times the C-4 that Sonny had used earlier to breach the doors—more than enough to put the utilities out of action.

When she left the basement, Eva went to the medical bay and laid another charge with an eighteen-minute delay, then returned to the atrium.

There were four large columns that took the weight of the upper floor. She planted a bomb at the base of each one, giving herself fifteen minutes to clear the area, then ran for the exit.

Outside, she jogged past the last of the prisoners to the head of the line.

"All set," she told Sonny, who was setting a reasonable pace, given the inmates' condition.

He didn't ask how long they had before the C-4 blew. They'd discussed the mission down to the last detail, and so far things had gone roughly to plan.

Which scared them both. Rarely did an operation go as smoothly as the planners hoped, but this one had. No civilian deaths, all the bad guys taken care of, and only a three-mile hike to the border ahead of them.

What could possibly go wrong?

CHAPTER 24

After ten minutes of walking, they came to the mouth of the valley that would lead them to China. The ten-foot-wide stream was frozen over. On either side, the wide banks quickly rose up the heavily forested slopes. It was also uneven, and the pace slowed to a miserable two miles per hour as the less nimble among them struggled to cope with the snow-covered rocks.

Everyone looked back as the sound of multiple explosions from within the prison reached them. They were so far into the valley that they couldn't see the building, but the sky above the eastern slope lit up for a few moments, then faded back to black.

Diversion over, they continued along the trail for another fifteen minutes before another halt was called.

A woman near the rear of the column had twisted her ankle. She'd misjudged her step and was now sitting on her backside, howling in pain.

"Shut her up!" Sonny told her companions, using the internationally recognized sign of a finger on the lips.

They managed to quiet her, but when they tried to help her to her feet, she collapsed once more.

"Ice it," Sonny said, and Eva translated for him. Thankfully, they had a plentiful supply of snow around them.

"We'd better take five," Eva said. "A few of the others are already looking a bit weary."

"Okay, but only five. We've been at it for half an hour and barely covered a mile. Have you got a signal yet?"

Eva checked her phone for confirmation that Wong would have the buses waiting by 3 a.m. Although at this rate she expected it would be closer to four by the time she got everyone across the river.

"Nothing yet. We should have more luck once we clear the valley."

Sonny took out the remaining chocolate bars and walked the length of the line, handing them to the children. As he went, he did a head count.

"Looks like just over two hundred," he said when he got back to Eva.

"One less than I'd hoped for."

The girl with the knitted doll would haunt her forever. There was nothing she could have done differently, but Eva knew she would always feel responsible for the child's untimely death. They couldn't have kicked off the mission any earlier, and there was no way she could have rescued her during her initial escape from Camp 33. Eva could only tell herself that she'd done all she could, and hope that by getting the rest of the prisoners to freedom, it would make amends in some small way.

A distant sound floated past her ears, and it warned her that the ordeal was far from over.

"You hear that?"

Sonny nodded, concern written on his face. "Chopper."

"Everyone, into the trees, *NOW!*"

The word spread down the column like wildfire. Bodies scattered like roaches, heading for the cover of the pines that covered the hills.

Sonny made sure everyone was hidden before dashing for cover himself.

"Tell them not to fire unless they hear me shoot first."

The prisoners were lightly armed with the sidearms collected from the dead. The only guards with automatic rifles had been the ones patrolling the fence.

Eva passed the word along, then put her NVGs back over her eyes. The sky was clear, but the noise from the beat of the rotors was edging closer. It wasn't long before the beast came into view.

It was huge, like a steel hornet, bristling with guns and rocket pods.

"That's a Russian Mil Mi-24 attack helicopter," Sonny said as the aircraft overflew their position. "If that gets us in its sights, we're fucked."

The chopper passed over the far side of the valley, heading for the prison.

"Then I suggest we move. We'll have to stick to the trees from now on."

"Okay. You take point," Sonny said. "I'll bring up the rear."

They ran in opposite directions. Sonny did his best to explain the situation to everyone he passed, pointing down to the frozen river, then shaking his head and crossing his hands over his waist to indicate the negative. They appeared to get the message: *Stay in the trees.*

Sonny hurried them along. They were still two miles from the river, and once the helicopter landed and those on board discovered that the prison was empty, the hunt would begin.

He didn't fancy their chances if it caught up with them.

Ground troops wouldn't be far behind, either. They'd left the prison around thirty minutes earlier. The Mil chopper could do about two hundred miles per hour but needed some prep time, which meant the airbase probably lay within sixty miles. If it housed soldiers too, they could be on the scene within forty minutes. No army facilities had shown up on the satellite images they'd analyzed, but given the DPRK's propensity for secrecy, that wasn't a surprise.

With the thought of imminent detection spurring him on, Sonny hurried the prisoners, urging them to pick up the pace. They responded for a few hundred yards, but the entire line came to a halt when a woman let out a shriek as she slipped down the hill towards the valley floor. A couple of prisoners followed her down, intent on helping her back up to the safety of the trees.

Their timing couldn't have been worse.

Sonny yelled at them to get back under cover, but his words were drowned out by the return of the attack helicopter. He couldn't see it through the treetops, but the downdraft was whipping up the freshly fallen snow, and the noise was deafening.

Worse was to come, as the Yak-B 12.7mm cannon on the aircraft's nose opened up, sending death to the valley floor. The woman was cut to pieces, and one of the men who'd gone to her rescue couldn't halt his descent in time. The cannon quickly switched its focus to him, splitting him in two.

The chopper wasn't running any lights, so Sonny guessed the weapons systems officer was using FLIR—forward-looking infrared—to choose his targets through the treetops. The body heat from the two hundred prisoners would show up as blobs on the WSO's scope, making them easy to pick off.

That fear was confirmed seconds later, when the trees began to split apart as hundreds of rounds poured down from above. The fire was concentrated twenty yards from him, and through the NVGs he could see the devastation it was causing. Men, women, and children exploded, eerie green eruptions jetting from their bodies as they fell.

If the carnage continued, they would all be dead in minutes.

Sonny wasn't going to let that happen.

He shrugged off the pack and pulled out the two remaining PF-89s, then ran down to the frozen stream to get a better shot. He made sure to stay to the rear of the chopper, in case the pilot saw him as a tempting target. Sonny dropped one of the rocket launchers to the ground and prepped the other. It was something he'd practiced beforehand, and he had it ready to fire in seconds. He lined up the sights on the rotor mast and fired.

Using an unguided rocket, all Sonny could do now was hope. He watched the projectile arc towards the helicopter, closing in on the sweet spot below the rotors, holding his breath as he anticipated the hit.

It didn't come. At the last second, the pilot, possibly warned by onboard sensors, jinked the metal beast forward. The rocket continued on into the night sky before dropping back to earth, its propellant spent.

All Sonny had achieved was to make himself the prime target. The chopper swung to face him, and rounds chewed up the ground as they inched toward his defenseless body. Sonny picked up the remaining PF-89 and threw himself to the right as the earth he'd been standing on splintered. Rocks and ice danced to the helicopter's deadly tune, but Sonny wasn't hanging around to witness the spectacle. He dived behind the nearest tree, safe for a few seconds, and the firing stopped as the chopper pilot maneuvered for a better shot. Sonny inched to the side, trying to keep the thick fir between himself and a bloody death, when he heard salvation in his earpiece.

"I'll distract him, you take the shot!"

Eva had opened up with her L119, peppering the helicopter's fuselage. The tiny bullets were useless against the armored beast, but the grenade from her underslung M203 got the pilot's attention. It exploded on the chopper's right flank, causing a little scorching to the armor plating but nothing more.

Sonny put his head around the tree and saw the aircraft turning to face the new threat, only seconds remaining before Eva was blown apart by the cannon. He threw the last of the rocket launchers onto his right shoulder, aimed, and fired.

Eva had the same idea, sending another grenade at the chopper. As Sonny's rocket left the tube, the helicopter banked to avoid another round from her M203. Sonny's last chance was heading impotently into darkness, until the pilot spun his vessel directly into the four-pound warhead's path. He readjusted too late, and the explosive head tore off two rotor blades. The remaining three, completely out of sync, had no chance of keeping the chopper airborne. It plummeted to the ground, hitting nose-first with a sickening crunch. No explosion, only the dead certainty that the pilot and weapons officer couldn't have survived the impact.

"Let's get the hell out of here!"

Sonny rounded up the survivors and pushed them onward. They had to navigate the kill zone, the spot where the chopper had made mincemeat of over three dozen prisoners, and a couple wanted to stay and mourn friends or loved ones who had fallen.

There simply wasn't time. Sonny hated to do it, but he pulled them to their feet and urged them ahead. He had to level his rifle at one man who didn't want to leave a woman's body behind. To the prisoner, it was probably a wife, possibly a sister, but to Sonny it was seconds wasted. There was no telling how many helicopters were based within range, and if another one showed up, they were well and truly fucked. They had probably ten M203 grenades between them, and no more shoulder-launched rockets. Not nearly enough to take on another Mi-24.

"How many did we lose?" Eva's voice came over the air.

"About forty."

Eva didn't respond. She didn't have to. The silence conveyed what they both felt.

Sonny stopped to help a woman who had tripped and fallen on her face. He helped her up and kept hold of her arm, dragging her along to catch up with the others. The prisoners probably thought it strange that their saviors would act so aggressively toward them, but to Sonny it was tough love. If he let them dawdle at their own pace, they would perish. Simple as that.

He kept both ears open for the sound of more aircraft, but whatever gods were watching them that night had seen enough entertainment.

A couple of hours later, Eva found a signal on her phone and called Wong. "We're near the river. We should be with you within the hour."

"Roger that."

They came in sight of the riverbank thirty minutes later, and freedom's proximity gave the prisoners the energy to run the last few hundred yards.

Eva was the first to the spot where the pulley system lay hidden in the snow. She dug it out and lifted it up to the hook on the pole that had been driven into the riverbank, then got some help to pull it tight so that the rope hung three feet off the ground.

"We'll send ten men over first," she told Sonny. "Once they get to the other side, they can pull from their end."

She chose the strongest-looking from the group and gave them instructions. They each put a hand through a loop attached to the rope and started walking. As they did, Eva ordered another dozen men to start pulling the rope from the near bank. On every tug, another prisoner joined the line. With the prisoners spread out by two yards, she had a hundred people on the move by the time the first ones made it to the other side. Some were carrying children in their free arm, which left only fifty remaining on the Korean side of the river when the ice gave way.

A woman screamed as she plunged into the freezing water. Since she'd been holding on to the rope, she only submerged up to her neck. With the next pull on the rope by the teams on either bank, she was dragged out onto the ice, cold but alive. The precaution Eva had insisted on had paid dividends, but now there was a problem for the remaining prisoners waiting to cross.

How to navigate the hole?

Eva ordered a halt to the pulling and ran out onto the ice. She got to with ten yards of the broken ice and told those waiting what to do.

"Straddle the rope and lay flat on it, then bring your right foot up and hook it over, so that your knee is dangling below you."

One or two were confused by the instructions, so she went to their aid. Pretty soon, everyone knew what to do.

"Only do this when you get close to the hole, otherwise it'll put too much strain on the rope. As soon as you're five yards past the hole, get back on your feet."

She ordered the teams on the banks to recommence, only this time slowly, and the line started moving once more.

Soon, only Sonny and Eva were left on the Korean side of the Yalu. They walked out onto the ice but didn't take the rope. Instead, they crabbed sideways, checking the Korean side of the river for signs of pursuit.

They were a third of the way across when they heard the sound they'd both been dreading. The rapid *thump-thump-thump* of rotor blades slicing the night sky—closing, and fast.

"Once you're over the hole, get off the rope and run!" Eva screamed at the prisoners.

Most of them didn't need telling twice. Those near the far bank released their handholds and sprinted for the shore, as did some closer to the ice hole.

The ones who had yet to reach the broken ice were the problem. Faced with being cut down or falling through the ice, two chose the latter. They ran as fast as they could, giving the ice hole a wide berth, but it didn't help.

They crashed through the ice within seconds of each other.

"Shit!" Eva cursed.

"Go help them," Sonny told her. "I'll hold it off for as long as I can."

To his surprise, Eva headed for the Korean side, but then he saw why. She tugged the inflatable dinghy from the bushes and turned it

over onto its base, then began dragging it toward the first of the struggling escapees.

Sonny returned his attention to the menacing sound of approaching death. It was coming from behind the hill they'd just descended,
so it had to be following the trail they'd left. A tinge of white above the
tree line confirmed that it was using a night light rather than FLIR to
track them.

Sonny checked his six. Only three more people had to navigate
the original hazard, and Eva was already helping the first of the fallen
prisoners out of peril.

No sign of the other one.

"Get a move on!" Sonny shouted. "We haven't got long!"

They had less time than he imagined.

A few seconds after Eva had the soaking, freezing man in the dinghy, thirty million candela turned night to day as the helicopter broke
over the crest of the hill. Sonny whipped the NVGs off his eyes and
started spraying lead towards the light, moving as he went to present as
difficult a target as possible. He was answered by gunfire from the chopper, but thankfully it wasn't the cannon he'd expected. It sounded like
GPMG—a general-purpose machine gun—which meant this chopper
was a transport craft, not an attack variant.

Sonny switched out his empty magazine as Eva joined the fight,
then sent another fifteen rounds heading skyward.

The light snapped out as rounds smashed into the lens, and when
he put the NVGs back into place, Sonny could see that it was a US-built
MD 500. It had no external weaponry, but the doors had been removed
and jump seats installed on the exterior. Two soldiers perched on either
side of the fuselage, and they were now firing blindly. Sonny answered
them, and when the first target slumped forward in his seat, the chopper banked back to the DPRK border. It dropped quickly, disgorged
the three remaining troops a few feet off the ground, then shot upward
and out of range of ground fire.

Sonny got a few bursts off, then moved position. He didn't yet know if the aggressors had night vision, but he would soon. He fired off another three-round volley, catching one of them in the chest, then sprinted to his left. The answering fire chewed at the ice where he'd been standing, which told him the bad guys were looking for muzzle flashes to pinpoint his location.

Fish in a barrel.

Sonny picked the remaining pair off with ease before they could send another round his way. Two quick bursts, one after the other, and both men fell.

The immediate threat was over, but they wouldn't be safe until they were across the river and past the tree line.

The last of the prisoners was now ten yards from the far shore, followed by Eva pulling the inflatable craft with its one passenger.

Still no sign of the other fallen inmate.

Sonny ran to the rope and followed it to the hole that had held them up and cost them another life. He straddled the line and yelled for the men on the bank to pull.

Nothing happened, so Eva translated and the rope began to move. After twenty seconds, Sonny was clear of the obstacle, and he jumped off and sprinted over to Eva. He grabbed one of the boat's lines, and together they dragged the last man to solid ground.

"Into the trees," Eva shouted. Most were already there, but a few had hung around to help their frozen compatriot.

Once everyone was accounted for and no stragglers remained on the icy Yalu, Sonny and Eva led them across frozen mud banks and through the stand of trees. Sixty yards away, a highway cut across their path, but at this hour it was clear of traffic.

That could change at any moment.

Sonny ordered everyone to get on their bellies thirty yards from the road, then crossed it and ran behind another bank of trees.

Wong had delivered as promised. A dozen buses were lined up, their doors open. The fixer himself was standing next to a coupe, smoking a cigarette.

Sonny gave him a thumbs up, then returned to the highway and called the first ten forward. These were the ones carrying or assisting the children, and he told them to run to the farthest bus and climb aboard. Once they were over and out of sight, he told the rest to cross. He'd sent the kids first in case a vehicle appeared and caused a panicked rush. The last thing he wanted was the children being trampled in a stampede this close to the finish line.

The precaution didn't turn out to be necessary, but he felt better for it.

Sonny saw Eva hand one of the escapees a phone and mumble some instructions. The man nodded, stuffed the cell into his underwear, then joined the line for the last of the buses.

"What was that?" Sonny asked.

"A way to let me know that they've reached Ulaanbaatar," Eva replied. "He's to text me one word if they get there safely, or a duress word if compromised. If Wong keeps his promise, they'll be there within a couple of days. If not, he'll lose his defector and a few of his own body parts."

"Do you think Hong's still alive? No food or water for three days . . ."

"Of course he is. He's sitting in a cushy apartment and his food is prepaid. The only thing he's likely to die of is boredom."

Sonny managed a tired smile. "I should have known."

"Yes, you should. Come on, I want to go to bed." Before Sonny could come up with a smartass reply, she added, "That wasn't an invitation."

"Never crossed my mind," Sonny lied.

He followed her to Wong's car.

"How did it go?" the ESO handler asked. "I heard a bit of a commotion."

"That *bit of a commotion* cost over forty people their lives." Sonny hadn't liked Wong from the start.

"That's unfortunate."

"No. Unfortunate is stubbing your toe on the bedpost. Unfortunate is a bird shitting in your hair as you walk into a job interview. Being cut in half by a twelve-mil cannon is as far from fucking unfortunate as you can get." The adrenaline from the battle had yet to subside, and Sonny was more than willing to expend one more round before it was over. "How about I call your wife and tell her I was firing my rifle and unfortunately you got in the way and I shot you in the head? What do you think she'd say, eh? 'Yes, that's unfortunate, thanks for letting me know?'"

"Enough," Eva said, getting between the two men. "I'm tired, I'm hungry, and I need a shower. Save the pissing contest for another time."

She took Sonny by the arm and pulled him toward Wong's car, opening the rear door and pushing him inside. She got in beside him.

"Don't antagonize him," she said. "I'm not finished with him yet. I still need information from him."

"Then tell him to stop being such a dick."

Eva elbowed Sonny in the ribs as Wong opened the driver's door and got behind the wheel. She gave the Englishman a look that ordered him to defuse the situation.

"I'm sorry," Sonny said, reluctantly. "It's been a tough few days."

"Forget about it," Wong said. "I shouldn't have been so insensitive."

Bridges mended, Wong started the car and maneuvered past the buses and out onto the highway.

Sonny leaned into Eva. "You're right. You do need a shower."

CHAPTER 25

Twelve hours after hitting the sack, Eva finally climbed out of bed.

It hadn't been her best night's sleep.

A lobster dinner, half a bottle of wine, and a twenty-minute shower should have knocked her out for days, but the face of the child with the knitted doll would not leave her.

She'd managed a couple of hours' sleep on the journey from the Korean border back to the Shangri-La. That had seen her through until four in the afternoon, when fatigue had finally caught up with her. She'd said goodnight to Sonny and headed to her room, only to be haunted by the innocent face every time she closed her eyes.

The clock on the wall read five in the morning. Knowing she wouldn't get any more rest, Eva did a set of sit-ups and push-ups, then took another shower. She was dressed twenty minutes before the hotel restaurant opened for breakfast.

Wong had told her the previous day that he was awaiting delivery of a file that would shed light on the Chinese end of the murderous trade. He might have received it while she was trying to sleep.

"Do you have anything for me?" Eva asked as a bleary Wong answered the phone.

"Yes. Can it wait?"

"No. Meet me for breakfast at six."

She put down the phone, not even slightly guilty at having interrupted his sleep.

Eva turned on the TV to catch the news. Unsurprisingly, there was nothing about their incursion into North Korea. She suffered through the sports report, caught the headlines at the top of the hour, then went down to meet Wong.

Sonny had beaten them both to it. He was already helping himself to the buffet, chewing on something while spooning noodles and bok choy into a bowl. Eva grabbed a plate and joined him.

"No need to ask if you slept well," Sonny said. "You look like shit."

"Thanks."

Annoyingly, Sonny looked great, as if he'd just spent a week on the beach rather than storming a prison, vastly outnumbered and in freezing conditions.

Eva loaded up on rice and what looked like minced pork, and led Sonny to a table in the far corner of the room.

Wong arrived five minutes late, and Eva surmised he'd spent the extra time on his appearance. Apart from the maître d', he was the only one in the room wearing a suit.

He took a seat at the table and told one of the waitstaff to bring him a coffee.

"This is what we were able to find on the operation."

He handed Eva a folder. It was disappointingly thin.

"I'll be back in a minute," Wong said, and headed for the door that led to the external smoking area.

As he braved the morning chill to get his nicotine fix, Eva opened the file and scanned the first page. She was still reading when the ESO man returned and sat down.

"His name's Chin Long Cheung," Wong said. "As you can see from the dossier, he's not quite the golden boy he's painted to be."

Eva had never heard of Cheung, but according to the file, he was a big name in China. At thirty-nine, he was the youngest billionaire in the country, having made his name and fortune in renewable energy. Aged seventeen, he'd sold solar panels for a local dealer. Four years later, he was manufacturing them. By the time he was twenty-five, Cheung had secured lucrative contracts to provide offshore wind turbines throughout East Asia. His solar farms dotted the globe, from the deserts of the Middle East to Australia's outback, providing cheap electricity to those who would otherwise have to do without. He was also a renowned philanthropist, donating millions to charity each year.

All in all, Cheung seemed like a decent guy. The next page suggested otherwise.

In the last few years, Cheung had branched out into healthcare. One of his subsidiary companies owned five hospitals and health centers across mainland China, one of them being the Jianguo Medical Center in Changchun.

Only a five-hour drive from the North Korean border.

The file contained a document listing funds transfers from the medical center to an offshore account. It didn't say who the recipient was, but the amounts were huge, comparable to the figures she'd found in the files at Camp 33.

"The last page lists his residences and his itinerary for the next three days," Wong said. "I assume you'll want to act quickly, so tell me what you need and I'll have everything ready for this evening."

Eva handed the file over to Sonny.

"How did you find him so quickly?" she asked Wong.

"I'd like to say it was great detective work, but we simply followed a refrigerated truck from the border as it made its last delivery. When it arrived at the Jianguo, we researched the company and everything led to Cheung."

That made sense. If the ESO hadn't cooperated with the venture, it would have been Eva's starting point, too. Before destroying the camp, that is. With the operation shut down, she would have to take Wong's word.

"What do you know about Cheung's security arrangements?" she asked.

"A three-man team. They go everywhere with him. Armed, of course."

It seemed straightforward enough. Choose a point in his schedule, scope it out in advance, hit him, and run.

"We'll need more information about every venue he's visiting over the next three days," Eva told Wong. "As for weapons, two suppressed assault rifles, two suppressed pistols, and a couple of knives for starters. We'll give you a comprehensive list once we've had a look at the target."

Wong drained his coffee. "I'll get on it." He stood to leave.

"How's the convoy getting on?" Eva asked.

"On schedule. I just hope Hong is still alive by the time they get to Mongolia. For your sake."

"He will be, as long as your people don't take any detours."

Wong seemed to consider replying, then decided against it, turned, and walked out of the restaurant.

"What do you think?" Sonny asked once he and Eva were alone.

"We're dealing with the ESO, and they're only helping because I've got them by the balls. I'm not ready to trust them."

"Good. I thought it was just me."

Eva took out the phone Wong had purchased for her on the way back from the border and opened the Shield app. "I think we're going to need a little help on this one."

She composed a message to Farooq Naser, asking him to delve into the background of Chin Long Cheung. She included the offshore account number that the payments from the Jianguo hospital had been made to. If anyone could follow the money trail, it was Farooq. She also added the name of the Chinese company printed on the invoices she'd taken from Camp 33 and asked for details.

Oddly, the North Korean invoices hadn't included account numbers. Perhaps that was in case they fell into the wrong hands, but Eva thought it more likely that they were settled in cash. Bank transfers left an electronic footprint that the US government could trace, and anyone paying such vast sums to the DPRK would be in hot water.

Whatever the reason for the discrepancy, it was at odds with what Wong's file suggested—that the Chinese medical company transferred funds to a payee. Another reason not to trust the man.

Farooq replied to let her know that he would get all he could on Cheung, but it would take some time to track the account down. Eva sent another message asking him to hurry, explaining that the clock was ticking.

"Do you want to wait for Farooq to get back to us, or make a start?" Sonny asked.

"Let's get moving," Eva said. "The itinerary said Cheung will be staying at his place in Changchun in a couple of days. Might as well check it out. We can take a look at the Jianguo while we're at it."

"Sounds good to me," Sonny said, and shoveled another load of noodles into his mouth.

CHAPTER 26

After getting a cash advance from Wong and renting a car, Sonny and Eva drove to Changchun. It was a little more than 180 miles from Shenyang, and they reached the outskirts in the early afternoon. Eva had chosen to drive, as she was the only one who could understand the Chinese satnav. Sonny had admitted to knowing only a few words, most of which involved beer and women.

The first stop was at the main railway station. Eva took her backpack from the trunk and walked inside the building, only to be consumed by a maelstrom of people. The place was packed, and everyone seemed to be in a hurry. She stuck to the wall and followed the signs to the luggage lockers, then chose a locker at random, took a plastic bag containing the North Korean prison documents from her backpack, and locked it away. She was back in the car a couple of minutes later.

They joined the highway that cut through the southern half of the city, then followed the signs for the Changchun Forest Botanical Garden. Cheung had built his mansion overlooking the idyllic park, no doubt paying the local authorities handsomely in order to secure permission for the site.

The road twisted through what would have been lush forest in the spring and summer, but was now a wooden graveyard, the leafless trees like giant hands reaching for the sky and the warmth beyond the clouds. It would be a couple of months before the thaw came to herald the next stage of the life cycle.

When they got to the turnoff that led to Cheung's residence, Eva drove on for a hundred yards until she found a place to park.

"Let's walk from here," she said. "It's only a mile or so east."

They bundled up against the biting wind and got out of the car. Deciduous beeches gave way to evergreen firs, which would make their approach a little stealthier. If they came across Cheung's security, they would pretend to be tourists out enjoying the view. They weren't armed and they carried the US passports Wong had acquired for them, so their story should hold up.

As they neared the building, it became clear that Cheung was a visionary.

From three hundred yards away, it looked like someone had dumped a load of shipping containers in a pile and walked away, but instead of steel, the building materials seemed to consist exclusively of wood and glass. As they got closer, Eva saw that the jumble of boxes had actually been thought through quite well. The sun flooded what appeared to be the living room with natural light, and the bedrooms overlooked the park and countryside rather than the sprawling city.

It was certainly an impressive building, but they weren't there to judge Cheung on his architectural taste.

"I see a few cameras, but that's it," Sonny said.

Eva saw them, too. Some sat atop the wooden fence that surrounded the house at a discreet distance, while others hung from the eaves of the building.

She took hold of Sonny's hand and they strolled parallel to the fence, keeping it seventy yards on their right. With their coats pulled up to their cheeks and hats covering their heads, they didn't fear being recognized. For now, Eva needed to ascertain whether the cameras were fixed or maneuverable. As they walked, Sonny put an arm around her and she nuzzled into his shoulder, playing the part of lovers out for a relaxing walk. When they reached the corner of the fence, they kept going until the house was out of sight.

"Those cameras can track us," she said. "If we go in here, we'll need a diversion. Something that'll get their attention but not require a call for backup."

"I'm sure we'll think of something. Let's see what the Jianguo has to offer."

Half an hour later, they parked in the lot of the Jianguo Medical Center. It was a seven-story structure, painted an unimaginative white.

"I'll let you do the talking," Sonny said. They'd worked on an approach on the drive over.

After Eva prepared for her scene, they walked into a reception area thankfully devoid of the hospital smell of disinfectant. She didn't know if that was a good thing or a sign of poor hygiene.

At the desk they were greeted by a young woman with tied-back hair and a corporate smile.

"Welcome to the Jianguo Medical Center. How may I be of service today?"

Sonny and Eva were clearly not Chinese, so the woman had spoken in English.

"We want to inquire about your . . . services," Eva said, pretending to hold back tears. "Our daughter. She's . . ."

Eva buried her face in her hands, and Sonny took over. "What my wife means is, our daughter needs a liver transplant. Urgently. This facility was recommended to us."

"I'm sorry, but there must be some mistake. We don't perform procedures of that nature. Our specialty is orthopedics and rehabilitation. Hip replacements, broken limbs, that kind of thing."

"Is there someone we can speak to?" Sonny persisted. "We've come a long way . . ." He hugged Eva, who played the part of a distressed parent in full meltdown.

"Certainly. If you take a seat, I'll get someone to attend to you."

Sonny led Eva to a couch and sat her down, putting his head close to hers. "Don't go over the top," he whispered.

"It's working, isn't it?"

Within a couple of minutes, an older man wearing hospital whites approached them.

"I'm Kenneth Li," he said, shaking Sonny's hand. "I understand you're looking for a service we don't provide."

"That's what your receptionist told us, but we were informed that we could get a liver transplant for our little girl for the right price."

Li looked concerned. "I don't know who gave you that information, but it is incorrect. For one, we only deal with corporate clients through an insurance system. We don't take clients off the street or referrals from other hospitals. We most certainly do not have the facilities to perform organ transplant operations."

On cue, Eva let out a heart-rendering wail.

"Are you sure you have the right facility?" Li asked.

"Yes," Sonny said, exasperated. "The Jianguo."

Li sighed. "I am sorry. Someone must be playing a cruel joke. I'm afraid I can't help you."

Sonny grabbed his arm, the instinctive act of a desperate father. "You must know somewhere that can help us. Money is no object."

Li studied him for a moment, seemingly conflicted. "What's the prognosis for your daughter?"

"Without an operation, she has a few weeks left to live."

Li nodded. "Come with me."

Sonny helped Eva to her feet and they followed the doctor to an office. Inside, Li closed the door and started writing on a notepad.

"This place might be able to assist you, but you did not get this from me, understand?"

"I understand," Sonny said.

"Good. Copy this down. I'm not giving you something with my handwriting on it." He pushed the pad across to Sonny.

"Is there any reason you don't want anyone to know?"

"My superiors don't like it when we refer customers to our . . . competition."

Sonny grasped Li's hand. "I'm so grateful. We're both grateful. I assure you, no one will learn of your involvement."

Sonny copied what the doctor had written—*Liang Xiao Clinic* and an address—then put the paper in his pocket and helped Eva to her feet. "Come on, let's go save our daughter."

He kept his arm around her until they got back in the car. "Nice performance. You almost had me convinced."

"That's because you're gullible."

Sonny smiled. "Thanks."

Eva sighed. "It's not a compliment, dumbass."

He gave her a wounded look. "I know. I was joking. On a serious note, though, it proves that the ESO are playing us. Li wouldn't send a job worth hundreds of thousands to his competitors if he could do it himself."

"Exactly. Give me the address you wrote down. I'll send it to Farooq and he can check it out for us."

Sonny handed over the scrap from the notepad. Eva noted that it was in Shenyang. That would make scoping it out much easier. "The ESO is still going to expect us to hit Cheung," he said. "If we don't, they'll know we've seen through them."

"That's a problem. Hopefully Farooq will be able to tell us why they want Cheung dead."

"My guess? He's pissed off the ESO somehow."

"That makes the most sense," Eva agreed. "Then again, the Jianguo might be a conduit. People are referred there first, then Li points them to where Cheung's secret services take place."

"I reckon we'll know more once Farooq has done some digging. Wanna check this other place out?"

"Sure. But first, let's eat. I'm starving."

~

Farooq got back to them while they were sitting in a restaurant. Eva and Sonny had just finished eating when the Shield app notified them of a series of messages. They paid the bill and retreated to the car before opening the first of them.

"Looks like we were right," Eva said. "The money does leave the Jianguo account, but Farooq found that it went to legitimate services. A new scanner, the very latest in prosthetic limbs, that kind of thing. Nothing points to the DPRK. The information Wong gave us was doctored."

"Why am I not surprised."

Eva typed a brief message to Farooq, then waited a minute for his response.

"Farooq says that the Liang Xiao Clinic is ultimately owned by Xu Wei. He's the polar opposite of Cheung. The bulk of his money comes from coal, oil, gas, and mining. And that's not all. He also happens to be behind the company that settled the Camp 33 invoices."

"Sounds like just the kind of person who would want to see Cheung out of the picture," Sonny said. "Competition, after all."

"Exactly. I bet you a million bucks he's ESO."

"He has to be. They want to protect one of their own, so they set us up to take out his competitor. We think we got what we wanted, and the ESO has one less financial headache."

Eva nodded. "You catch on quick."

"I'm not just a strikingly handsome face."

Eva looked at him, and saw something new. Up until recently, he'd been a soldier and an accomplice, nothing more. Now, she thought back to the evening before they'd stormed the camp. As well as being intelligent and having a lifetime of experience under his belt, Sonny spoke consistently of loyalty and comradeship. Despite his murderous skills, he didn't come across as the violent type. He'd mentioned his future dreams, and though they'd sunk more than a few beers, he hadn't been a belligerent drunk. The banter had been full of wit without the innuendo she'd been expecting.

In the sober light of day, she saw a lot of Carl Huff in him.

That scared her.

Could she really be thinking of Sonny in this way? He certainly wasn't bad looking, and in his early forties he was still in his prime. There might be a few creases in the boyish face, but he had all the other attributes she'd want from a lover.

Stop it.

"Let's go check out the clinic," she said, trying to put some distance between herself and her thoughts.

Eva entered the destination into the satnav and pulled out into traffic. They'd only traveled a mile when Eva took a left turn, ignoring the machine's directions.

"What're you doing?"

"Just checking to see if we picked up a tail. The gray sedan's been three cars behind us since we left the restaurant."

A novice would have spun around in panic, but Sonny knew not to look back in case it alerted the pursuers. "Are they still with us?"

The car was directly behind them now, but hanging fifty yards back. "Damn it," Eva said. "My guess is it's Wong, or someone working for him."

"Then let's play it cool," Sonny said. "Head back to Shenyang as if we haven't seen them."

The sedan stayed with them all the way. There was little point trying to lose them on the freeway, so Eva kept the speed steady and made it easy for the pursuers to keep track of them. By the time they reached Shenyang, Sonny had a plan.

"Take us to within a couple of blocks of the clinic, then park up and get out. I'll take the car four blocks down the street and hope they follow me. Once you've been to the clinic, come and meet me."

"I like it."

Eva threw in a couple more turns to confirm her suspicions. Once there was no doubt that they were being followed, she pulled over near a shopping mall and got out. Sonny slid behind the wheel and Eva leaned into the window. Sonny opened it.

"Give me half an hour," she said, looking in the side-view mirror. The gray sedan had stopped, and one of the passengers climbed out of the back of the car. He stepped over to a store window and pretended to inspect the goods on offer.

"Okay, take off."

Eva tapped the roof of the car and Sonny pulled casually into traffic. She walked into the mall, using the glass storefronts to keep an eye on the man following her.

The ESO had put tails on her before, and they'd been good. She hadn't known about them until it was far too late, but thankfully they'd only followed to make contact with her, not take her out. This guy wasn't in their league. It looked like he'd learned the trade from some 1950s B-movie. Eva toyed with him for a few minutes, frequently stopping to check out the window displays, until she found a store that sold women's underwear. She strolled in, knowing the tail would wait for her outside.

As Eva pretended to shop, she made a point of looking through the huge windows every now and then, sometimes making eye contact with the tail, a middle-aged Chinese man in a long coat. She knew that if she did this often enough, he would eventually move out of her view, and within a few minutes he did exactly that.

The moment he stepped away from the window, Eva dashed to the back of the store and through a door marked "Employees Only." She ignored the protestations of the staff in the back room and found the fire exit. An alarm sounded as she pushed the bar to open it, but she had enough of a lead that she was confident of losing her hapless tail.

Eva bounded down a flight of stairs and pushed through another door, which led to an alleyway. She ran to her right and emerged onto a main street that paralleled the one she'd got out of the car on. She stole a glance back down the alley but saw no sign of pursuit.

Slowing to a walk, Eva crossed the street and took a left, always with one eye on store windows to see if the ESO man had picked her up again, but he was probably still standing outside the lingerie store looking like a bored husband waiting for his wife to finish shopping.

The Liang Xiao Clinic came into view, another all-white affair that rose six levels and had a parking lot for at least a hundred vehicles.

One of them caught her eye.

It was the same kind of refrigerated truck that she'd seen at Camp 33. The type used to transport organs over the border into China. Which Wong claimed the ESO had followed to Cheung's medical center.

But this was its ultimate destination.

Knowing she had the right place, Eva decided against going inside. Instead, she continued down the street until she came to an alley that led around the back of the clinic, taking in the security measures that she would have to overcome. The truck was proof enough for her, but the international community would need more than that and the North Korean files. Which might mean breaking in and gathering evidence.

She preferred not to have to do that. She would ask Farooq to try to work his magic first, but if he were unable to gain access to the servers, she would have to do things the old-fashioned way.

She found a camera at the rear of the building, but it appeared to be fixed and easy enough to avoid. The back entrance was probably alarmed, but a couple of drainpipes provided access to the upper windows.

Eva took out her phone as if she'd heard it ringing. She hit the button to open the camera and set it to record, then put it to her ear and started talking as she made a video of the building. It would be much easier than trying to describe it to Sonny later.

Once she had enough footage, Eva walked a couple of blocks, found a store that sold clothing, and purchased a new set of underwear and a couple of sweaters. She also found a couple that would look good on Sonny, and put them in her basket.

What are you doing, dressing the guy now?

Eva dumped the menswear back on the shelf and paid for her own clothes, then strolled back to where she'd arranged to meet Sonny. On the way, she pondered their next move.

They would have to convince the ESO that Cheung was dead. The easiest way to do that would be to actually kill the man, but enough innocent people had lost their lives in this venture. What she needed was a way to convince the ESO that Cheung was out of the picture permanently, but in order to fake his death, Cheung would have to be in on it. It was a plan that needed much thinking through.

Eva found Sonny parked outside a grocery store with the engine running, the gray sedan fifty yards away on the other side of the street.

Sonny got out as she approached the car and took the bag from her, putting it in the trunk before getting into the front passenger seat.

"How did it go?"

"The Liang Xiao is the place, all right. The truck that took the body parts from Camp 33 was parked outside. All we need to do is get inside and find paperwork that leads to Xu Wei. I took a video of the back entrance. I'll show you when we get to the hotel and we can figure out a way in."

"Sure, but that can wait. If we don't deal with Cheung soon, Wong'll be suspicious."

"I know, I've been thinking about that. How do we convince a man of Cheung's stature to fake his own death and disappear? His companies would go into meltdown if he vanished off the face of the earth, so he's unlikely to agree—and without his cooperation, our only option is to kill him."

"It shouldn't have to come to that," Sonny said. "He only has to hide out for a few days, like Hong. Once we've dealt with Xu Wei, Chin'll be free to show his face."

"Think we can get him on board?" Eva asked.

She received a huge, shit-eating grin in response. "Trust me."

CHAPTER 27

They decided to go in the following night.

After driving back to the Shangri-La, Eva gave Wong a list of items to source for Cheung's takedown, then went to her room with Sonny. Eva turned the television up to drown out their conversation and sat on the bed next to him.

"You do realize that once Xu Wei is dead and Cheung turns up alive, the ESO are gonna be pissed," Sonny pointed out.

"Tell me about it."

"They knew how to find you, they've got access to your money, and they've clearly been watching me for some time. There's no way we can run from them."

"I know. Once they know we've crossed them, there'll be no hiding."

"What do you suggest?"

Sonny's body was so close to her. She could smell his cologne; different from the one Carl wore, but evoking the same feelings.

Get a grip, woman.

"I have an idea, but we need Farooq to join us. We don't need his skills, but he has to be with us or it'll be for nothing. Ideally, I'd want Rees too, but he's stuck in the hospital."

"Wanna let me in on it?" Sonny asked.

"Not yet. It's a work in progress. For now, just concentrate on finding an excuse to get Farooq to join us. We'll work on it from there."

Sonny thought for a moment and began throwing suggestions at her. One of them stuck. After a bit of tweaking, Eva decided to use it.

They ordered room service and made small talk while they ate.

Two hours later, Wong arrived at the room with a large bag.

"I understand you paid a visit to the Jianguo hospital earlier today," he said. "Care to tell me what you did there?"

Eva had concocted a story on the drive back to the hotel, knowing Wong's men might have seen them there.

"I was checking the place out," Eva said. "We plan to destroy it once Cheung is dead, so I was looking for security measures we'll have to overcome. We can't just walk in with a case full of C-4 and start laying charges."

"And what did you learn?" Wong asked.

"Two security cameras, one outside covering the entrance, the other above the front desk. The clinic is empty after six in the evening, so no collateral damage."

Wong seemed to accept her lies.

"Why the dart guns?" he asked, as Eva emptied the contents of the bag onto the bed. "I thought you planned to kill Cheung."

"I will," said Eva. "But not quickly. The people in Camp 33 suffered while they died. I'm going to do the same to Cheung. As for his guards, we'll try to incapacitate them rather than kill them. Too many innocent people have died already. I don't want to kill anyone I don't have to. That's why I asked for the stun grenades, too."

Eva held up the clothing Wong had brought her. The black sweater and pants looked to be a good fit, as did the balaclava with holes cut out for the eyes and mouth. The suppressed pistols and knives were the ones that Sonny and Eva had taken to North Korea but hadn't used.

"What's your plan?" the ESO man wanted to know.

"Once we've disabled his security, I'm going to do a number on Cheung. Once I'm through with him, we'll take what's left of his body and dump the bits in the reservoir."

"Why not leave them at his house? Why go to all that trouble?"

"Because he's a big name in China," Sonny said. "If someone discovers his dismembered corpse, do you think they're going to leave the investigation to a couple of beat cops? No, they'll throw everything at it, and I'd rather not be around when that happens. If he disappears, it at least muddies the waters."

"We need a few more items from you," Eva said. "A large plastic sheet, say, ten feet square, to catch all the blood and wrap up the body parts, plus a cleanup crew. There's bound to be blood spatter, and anyone investigating Cheung's disappearance will see it. We need people with luminol and black lights to go over the entire place once we're gone. If they see signs of blood, they need to remove it."

Wong simply nodded, as if cleaning up murder scenes were a daily occurrence.

"What about Hong?" he asked. "My superiors are getting anxious."

"I'm waiting to hear from the survivors of Camp 33. Once they reach Ulaanbaatar, I'll give you Hong."

"That should be within the next couple of hours," Wong said, looking at his watch.

"Let's hope so. In the meantime, Sonny and I will get ready. We're heading to Cheung's place in Changchun tomorrow evening. That should be plenty of time for you to get Farooq Naser here."

"What do you need him for?"

"Cheung has cameras watching the grounds of his house, so I'm assuming he has other security measures in place. I need Farooq to neutralize them."

"I can get someone local," Wong said.

"I'm sure you can, but I'm going with Farooq. I only work with people I trust."

If Wong was hurt by the barb, he didn't show it. "Fine. Get him here."

"I'll need a contact number for him," Eva said.

"I'm sure you can get in touch with him if you—"

"Just get me his number," Eva cut in. She could indeed contact Farooq via Shield, but the more she used it, the more chance they had of intercepting the signal and working on a way to crack the code.

Wong's face remained unreadable for a moment, then softened. "Sure. I'll have it in the next ten minutes."

He left, and Eva went into the suite's bedroom and tried on the clothes Wong had brought her. As she'd suspected, they fit perfectly. She took them off again and ran her finger along every seam, looking for a hidden tracking device. She found one in the collar of the tight-fit sweater, and another in the waistband of the pants.

Perfect.

She assumed that they would've also bugged the rental car by now, the mistrust clearly mutual.

Wong returned within ten minutes. Sonny let him in, and he gave Eva a piece of paper with a cell number. He left again without saying a word.

She used the hotel phone to call Farooq. Wong was surely listening in, so it didn't matter if she used her cell or the landline.

"Hello . . . ?" He sounded tentative, as if not used to receiving phone calls.

"Hey, buddy. Long time, no see."

"Eva! What the hell are you doing calling me on a landline? And how did you get this number?"

"Relax. I got it from the ESO."

Silence from the handset. It lasted longer than she expected.

"Please tell me you're joking," Farooq finally said, his voice shaky, bordering on petrified.

"Sadly, I'm not. I don't know how long they've been onto you, but they seem to know everything Sonny and I have been doing for the last few months. Don't worry, though, they're not out to get you. I need your help doing a job for them.".

More silence, though this time not as lengthy. "You're . . . working for them?"

"I know. It's complicated. I'll explain when you get here."

"What? Wait . . . you want me to go to . . . Shenyang?"

He was either tracing the call or had looked up the area code of the hotel's number. Either way, he was still sharp, despite the shock. Eva liked that.

"As soon as you can," she said. "I'll book a room for you at the Shangri-La. Shall we say . . . twenty-four hours?"

"I . . . I guess I can do that."

"Good. See you then. Call me in room 1803 when you get here, and try to get some sleep on the plane."

Eva ended the call.

"Does that mean I get the rest of the day off?" Sonny asked.

"Sure. Got any plans?"

Candlelit dinner, bottle of wine, screw my brains out . . .

"I thought I'd hit the gym," Sonny said.

"Great idea," she said quickly, hiding her disappointment. "I might treat myself to a massage at the spa."

After a cold shower . . .

CHAPTER 28

Eva reached for the end of the pool and spat water. After fifty lengths she was barely blowing, but she didn't want to overdo it. She still had a couple of hours planned in the gym, including more cardio on the treadmill followed by a stint at the weight station. She'd already decided to leave the massage until the following day.

In the changing room she swapped the swimsuit for shorts and a sports bra, then set her iPod to her favorite running tracks.

After two miles and a handful of songs, she turned it off. She couldn't hear the music over the thoughts rattling around inside her head.

They were all about Sonny.

What the hell is happening to me?

If this were some biological stage that every woman went through, it was a new one for Eva Driscoll. She'd never been one to crave intimacy, except during her time with Carl. But after the few weeks with him, she'd spent the years alone, dedicating herself to her career as a CIA operative. It was only after he'd turned up again a decade later that her desires had resurfaced.

It had been two years since Carl's death, and in that time she'd never thought about another man.

Until Sonny showed up, all smiles and charm.

Eva kicked up the pace to ten miles per hour, hoping the exertion would take her mind off the subject, but it proved pointless. After another mile, she gave up on the treadmill and walked to the weight benches. The gym sadly lacked a punch bag, or she would have been able to take her frustrations out on that. Instead, she picked up a couple of twenty-pound dumbbells and pretended she was using them to smash Wong's face in.

After twenty minutes, Eva was spent. She took the elevator back to her room and showered, then picked up the room service menu. It was almost time for dinner, and she didn't fancy sitting alone in the restaurant. Still, it would be better than sharing a table with Sonny. At least by herself she might be able to figure out what was behind this new infatuation.

Eva was trying to decide between the steak and sea bass when a knock came at the door. She pulled the complimentary bathrobe around her and tied it at the waist, then picked up the suppressed Sig Sauer Wong had given her.

"Who is it?" she called as she stood to the side of the door.

"Schrödinger. Have you seen my cat?"

Eva swung the door open. "Get in here, you idiot."

Sonny walked in and held up a bottle of wine and a bucket full of ice and beer. "Celebration time," he said. He dipped into the bucket and popped a cap.

"Really. What's the occasion?"

"It's the two-year anniversary of Carl and Len's decision to watch the rest of the show from the balcony seats."

Eva had the date firmly embossed in her mind. She'd shed more than a few tears a year earlier, and this year the plan had been to work through the pain alone. Again.

Sonny clearly had different ideas about the grieving process.

"It isn't until tomorrow," she said.

"I know," Sonny told her, pouring a glass of wine and handing it to her. "But we'll be busy come tomorrow night. Today, however, we have all the free time we need."

He held the bottle up, and Eva clinked her glass against it.

"To Carl and Len."

"Carl and Len," she echoed.

She sipped the wine, taking her time so that Sonny wouldn't see her forcing back a tear. She stood and said, "Gotta pee." In the bathroom, she splashed cold water on her face and tried to compose herself. Once she was sure she had her emotions in check, she flushed the toilet and went back into the living room.

"I got a call from one of the Camp 33 prisoners just before I hit the gym," she said. "They reached Mongolia safely."

"Excellent. Have you told Wong?"

"Yeah."

Sonny laughed. "I bet he was pissed when he found out Hong had been staying in an apartment a couple of miles away."

"Let's just say I'm no longer on his Christmas card list."

She guessed that Wong might be listening in to their conversation, but didn't care. She would only take precautions if the topic moved on to operational matters.

Sonny dropped his empty beer bottle in the trash and opened another. "So, tell me about Carl," he said. "You never told me how you two met. I know you were both CIA, but that's about it."

She realized he was right. The first time she'd met Sonny, they'd been too busy fighting the ESO to discuss their pasts, and their last mission—the one Carl and Len hadn't survived—had been all business, too. Even when they'd shared a few too many drinks before the DPRK mission, the subject had never come up.

"We met the first day of boot camp. One of the first things they told us was that relationships between candidates were strictly forbidden, and for some reason the instructor looked at me when he said it."

"Because you were the only woman?" Sonny asked, topping up her glass.

Eva chuckled. "No, there were two others, but I guess my profile suggested I liked a challenge."

"And not being one to disappoint . . ."

"Actually, that's not what happened. I did hook up with someone, only it wasn't Carl. It was Bill Sanders."

"*The* Bill Sanders? Head of the CIA?"

"Yeah, only he was just head of clandestine ops at the time. I must have caught his eye, because he invited me to his log cabin one weekend. I hardly felt I could refuse."

"You hussy!"

Eva managed a full laugh this time. "Call me what you will, but it was all about survival. I knew what his intentions were, so I took advantage of the situation. I used the CIA's own surveillance kit to record our . . . activities for posterity, and I let Sanders know that if the company ever got tired of me and decided I needed to meet with an accident, it would all come out. His career and marriage would have been ruined."

"Ah." Sonny nodded sagely. "That's why he sent Carl to help us against Langton. To prevent the shit sticking to him."

"Exactly," Eva said. "Anyway, a few weeks after that, we had a five-day evade-and-survive test. At the end of it, when everyone was hitting the bunks, I went to the nearest bar to tend my wounds. And who should be there but Carl Huff."

"And the rest is history."

Eva nodded.

"Sounds just like me and Len," Sonny said. "Only without the hot sex."

Wine shot out of Eva's nose, and she slapped Sonny on the arm before going to the bathroom to clean herself up. When she got back, her glass was full once more. Sonny had moved to the couch and had one arm resting along the back of it. Eva sat next to him.

"Do you miss Len as much as I miss Carl?"

"Every single day."

They descended into silence, and she was grateful to Sonny for not breaking it with idle chatter. His excellent choice of wine put another checkmark in his column.

She turned to look at him, and he did the same to her.

"Why does it still hurt so much, even after all this time?"

"Because they were special," he said.

Eva ran her finger around the rim of her glass. That they were. And as much as she missed Carl, she suspected the hurt was equally deep for Sonny. He'd lost a soulmate he'd known his entire adult life. Not an easy void to fill.

"Cheer up," Sonny said. "They wouldn't want to see us moping around down here." He polished off his second beer and opened a third. "Time for some music."

He turned on the TV and found a cable channel dedicated to tunes, though the menu told them not to expect anything penned this century.

As a classic erupted from the TV's speakers, Sonny took Eva's hand and pulled her to her feet. "Just pretend you're at your high-school prom."

"*. . . I never stood a chance. You were straight down to the lovin'. . .*"

Everything was forgotten as she watched Sonny shake his groove, and she lost herself in the music, gyrating her hips in time to his. He was a decent dancer, and that smile never left his face.

The track faded out as the next song began, and Sonny crooned along to a familiar love ballad by Foreigner.

And he can sing, too . . .

Sonny moved closer, gently swaying his hips, and Eva put her arms around his neck, moving in time with him.

His face came within inches of hers, and all thoughts but one slipped from her mind. She closed her eyes and planted her lips on his, and Sonny put his hands on her hips, bringing her closer.

Eva was lost in him. She felt him stiffen against her, his hands roaming up her back and down her sides. She gripped his hair, thrusting her hips forward while her tongue battled his. The music on the TV had given way to adverts, but she and Sonny were dancing to their own tune now.

It was as if someone had thrown a switch.

Eva pushed herself away from him, horrified at what she'd done. At what she'd wanted to do.

"I'm sorry," she said. "I . . . I can't."

Sonny smoothed his hair back into place. "I understand."

"I shouldn't have done that."

"It wasn't just you," Sonny pointed out. "But honestly, it's no big deal. I'm not sure I could have gone much further with Len watching, anyway."

He seemed okay with the situation, which made her feel a little better. Some men would have been angry at being led on, but Sonny looked genuinely tranquil.

He switched the TV off and they stood in awkward silence.

"I should go," he said eventually.

"No." It came out a little too quickly.

"I'll tell you what. I'll go for a walk. Call my room in half an hour if you want to watch a movie or something."

He kissed her on the cheek on the way out, and Eva sank into the couch as the door clicked shut.

What the hell were you thinking?

The simple answer was: she hadn't been thinking. Her carnal desires had overruled her heart and head, causing her to act like a hormonal teenager. Thankfully, she'd managed to break the spell before things had gone too far.

Eva took the glass of wine through to the bathroom, poured the contents down the sink, then brushed her teeth. When she got into bed, she cuddled the spare pillow and cried herself to sleep.

CHAPTER 29

Farooq looked like he hadn't slept in a year, never mind the nineteen hours since she'd last spoken to him.

Eva's night hadn't been that great, either, but at least the bed had been comfortable.

"I told you to get some sleep," she said as he collapsed into a chair.

"You know I can't sleep on planes. I took two diazepam, but they didn't help. All I've had is twenty minutes in the taxi from the airport."

"Then go lie down," Eva said. "We're going to be leaving here at ten this evening, so you should be able to get at least seven hours."

"I will, but first can you explain what the hell's going on?"

"The short version is: I need you to defeat a security system. That's all you're getting for now. I'll give you a full briefing on the way."

"But what about—"

"I said that's it." Eva glared at Farooq. It was the first time she'd ever been firm with him, and he seemed more shocked than subjugated.

"Okay. I'm gonna hit the sack. You can fill me in later."

He picked up his bag and left her room.

Eva sighed. She hadn't wanted to be harsh with her old friend, but there was no way she could discuss it with him while he was so ragged.

He needed a clear head so he could follow the security protocols they'd need to use while talking shop in the hotel.

With several hours to kill, she headed to the gym.

~

When Farooq knocked on Eva's door at nine that evening, she let him in and immediately put her finger over her lips, then handed him a sheet of paper. He looked confused, but sat down and read it.

> *The room is bugged. I'm going to ask you to defeat a home security system. Just say you can do it. The ESO want me to kill Cheung, so play along. Feel free to sound concerned about working with the ESO, but don't lay it on too thick.*

"So, can you tell me what this is all about now?" Farooq said.

"Sure," Eva replied. She took another sheet of paper from her pocket and gave it to him to read—this one had instructions that needed to be carried out as soon as possible. While he absorbed the contents, she started at the beginning, from her first meeting with Johnson in Melbourne, the failed attempt to get Hong out of the country, their spell in Camp 33, and the attack that liberated the prisoners.

She then told him what she planned to do to Cheung, the man the ESO said was behind the organ racket.

"Jeez, Eva, you ever heard of a concept called 'none of your fucking business'?"

"That's easy to say when you read about it in a newspaper, but I've been there. I've seen the faces of the people sentenced to an excruciating death simply because they're healthy enough to provide living tissue to rich people in need. Including *kids*, for fuck's sake."

Farooq hung his head.

"I have to finish this," Eva said. "If I walk away now, they'll just move the operation to another facility in the DPRK, and Cheung will continue to profit from it. If I don't kill him, I won't be able to live with myself."

"I'm sorry." Farooq looked up. "I should have expected nothing less from you. I just hate the idea of working with the ESO. They tried to kill us."

"I don't like it either, but we've got no choice. They've shown that there's nowhere for us to hide. We're only alive because they need our skills and we're providing them. If we don't play along, we outlive our usefulness."

Farooq put his head in his hands. "I need a drink."

"You back on the bottle?" Eva asked, concerned.

"No. I haven't touched a drop in over four years."

"Good. I need you sober tonight."

Eva went into the bedroom and came back with a sweater, which she tossed to Farooq. While he sat looking quizzical, she wrote on a scrap of paper:

There's a device sewn into the lining. Is it location, sound, or both?

Farooq took a letter opener from the desk and made a small incision in the garment, then pulled out the tracker. He studied it for a moment, turning it in his fingers, then put it back in place and wrote on the paper.

Location only.

A knock came at the door. Eva took the gun from her waistband and checked to see who it was.

"It's me."

Wong entered when she undid the lock. "The extra items you requested are ready. If you give me your car keys, my man will put them in the trunk."

Eva tossed him the keys. "Do you have a team on standby?"

"They'll be half an hour away," the ESO man said. "Once you're done, call them at this number and they'll clean the place up."

He handed Eva a slip of paper with a cell number written on it, and she entered the details into her phone.

As Wong left, he passed Sonny in the doorway.

"Hey, buddy," the Englishman said to Farooq. "Long time, no see. How you doin'?"

"Wishing I could wake up from this nightmare," Farooq said, rising to shake Sonny's hand.

"It's a bitch, ain't it? So what have you been up to for the last two years?"

"Hiding. But not very well, apparently. I've spent the last eighteen months moving around South America, using Airbnb, never staying in the same place for more than a few weeks. They still found me."

"And they always will," Sonny said, hewing to the planned discussion, but also pointing out a painful truth. "Running is pointless. We have to do as they say, or it's lights out. You better get used to it."

Wong returned a few minutes later. He gave Eva the car keys.

"What do we do once Cheung is dead?" she asked. "I assume you're going to come calling regularly, so do we check in with you every time we move, or just wait for you to find us?"

"Makes no difference to me," Wong admitted. "I'm just a small cog in the machine. If you want to leave a forwarding address, I'll pass it on. If not . . ." He shrugged.

"I don't know about you guys," Sonny said, "but my money's been burning a hole in my pocket. I think it's time to start spending it. Anyone fancy a few weeks in Bora Bora when this is all over?"

"Count me out," Farooq said. "One flight a year is too much for me. It's at least three to Bora Bora."

"Then we can hire a plane and fly direct from here," Eva said. "Get on your laptop and find one that can make it without stopping." She turned to Sonny and smiled. "I've always wanted to go there."

To his credit, Sonny hadn't mentioned the previous evening since they'd parted company. He was behaving as if it hadn't happened, which was what she'd hoped for. The last thing she needed was Farooq spotting something between them and adding his two cents.

Farooq completed his search in less than a minute. "The Four Seasons Resort on Bora Bora has its own charter service. They use the Gulfstream G550, which has a range of over twelve thousand kilometers, and it's just shy of eleven thousand from here."

"Great. Charter one for tomorrow."

"They only run it from Los Angeles," he said. "We'll have to charter our own from here. It'll cost a fortune, though. A Four Seasons shared charter is over thirty grand a person. Expect to pay three hundred grand."

"I'll cover it," Eva said. "The ESO owes me another twenty million for rescuing Hong. I'll enjoy it more knowing it's on their dime."

Farooq went back to work and found a company that could provide the plane they needed.

"I need to call them," he said. "I can't do this online."

"You'll have to do it on the move," Eva said. "We gotta go."

Eva put her jacket on, picked up her bag, and led them out of the room. Wong peeled off and returned to his room while the others took the elevator. On the way down, Farooq reached the charter company and booked the flight for three days' time. When it came to payment, Farooq took out a pen and jotted down the firm's bank account details, promising that the money would be there within the hour.

When they got to the car, Farooq got in the back while the black-clad pair took the front seats. He hooked up the cell phone to his laptop and navigated to Eva's bank. He gave her the laptop so that she could log in, then read out the account to transfer the money to. After parting with almost four hundred grand, Eva passed the laptop back to Farooq.

"Book somewhere to stay on Bora Bora," she said. "I want at least a month, and make sure they're the best rooms available."

Once Farooq confirmed their bookings, they drove the 120 miles to Changchun in silence. They knew the car was likely to be bugged, and Eva didn't want them stumbling onto subjects better kept from prying ears.

Sonny parked the car a mile from Cheung's house. A cloudy night sky kept them hidden on their approach, and when they were within fifty feet of the fence that encircled the building, Eva took a knee. She scanned the entire area through NVGs—not just the house, but also checking to see if the ESO had sent people to watch the operation go down.

No sign of anyone.

Inside the house, she saw a figure walk past a lit window, one of three illuminated on the first floor. The two upper floors remained in total darkness.

"We've got two options," she whispered. "Stealthy approach or direct."

"We could disable one of the cameras on the fence at the back, where there's no lights," Sonny suggested. "Jump over, get in the rear entrance, and take out the guards."

"Or we could just knock on the door." Eva smiled.

"Seriously?"

"Why not? We're here to gain his trust, after all."

She'd come up with the idea of a non-threatening entry on the drive over, and now that they were on target, it made a lot of sense.

To her, at least.

"You think they're just going to welcome a pair of strangers into the house at"—he checked his watch—"one in the morning?"

"No. That's why I'm going in alone. You can cover me."

"I don't like it," Sonny said. "If we storm the place and disable his bodyguards, he'll know we could easily kill him. If we then explain the reason for being there, he might believe us. If you just knock on the door and tell him that a shady organization wants him dead and could he please comply, he'll think you're crazy. They might even shoot you the moment you set foot on his property."

"Unlikely," she replied. "Still, if it makes you feel better, let's compromise. I'll approach the front door while you scale the fence at the back and wait by the rear entrance. If you hear a commotion, get inside and assess the situation. Don't shoot unless you absolutely must."

"That still leaves you vulnerable," Farooq told Eva.

"I'm a big girl. I can look after myself."

She tucked the dart gun into the back of her waistband, next to the suppressed Glock. In her belt she carried three spare cartridges for the non-lethal weapon, the only drawback of which was that she had to manually load each round. If things got dicey, that would be a problem, but she had the Glock for backup if the need arose.

"Give me and Farooq a couple of minutes to get into position," Sonny said, resigned to following her lead.

The men trotted off. She watched them approach the fence below one of the CCTV cameras. The device was pointing along the fence, so anyone climbing over would be spotted. She saw Farooq take out a handheld machine and connect it to the wire feeding the camera, then tap Sonny on the shoulder. The Englishman was up and over in a few seconds, and Farooq removed the device and crouch-jogged back to Eva.

"Wait here," she said. "We'll come out and get you when it's safe."

Without waiting for a reply, she took off her night-vision glasses, unzipped the black jacket, and walked calmly toward the front gate.

Unlike the eight-foot fence that surrounded the building, the gate was made of ornate ironwork, not wood. Through it she could see the front of the house, where huge double doors were flanked by alabaster dragons on marble plinths.

She tried the gate, but it was locked. A speakerphone was built into the wall on one side, but she chose not to use it. Instead, she climbed over the gate and dropped to the ground. The moment she started walking towards the house, the front door opened.

The guard was huge, like a jacked-up sumo wrestler. Eva was glad she'd brought along the most powerful tranquilizer available, though she wasn't sure the dosage would be enough to take him down.

She would soon find out.

As he waddled toward her, she could see a gun in a shoulder holster every time his jacket flapped open. Her diminutive figure worked to her advantage once more, as the heavy clearly didn't consider her a threat. If he had, the pistol would have been in his hand by now.

"Get out of here!" he shouted, pointing back at the gate. "This is private property!"

Although he'd spoken in Chinese, Eva stuck to English. "I need to speak to Mr. Cheung. His life is in danger."

As she spoke, she continued walking toward the bodyguard. Twenty feet. Fifteen . . .

Because his words didn't seem to be registering, the man-mountain put his hand inside his jacket and pulled the pistol free.

Eva froze ten feet from him and threw her hands in the air, playing the petrified lost tourist to perfection. Her face was a mask of shock, and she started stammering as she spoke.

"P-please, I'm sorry, don't sh-sh-shoot."

The bodyguard continued toward her, obviously not seeing her as a threat. The gun rested alongside his hip as he pointed at the gate with his other hand.

When they came within two feet of each other, Eva struck. His physique suggested he could absorb a lot of blows, but there were still a couple of vulnerable points. She punched him in the throat with her right hand, while her left reached for the dart gun. As the goon put his hands to his neck, she pistol-whipped him with the grip, then fired a dart into his thigh. Rather than knock him out, it enraged him. He swung the gun round at her, but she blocked the arm and a shot rang out, missing her head by inches. She trapped his arm against her side and brought a knee up into his stomach; it was like hitting a brick wall. A hand like a vise gripped her throat, cutting off her oxygen supply. She used her knee to hit him again and again, hoping to connect with his groin, but he maneuvered to protect his privates. Eva clawed at his fingers, trying to break his grip, but it was a losing battle. Darkness was enveloping her, the moon-shaped face before her fading . . .

Suddenly, she could breathe again. The hulk's hand fell away, and he collapsed to the ground. As his huge frame fell, it revealed Sonny, holding the piece of wood he'd used to clobber the giant.

"Get to the door, now!" he whispered.

Eva gulped air as she inserted another dart into the gun, then followed him as he ran for the house. They were twenty feet away when the doors flew inward and another bodyguard was framed in the light pouring from the opening. Sonny and Eva fired darts in unison and dodged sideways, forcing the man to choose which one to aim for. He picked Sonny and fired off a couple of rounds, but both went wide as the sedative took hold. He raised his arm to aim once more, but he couldn't find the strength to pull the trigger. He collapsed to his knees, stayed there for a moment, then toppled sideways.

Sonny and Eva reloaded, then stood either side of the open door.

If Wong's intelligence was correct, there was only one remaining bodyguard.

The problem was, there was no sign of him.

~

Sonny indicated that he would go in first. He stepped around the doorway and into the vast hallway. One door was slightly ajar, and behind it Sonny could see light. He gestured for Eva to enter the house and cover the stairs that ran up the left wall to the upper levels, while he approached the open door.

Sonny eased himself silently up against the wall. There were voices coming from within the room, but he could only hear one side of the conversation. It had to be someone making a phone call, probably for backup.

Sonny pulled the pin on an M84 stun grenade and threw it into the room. It was primed to detonate two seconds after the lever was released, and right on cue, a deafening explosion shook the first floor. Sonny was moving the second the noise reached him, and inside the room he saw two men lying on the floor by a set of French windows. One of them had his hand a few inches from a gun, and Sonny gave him a dart in the backside, then kicked him over.

It wasn't Cheung, but the other person was. Late thirties, thin as Farooq, with a birthmark under his lower lip, he matched the photo Wong had given them.

Sonny dragged him to his feet and pulled him into the hallway. Eva had already closed the front doors, and she pointed to a chair. Sonny dumped Cheung into it.

"Go and bring the guards inside," Eva said.

"You want me to lift that huge sack of shit by myself?"

"Okay, put him in the recovery position and bring the other one in. I don't want them swallowing their tongues. We'll lose his trust if one of them dies."

Sonny was okay with that. He stuck his head out the door, saw no danger, and left the building.

~

"Come on, wake up," Eva said, gently slapping Cheung's thin face.

Sonny was back by the time Cheung started to respond. He pulled the smaller bodyguard into the hall and shut the door, then went to attend to the one who'd been stunned by his grenade.

"If you want money, the safe is upstairs," the businessman said groggily, in his own language.

"Speak English," Eva said. "I know you're fluent."

Cheung looked up and saw her for the first time. "The safe's upstairs," he repeated.

"We're not here for your money. Someone wants you dead."

The color drained from Cheung's face. "You're here to kill me? Why?"

"Relax. If I wanted you dead, you wouldn't be talking to me."

"But you killed my men," Cheung said.

"They're drugged, that's all," Eva assured him. "The big one might have a headache and a sore throat, too, but other than that they're fine."

"Then what do you want?"

"To save your life."

Sonny returned from the other room. "I heard someone on the phone," he said. "We should expect company soon."

"Who were you calling?" Eva asked.

"The police," Cheung said. "They'll be here in a few minutes."

"Go get the phone," Eva told Sonny. While he was gone, she said to Cheung, "Call them and tell them it was a mistake. Everything's fine. False alarm."

"So you can spend the whole evening torturing me? No thanks. I'll take my chances."

Stubborn son of a bitch.

"How can I make this simple so you understand it? Someone has tasked me with killing you. I don't want to do that. If you don't call the police off, I'll shoot you in the head. If you do, we'll have a nice chat and you'll hopefully live a long life. Time's running out, so make a decision."

"Who?" Cheung asked. "Who wants me dead?"

"If I told you, you wouldn't believe me."

"Try me."

Eva did her best in the limited time available, but Cheung looked skeptical throughout. She couldn't blame him. Trying to elevator-pitch the concept of the ESO in less than a minute was impossible. Even though the US president had publicly launched an investigation into the organization a couple of years earlier, she realized that convincing Cheung would be difficult.

"What else can I tell you?" Eva asked. "We know the police are on their way. If I was here to kill you, I would have done it by now. If I wanted to torture you, I would have drugged you, taken you to my car, and driven to a remote location. Yet I'm still here, and so are you."

Cheung massaged his temples, as if trying to coax his brain into making a decision.

"Time's a wasting," Sonny said, now back with the phone. "Give him five more seconds, then shoot him. If the dumb bastard wants to die, that's fine with me."

"Five . . ." Eva said, looking Cheung in the eye.

As the countdown reached one, he held out his hand. "Give me the phone."

Sonny handed it over, and Cheung dialed. When he was put through, he spoke in Chinese. Sonny glanced at Eva to see if she detected any sign of deceit. She shook her head.

"Done," Cheung said, ending the call and tossing the phone back to Sonny. "Now what?"

"Get the stuff from the car, and bring Farooq in," Eva told Sonny. She instructed Cheung to find somewhere more comfortable so that they could talk, and he led her through to the living room. As in the hallway, the decor here was minimalist, the furniture all glass, chrome, and white.

Cheung sat on one of two sofas facing a round glass table. Eva positioned herself opposite him.

"Why does the ESO want me dead?" Cheung asked.

"Because I told them I wanted to kill the people behind a North Korean organ-harvesting racket. The ESO pointed me in your direction, but I think the real kingpin is Xu Wei."

"If that's the case, why are you here? Why aren't you at Xu Wei's place right now?"

"We think Xu Wei is ESO," Sonny said as he entered the room. He dumped the folded plastic sheet on the floor.

Farooq followed him in and offered Cheung a timid wave.

"I'm assuming that if you don't kill me, the ESO won't be happy with you. I take it you have a plan?"

"I do," Eva said, "but it needs your willing participation."

"It's not as if I have much of a choice."

Eva stood and took out a knife that had a razor-sharp, six-inch blade. She walked over to Cheung, who shrank back into the sofa.

"Relax," she said. "I just need a little blood. Hold out your hand."

Cheung looked reluctant, but gingerly offered her his left hand. Eva took his wrist and sliced the palm, and the two-inch cut started bleeding immediately. She waited until a little had pooled, then flicked his hand to the side. Crimson spots dotted the hardwood floor and oriental rug.

"Show my friend where the kitchen is," she told Cheung, "and bring something to clean this mess up."

Cheung held his hand to his chest, and Sonny followed him out of the room. A few minutes later they returned, and Sonny had done a good job of bandaging the wound. He was carrying a box filled with rags and cleaning solutions.

Eva took a cloth and a bottle of bleach and removed the blood from the wooden floor. She deliberately left a spot under a table, knowing the ESO's hired clean-up squad would be looking for signs of Cheung's demise. If they had the capability to match DNA, so much the better.

"What now?" Cheung asked.

"We sit and wait," Eva said. She hadn't seen anyone watching the house, but that didn't mean they weren't. The ESO would expect her to take at least an hour to torture and dismember Cheung, so she used the time to explain the rest of her plan.

"Are you claustrophobic?" she asked.

Cheung shook his head.

"Good. In about an hour, we're going to wrap you in the plastic, then the rug, and put you in the trunk of our car. We'll drive to the lake, but once we're sure we're not being tailed, we'll stop on the way to let you out. You'll have to find your own way from there, so take plenty of cash. No bank cards, they can be traced."

"Where do I go?"

"Anywhere," Eva said. "Just stay hidden for three days. That'll give us time to do what we need to do."

"Which is . . . ?"

"It's best you don't know," Sonny said, "You got any coffee?"

Cheung nodded toward the kitchen, and Sonny went to make a pot.

~

At 2:15 in the morning, Sonny spread the plastic sheet out on the rug. "It's time."

"What about my men?" Cheung asked.

"They'll be coming to soon," Eva said.

"But when they wake, they'll report me missing."

"No they won't. They're coming with us. We'll put them in your car, and when we drop you off, they can join you. We'll drive your car into the lake to add to the mystery. By the time the ESO figures out what happened, we'll be long gone."

"I hope you're right," Cheung said.

211

The first of his bodyguards started to stir. He let out a moan and pushed himself up onto his knees, his head on his chest. He looked up with some effort, and the sight of strangers in the house gave him a fresh burst of strength. He leapt to his feet and reached for his weapon, but the holster was empty.

"It's okay, Cho," Cheung said. "These people are friends. Go and see how Lee is. He's in the study."

The henchman pulled himself together, then went to check on his colleague. Eva stopped him and asked him to open the gate. He looked at Cheung, who nodded, then pulled a small device from his pocket and clicked a button.

"Go get the car," Eva told Farooq.

When Cho returned with Lee, Cheung explained what they were going to do. The pair didn't look happy with the idea, but Cheung told them to do as he ordered, then lay on the edge of the plastic sheet.

Eva and Sonny wrapped him up loosely—she didn't want him to suffocate—then rolled the rug around him. She got the bodyguards to help carry him to the front door, then told them to wait.

The sound of a horn told them that Farooq was back. Eva and Sonny carried the rolled-up rug to the vehicle and dumped it in the trunk, then asked Farooq to help them with the huge bodyguard, Tong. Between them, they dragged him inside the house in order to wake him up in private. She would have asked the other guards to help, but if the ESO had people watching, they would see through her ruse.

Eva got a glass of water from the kitchen and threw it into the big man's face.

Tong sputtered and wiped his eyes. When he saw Eva looking down at him, his face contorted with rage. He was on his feet in a second, surprising everyone, but before he could launch himself at Eva, Cho stopped him.

"Tong! She's on our side."

The giant hesitated, and when he saw that his colleagues were unharmed, anger gave way to confusion.

"You can explain on the way," Eva said. "Get in your boss's car. We have to go."

She followed them into the garage, where an electric version of a luxury car gleamed under the LED lights. Cheung's men got in, and she ordered them to stay down until someone told them otherwise.

Eva opened the garage door, and Farooq walked in and got in Cheung's car.

"Stay close behind me," Eva told him, then jogged to the rental and got behind the wheel.

She drove out of the compound and followed the main road, which was thankfully empty. There was no way the ESO could put a tail on her, but there were still the trackers on the car and her clothes to consider. It would take at least a minute to get Cheung out of the trunk, and her minders would notice the car being stationary all that time. A railroad crossing would have helped, but she'd checked the map ahead of time and there were none in the area. She would have to rely on her backup plan.

As they approached the edge of town, Eva checked the mirrors once more.

"Shit!" she said for the benefit of any listening devices in the rental, then pulled over. Farooq parked up a couple of yards behind her. Eva got out and took a beer bottle from the glove box, then gestured for Sonny to get into the driver's seat. She'd brought the bottle from the hotel, and it was time to make use of it. She threw it on the road and it smashed into pieces. Having found a suitably large, strong shard, she placed it in front of the rear wheel and signaled for Sonny to move the car a couple of feet.

The vehicle crept slowly forward, and she was rewarded with an angry hiss as the glass dug into the rubber. She slapped the side of the car, and Sonny put it in park and turned off the engine. He got out and helped Eva drag Cheung from the trunk and unwrap him.

"How are you doing?"

"I'm okay," Cheung said, gulping air. Sweat ran from his head, and his shirt was soaking.

"Good. Find a hotel, rent a car, whatever. *Cash only.* Then stay hidden for the next three days. After that, go to the Jianguo Clinic in Changchun. Hopefully there'll be something waiting for you."

Cheung's bodyguards were already out of the other car, and Eva watched the quartet trudge toward town before she took out the spare and began changing the tire.

CHAPTER 30

Wong was outside Eva's room when they returned to the Shangri-La. He waited for her to insert her key card, then followed them in without being asked.

"How did it go?" he said.

"He's dead, if that's what you mean."

"And his bodyguards?"

"We disposed of them, too," Sonny said. "We thought about leaving them alive, but once they came round they would have alerted the authorities. We didn't want that."

Wong stood with his hands on his hips. "The cleanup crew didn't see any sign of them being injured."

"That's why we used the tranquilizer darts," Eva told him. "We put them in Cheung's car while they were still out, and drove it into the lake."

That was partly true. The vehicle was now under ten feet of water, but no one had perished inside.

"Any problems getting to the lake?" Wong asked.

You know because you were tracking us, Eva thought. "We had a flat tire that stopped us for about ten minutes. Apart from that, no issues. Speaking of which, can you ask someone to get the tire repaired? We had to drive all the way back on the spare."

She tossed him the keys.

"The rental company will do that when I return it."

"This morning would be better," Eva said. "We've got another couple of days until our flight, so we're going to need a car to get around."

Wong looked put out but agreed to have the car ready for use by the time they woke up. He left the room, and once she was sure he wasn't going to return, she took a sheet of paper from the notepad on the desk and wrote on it.

All talk from now on about Bora Bora. If we need to talk about the mission, we'll do it outside only. When we wake, meet in the lobby at 2pm.

Once they'd read it, Eva used an ornamental lighter to set fire to the note and dropped it into an ashtray. When it had burnt out, she washed the ashes down the sink.

"Get some sleep," she told the others. "Let's meet at two and see a bit of the town before we leave."

"Sounds like a plan," Sonny agreed.

Farooq simply yawned and got to his feet. As they opened the door to leave, Eva called Sonny back.

"I just wanted to thank you for helping me back there. If you hadn't shown up . . ."

Sonny gave her his most disarming smile. "Always a pleasure."

He closed the door behind him, leaving Eva alone, physically and spiritually. She stripped and got into the shower, and ten minutes later she slid beneath the sheets and fell asleep in seconds.

When she woke at one in the afternoon, Eva brushed her teeth, then looked through the sparse wardrobe she'd been provided with and picked out slacks, a T-shirt, and a sweater. Before she put them on, she ran her fingers over every seam. It wasn't long before she found what she was looking for.

As with her prior outfit, Wong had sewn trackers into all three articles of clothing. She expected everything else in the closet had been given the same treatment, probably while they were dealing with Cheung. That would work in their favor later.

She put the clothes on and called Sonny's room. He was already awake, and said he would check on Farooq and meet her in the lobby in thirty minutes.

Half an hour later, Eva headed downstairs. She wasn't surprised to see Wong waiting with Sonny and Farooq. He tried to strike up a conversation with her, but Eva was keen to get going. She asked him for the car keys, and when Wong handed them over she turned to Sonny and Farooq.

"Shall we?"

The trio walked out into the cold and found the vehicle in a reserved spot.

"Where to?" Sonny asked.

"Shopping," Eva replied, and handed him a note she'd written earlier. "I need a few outfits for Bora Bora."

"Good idea. I left my mankini in New Zealand."

"You buy one of those, I'll feed you to the sharks."

Sonny read the short missive, which instructed him to buy new pants and a sweatshirt and wear them immediately because his own clothes were likely bugged. He passed the paper to Farooq without comment, and he in turn gave it back to Eva.

No one spoke as they drove to the nearby mall. Inside the huge complex, Eva found a store where the boys could get their new clothes while she shopped to meet her needs. They met up thirty minutes later, all wearing new outfits. She was pleased to see that Sonny and Farooq had remembered to purchase suitable apparel for the upcoming trip to French Polynesia, too.

Eva suggested they take a walk to the nearby park. On the way, they dumped their bags of new clothes as well as their bugged outfits in the trunk of the rental.

The sky remained cloudy, but at least the rain was holding off. They strolled leisurely through the ornamental gardens, chatting about nothing in particular as they kept an eye out for Wong's men. A couple had tailed them for a short while, then had peeled off to sit on a bench and sip their coffees a few minutes ago. Those men aside, she saw no one who caused any concern.

"I need you to hack into the servers of the Liang Xiao Clinic and get any documentation you can relating to North Korea," Eva told Farooq. "Emails, invoices, inventory, etc. When we leave here, find an Internet connection and get to work."

"Will do."

"I also need you to find an address for Xu Wei. He owns the clinic, so start there. That way you'll know you've got the right person. Sonny and I will split up, so if anyone's following us, we'll draw their resources. We'll meet back here in three hours."

"That should be plenty of time," Farooq said. With his laptop tucked in his backpack, he headed back the way they'd come. Eva watched to see if he picked up a tail, but he left the park without attracting any unwanted attention.

"I want to thank you for not dwelling on what happened the other night," Eva said once Farooq was out of sight.

"Grief and booze is a bad combination. It makes us do things we normally wouldn't consider."

"I'm not sure it's fair to blame it on the moment." It hadn't been an impulsive move, and Eva knew it. After two years alone, it was time to move on. She was still young, in her mid-thirties, and she couldn't spend the rest of her life in mourning. Carl wouldn't have wanted her to. If he were indeed looking down on her, he'd be screaming at her to find someone new. Someone like Sonny, who shared many of Carl's attributes, though height was definitely not included.

Eva felt like a shy teenager about to reveal her feelings to her high-school crush, but it had to be done. She'd sent out a strong signal to Sonny, and now she needed to clarify her position. It wasn't fair to leave him dangling, not knowing where that first kiss would lead—if anywhere. She also needed to know if he felt the same way.

She turned to look at Sonny. "I've been feeling that way since you arrived. I just think the timing sucked."

He took her hand, gave it a quick squeeze, then let go. "Me too," he said. "I'm here whenever you need me."

"Thanks."

An awkward silence fell on them. It was Sonny who broke it.

"I'd better . . . you know . . . take a walk. See you back here at six."

"Sure. Keep an eye out for the bad guys."

Sonny smiled as he walked away, and it was infectious. Eva beamed as she dug her hands in her coat pockets and walked in the opposite direction.

~

It was dark by the time Eva walked back into the park. She'd spent the last three hours window-shopping and looking for signs that Wong had them under surveillance. Either his men were the best in the business, or Wong wasn't interested in their movements anymore.

And why should he be? Cheung was gone, her personal mission seemingly complete. She and the boys would be on a plane to Bora Bora in a couple of days, so the ESO knew where to find them, leaving no need to stalk them 24/7.

She hoped not, anyway.

Sonny and Farooq were already waiting at the rendezvous.

"What did you find?" Eva asked her old colleague.

"Plenty and nothing. I got into the clinic's system, but there doesn't appear to be anything that relates to North Korea or organ transplants. They're probably keeping them off the books in case they're audited. The clinic itself doesn't mention such procedures on its website or in any corporate literature."

"So what *did* you get?"

"Xu Wei's home address. It's a penthouse apartment about a mile from the clinic."

That wasn't good news. It wouldn't be easy to assault, unlike Cheung's remote place in the countryside.

"Did you get an itinerary?" she asked, but Farooq shook his head.

"Any personal security?" Sonny wanted to know.

"I found a few photos of him online, and there are two men who are always hovering nearby. They could be his bodyguards. I also got blueprints for the building. His apartment is on the eighteenth floor, and there are security cameras in the hallways."

"Is the lobby manned?"

"Yeah, one man on the desk and another in the CCTV room. There's an apartment on the eighth floor for sale; I got the information from the online sales brochure. I did a walk-by, just to make sure the information was up to date."

"What do you reckon?" Sonny asked Eva.

"It's not going to be easy to get at Xu Wei," she conceded. "Our priority, though, is confirming that he's our man. The paperwork we need will be in the clinic, so that's our first target."

"Then we'll have to make a move tonight. If we find what we're looking for, we take out Xu Wei tomorrow."

"I think Wong's going to notice us leaving the hotel both nights," Farooq pointed out. "What do we do about him?"

Eva frowned. It was a good point.

"I'll come up with something."

CHAPTER 31

Eva decided that they'd all catch a movie. The local cinema was showing the latest in the *Fast and Furious* franchise with Chinese subtitles, so they made arrangements to take in an evening showing.

Eva dressed in some of the new clothes she'd bought—cargo pants, flat shoes, and a wool sweater, all black—then put a bugged pair of loose pants and a jacket on top. She knew Wong would be tracing her via the trackers sewn into the linings, and she would turn that to her advantage. The footwear wasn't ideal for the weather conditions, but were much easier to climb in than sensible boots.

Sonny and Farooq knocked on her door at seven thirty. She picked up her purse, which contained the small device she'd purchased on the way back to the hotel. The bag went over her shoulder as she followed her friends to the elevator.

It was a short walk to the Huachen Cineplex. Eva paid for the tickets, and as soon as the doors opened, they took their seats at the back of the theater.

"How long until the film starts?" Eva asked as she wiggled out of her extra pants.

"About twenty-five minutes."

The movie was due to last 115 minutes, which meant she had at least two hours. It should be more than enough.

She took off her jacket and folded it on her seat, then headed to the restroom. She found all three stalls were empty, but the only window was blocked by three metal bars.

Not leaving that *way, then.*

Eva walked back into the hallway, past a couple of disused concession stands, until she came to the fire exit. As in movie theaters around the world, the door boasted an alarm to prevent patrons from sneaking in the back way. All she could do was hope the age-old setup was merely a deterrent, not an active system. She pushed the bar and stepped out into the street.

No alarm, though it could have been a silent one that only notified employees. Eva didn't hang around to find out. She pushed the door shut and jogged in the direction of the Liang Xiao Clinic.

She reached the alley behind the building in fifteen minutes, and took a few moments to catch her breath as she considered her approach. There were two drainpipes leading up the side of the clinic to the roof. The nearest one passed close to a window on the fifth floor. She chose it after double-checking that no one would witness her ascent.

When Eva reached the third floor, she saw that the window five feet to her left was covered with a heavy curtain to prevent the light behind it pouring out. She suspected the room was for surgery recovery.

If the files she was looking for were on that floor, she was in trouble.

She shimmied up the pipe to the fifth floor. The window ledge was six inches deep, allowing her a foothold while she used a pocketknife to prize the window open with one hand.

She found herself in some kind of storeroom. It was full of medical supplies, promotional leaflets, surgical gowns, and staff uniforms. Eva checked a few of the boxes to see if any contained paperwork, but saw nothing to incriminate Xu Wei.

Eva quietly opened the door and peered out into the hallway. She didn't expect the building to be alarmed or populated, but she might encounter security personnel. Here, at least, the coast was clear. She stepped out of the room and saw three more doors to check on this floor. She put her ear to the first one but heard nothing, so she eased it open.

No point going inside. The room was filled from floor to ceiling with furniture, no space for any paperwork.

Three minutes later, she'd checked the other rooms and come up empty-handed. A further five minutes on the top floor turned out to be equally fruitless, so she took the stairs down to the fourth and met her first obstacle.

As she stood in the stairwell and looked through the glass built into the door, she noticed the hallway lit beyond. No sign of anyone, but she could only see so far. If she ran into a guard, the mission would be a bust. News would get back to Wong, and he would guess her intentions.

Then again, if she backed off now, she wouldn't be able to confirm Xu Wei's guilt, and she couldn't kill the man without good cause. But letting the man responsible for the horrors of Camp 33 live was not an option.

She had no choice but to push ahead.

Eva pushed the door open a couple of inches and stuck her head through. The hallway was empty, but she heard sounds from the first door along. It sounded like a television, so possibly a guard station.

That was enough to convince her to abandon the fourth floor unless forced to return.

Eva ducked back into the stairwell, then ran up the stairs in her silent rubber-soled shoes. On the fifth floor, she went into the room containing the staff uniforms and picked out a white coat in her size. She was back in the stairwell seconds later, jogging down to the second floor, and pleased to see the entire corridor enveloped in darkness. There were many more doors here, most of them marked with the names of doctors. She tried the first one, and wasn't surprised to find it locked.

Eva took out her pocketknife and the two thin picks she always carried with her. The door clicked open half a minute later and Eva slipped inside the room. A desk dominated the space and the walls were adorned with certificates, but it was the filing cabinet that caught her attention.

Eva had the cheap lock open in seconds, and inside she found hundreds of patient records. Quite a few had foreign-sounding names; she plucked one such file at random. The patient's address was Long Beach, California, and the procedure was a liver transplant. Eva flicked through the file until she came to the billing information, and saw that payment had been made in advance via wire transfer from a US account. The only thing she needed now was the details of the donor, but no name was given. Instead, she found another file number.

Clearly, the information regarding the unwilling donor was being stored separately, which meant her hunt was far from over.

Eva took the small portable scanner from her pants pocket and ran it over every document in the file, then replaced it in its original position. She repeated the process with two other random records, then she secured the cabinet by pushing the lock back into the frame and left the room. She couldn't lock the door from the outside without the key, but that wasn't a problem. With nothing missing, it would simply be seen as an oversight by the doctor.

She checked the nameplates on the other doors on the second floor. All doctor's offices, except the farthest room from the stairwell. This one had no name on the door, and she was glad to see that it was protected by two Yale locks. Eva got to work on them immediately.

She was inside the small room in a minute. It was no bigger than a cleaning cupboard and dominated by three filing cabinets. Seconds later, she had the first one open, and Eva realized she'd struck gold.

The first record she took out looked identical to the ones she'd stolen from Camp 33, only this one included financial information. It broke down the cost of each organ delivered, and although it didn't give bank account details, the link to Xu Wei's hospital was now undeniable.

Eva scanned the contents of three files, then left the room. The door automatically locked behind her, and she jogged back to the stairwell and ran up to her entry point on the fifth floor, leaving the white coat where she'd found it.

Eva couldn't lock the window after squeezing out onto the ledge, but it was unlikely that anyone would notice it in the next couple of days. She had to wait a minute while an employee from the restaurant opposite threw the trash out, but as soon he went back inside, she slid quickly to the ground and checked her watch. The film was due to end in about an hour, so she didn't have to rush.

Back at the cinema, she took her ticket stub from her back pocket and showed it to the attendant, explaining that she'd been out for a cigarette, then took her seat with the others as another car chase exploded onto the screen.

Sonny squeezed her hand and looked at her quizzically.

She replied with a nod.

Job done.

She slipped her ESO slacks back on and watched the last few minutes of the movie, then walked back to the hotel with the boys to prepare for the next stage of the plan.

CHAPTER 32

The boys were already tucking into breakfast by the time Eva entered the restaurant. She helped herself to some food from the buffet and joined them at the table.

"Morning." Sonny smiled. "Got any plans for today?"

"Just to see a little more of the city before we leave," Eva said.

In truth, their schedule was already set. On their way home from the movie, they had discussed what they planned to do the following day. They would scope out Xu Wei's place that morning and look for the best way in, then shop for the items they would need for their flight to Bora Bora. Farooq was to disappear for an hour and make the final arrangements for their journey.

"I need to get some sunscreen," said Farooq.

"No problem," she said. "We're all going to need it, so get plenty."

Eva wished she could talk openly, but couldn't take the chance. They had to pretend to be preparing for their vacation, nothing more, in case Wong was listening in.

Sonny spent a few minutes detailing what he planned to do once they reached the island, which amounted to scuba diving, jet-skiing, and lots of beer while reading on the beach. Farooq said he'd spend most of his time in the water, while Eva mooned over the luxury spa.

Once breakfast was over, they returned to their rooms to change, then met up in the lobby at nine. The sun was shining outside, yet the temperature remained at the freezing mark. Eva was glad to be wearing two layers of clothing once more.

They strolled west, stopping occasionally to look in shop windows. Half an hour later, they entered Zhongshan Park. Eva took out her phone.

"Let me get a picture of you two," she said, and the men struck a pose. She snapped a dozen shots, but she wasn't interested in the male models. She'd framed them against the eighteen-story building in the background, the top floor of which was Xu Wei's penthouse apartment.

Sonny suggested they grab a coffee, and the others liked that idea. They walked past Xu Wei's tower block on the way to the Costa, taking in the neighboring buildings, access points, and security measures as they walked. Eva counted two cameras that they would have to avoid, and through the glass doors she could see that it would be impossible to slip past the concierge unnoticed. The lobby was some forty feet wide, with the desk set twenty feet from the entrance. As the plan was to hit Xu Wei without anyone noticing—at least for a day—taking out the doorman was not an option.

She looked down the side of the building as they passed. The side street was narrow, and across from Xu Wei's building stood another apartment block. Trying to scale the outside would be extremely risky, even in the middle of the night.

They reached the coffee shop and Sonny ordered while the others found a quiet table. Eva waited until the drinks arrived before discussing the recce.

"We can't go in the front way, and climbing the outside is too risky."

"And we can't zip-line from the nearby buildings because they're not tall enough," Sonny added.

Eva looked at Farooq, who simply shrugged, bereft of ideas.

She sighed. Even with a few more days to prepare, there was no way to get at Xu Wei. She would have to be content hoping that the evidence she'd gathered would be enough to halt the trade and perhaps see him face jail time—though if he were ESO, the latter seemed unlikely. He'd probably throw some poor employee under the bus while denying any knowledge of the practice, and his connections would ensure he walked away clean.

Cheung would be okay. She'd leave him instructions on what to do once he returned from his short exile, which would include sending copies of the evidence to all international news outlets along with a timeline of events, including the ESO's involvement. The shadowy organization would be foolish to target him after the story broke, as it would only prove Cheung right and draw unwanted attention to the group.

"Then we call it off and get on the plane as planned." To Farooq she said, "Make sure everything's ready for the flight tomorrow."

"Will do. I'm going to find something to eat first," he said in reply.

"You just had breakfast," Sonny pointed out.

"I know, but I always get nervous the day before a flight. Eating's my coping mechanism."

"I wish I could eat as much as you and never put on weight."

"I wish I could get the hot girls," Farooq said with a wink, "but we can't have everything." He stood, picked up his laptop bag, and left the coffee shop.

Eva and Sonny looked at each other.

"Was he talking about us?" she asked.

"I have no idea."

Eva hoped her feelings for Sonny weren't so blatant. Had Wong noticed it, too?

If he had, it didn't matter. This time tomorrow, they would be on a flight to Bora Bora, never to see Wong again.

Sonny got a fresh drink while Eva found the restroom and removed her outer layer of clothing. She placed the bugged clothes in a bag and dropped it next to the table, throwing Sonny a seductive eyebrow-waggle.

She smiled at his reaction as she walked out into the street and took a taxi to the railway station. She bought a round-trip ticket for the fast train to Changchun, then purchased a notepad and pen from one of the outlets. It would be a three-hour journey, plenty of time to write a detailed letter to Cheung with instructions on what to do with the evidence she was about to present to him.

When she arrived in Changchun, Eva went straight to the lockers and found the one where she'd dumped the files taken from Camp 33. She added the device that she'd used to copy the records from the Liang Xiao Clinic, along with the letter. After locking it once more, Eva took a taxi to the Jianguo Medical Center. She asked the receptionist for an envelope, then sealed the locker key and letter inside and wrote Cheung's name on it along with the name of the railway station.

"Make sure he gets this," she said. "He's expecting it."

If the receptionist recognized Eva from her earlier visit, it didn't show. She promised to pass the envelope on and asked if there was anything else she could do to help.

"No, thank you."

Eva took another taxi back to the railway station for the long journey back to Shenyang.

CHAPTER 33

"I don't trust them," Wong said when the call connected. He didn't know who he was speaking to, only that his employers represented the most powerful people in the world.

"You've been saying that ever since Driscoll showed up," the voice said. As always, it was masked, as if speaking at 80 percent speed inside a tin can. From what Wong could tell, the person sounded bored. Wong also thought he detected a hint of displeasure.

Not a good sign.

"What is it this time?" the voice asked.

Wong hesitated. His reasons for calling suddenly seemed trivial, and he didn't want to piss his superiors off any more than he already had. But he was committed now.

"I can't put my finger on it, but they're acting too . . . normal."

"What the hell does that mean? They've completed their mission. How are they supposed to act?"

Wong swallowed hard. "I don't know, but yesterday they all bought new clothes and wore them immediately. I saw how they were dressed when they returned from a day out, and they'd discarded the clothes that we'd sewn trackers into."

"Meaning . . . ?"

"They obviously knew about the devices."

"Which suggests to me that you didn't do your job properly."

Wong wished he'd never picked up the phone to share his observations. "I had no choice," he said. "We put people on them when they left the hotel, but Driscoll spotted them and lost them. Remote tracking was the best option left to us."

The phone went silent, and the longer it lasted, the more nervous Wong felt.

"I can't say I'm pleased with your performance," the voice said. "As for Driscoll losing your team, what would you have done in her situation? She doesn't have any reason to trust us, and every reason to despise us. I'd want to put a little distance between us if I were in her shoes."

"There's also the Cheung matter," Wong offered, trying to dig himself out of the hole he'd created. "I'm not happy with her explanation."

"You mentioned that yesterday. She visited Cheung, and now he's gone. Blood found on the floor matched his DNA. What else is there to explain?"

"My concern is that her story kept changing. First, she was going to kill the guards, then just stun them, and in the end she did both. I thought she was an expert in preparation."

"Situations like that are fluid at best. Her expertise is in adapting to whatever situation she finds herself in. You said yourself: Cheung is gone, his car is gone, his men are gone. We tracked his phone to the bottom of a lake. What more do you need?"

Wong was fighting a losing battle, and he knew it.

"Just keep an eye on them until they fly out tomorrow. After that, your work is finished."

Wong read between the lines as the call ended. Once Driscoll and her cronies were gone, his time was up. If he was lucky, he'd be reassigned to a surveillance role. The worst-case scenario didn't bear thinking about.

What he needed was proof. Concrete evidence to show that Driscoll was lying.

There was one way to get it.

~

When Eva returned to the Costa shop in Shenyang seven hours later, Sonny was still there, although he'd moved to a seat near the back. He was engrossed in his Kindle but seemed to sense her entering the café. He looked up and smiled as Eva approached.

"How did it go?"

"Boring," Eva replied. "Farooq?"

"Everything's in place and he's back at the hotel. Probably stuffing his face again."

"Sounds like a plan. I'm just going to the restroom," Eva said, "then we'll head back, too. I'm gonna have the salmon tonight." She took the bag of bugged clothes with her and dressed in them once more. When she returned to the table, Sonny was ready to go.

It was a pleasant stroll back to the Shangri-La, especially knowing that Farooq had made the final arrangements. With everything set, she could finally relax a little. The flight was scheduled for ten the next morning, and Wong had promised to ease their passage through security.

Back at the hotel, they had the rest of the night to themselves. Eva briefly considered inviting Sonny to her room for a nightcap, but decided against it. She knew where it would lead, and she didn't want her first intimate moments with Sonny to be recorded by Wong and the ESO. Instead, she said goodnight and told him to be in the lobby at seven the next morning.

In her room, she undressed, threw on the complimentary robe, and opened a bottle of wine. Then she put the TV on in the background as she dreamed of the new life that lay ahead.

~

Four hours after his last call to his superiors, Wong dialed the same number with a lot more confidence. The report he'd received moments earlier vindicated his mistrust of the Driscoll woman, and should earn him some bonus points with his employers.

"What?" the voice asked.

"Driscoll deceived us," Wong said. "Cheung is still alive."

"How do you know?"

"I ordered my men to take a boat to the lake and look for his body. They used the last known signal from his phone as a marker and sent two divers down. They found a rug, and inside that was a plastic sheet filled with rocks. No sign of Cheung." As he waited for a reply, Wong took the opportunity to show how thorough he'd been. "I then told them to locate Cheung's car and see if his security team were inside. They were not."

Wong thought the line had gone dead when the silence dragged on, but eventually the voice spoke once more.

"Leave it with us."

The call ended. No praise for a job well done, nor any indication that his services would be needed in the future.

All Wong could do was wait, and hope he'd done enough to deflect their ire.

~

"It seems Driscoll doesn't want to play the game fairly," Vincent May said to the others gathered in the boardroom. It was just after nine in the morning at the Washington, DC headquarters of one of America's most illustrious hedge funds, thirteen hours behind Shenyang, China, where Wong had just called from.

"I warned you from the start," Larry Carter said. "We should have tipped off the Koreans when she decided to head back in-country."

"Your opinion is noted," May said, his voice relaying his displeasure at the MIC representative's input, "but the past cannot be changed. I'll be the first to admit that I was wrong. I thought I could control her, but that wasn't the case."

What concerned him now were Driscoll's intentions. She hadn't disposed of Cheung as they'd hoped, which meant she'd seen through their ruse. Did that mean she knew about Xu Wei? If she did, the Chinese national would be in her sights.

That wasn't part of the plan.

"We should end our . . . . relationship with her now, while we have the chance," he said.

It pained him to do so, but any hopes of taming Eva Driscoll were now extinguished. Few could have pulled off the rescue mission in North Korea. In fact, few would have even attempted it. And to be imprisoned, tortured, and still escape the DPRK showed how special she was. It was a shame to have to kill her.

"Is Wong up to the task, or should we bring in additional resources?" James Butler asked.

"We don't want a showdown," Ben Scott added. "Driscoll brought our organization to the world's attention, and we're still recovering from that. If she's killed in a gunfight, questions will be asked and fingers pointed. We need to be subtle, make it look like an accident."

"Involving all three of them? That won't be easy to achieve."

"Actually, it might," May said. "She has unwittingly provided us with the perfect opportunity."

He called back Wong, who picked up on the first ring.

"You did well to uncover her deception," May told him, "but I'm not happy that it took so long." He let his words hang for a while. "However, you have a chance to redeem yourself."

"I'll do whatever it takes," Wong replied hastily.

Yes, you will.

May gave him instructions, which included sending a team to protect Xu Wei, and after hearing Wong's assurances that there would be no mistakes, he hung up and looked around the room.

"Cheung's too big to disappear for good. When he shows up again, there's bound to be speculation. I want to deflect it away from us, is that understood?"

He got nods all around, then moved on to the next item on the morning's agenda.

CHAPTER 34

Wong was waiting in the lobby when Driscoll and the other two came down to check out. He met them at the reception desk.

"The bill has been settled," he said, then smiled. For once, he didn't have to force it. He took genuine pleasure in knowing that their time on the planet was almost at an end. The woman had shown him no respect since the day they'd first met, treating him like a servant. The Englishman was no better. It was a pity he wouldn't be able to witness their final moments, though he would be tracking it from his office near the hotel.

The plan was simple, though it hadn't been easy to execute. "Put a bomb on the plane" worked like magic in novels and films, but in real life it was never straightforward. Wong's first challenge had been to find someone with the skills to create the detonator to his superior's specifications. It had taken four hours to track that person down, and another three to create the device. There was no chance to check that it worked, of course. It was set to go off six hours after the aircraft reached cruising altitude, not something they could easily simulate. Wong would have to take the creator's word that it would do the job as expected. Sourcing the explosives themselves was no problem, though, and having a couple of people working security at Shenyang Taoxian International Airport helped to smooth the process. The bomb, consisting of thirty pounds of C-4, had already been loaded onto the Gulfstream G550. All that remained was to ensure Driscoll and her companions got on board and took off.

"Are you going to take the car or would you like me to call for a taxi?" Wong asked.

She opted for a taxi, and Wong told one of the receptionists to organize it.

Driscoll tossed the keys to the rental on the desk. "We'll get our own," she said, and the trio dragged their luggage out into the street.

Wong was tempted to give them a piece of his mind while he had the chance, but he kept his mouth shut. His moment of satisfaction wouldn't wait long.

He let them go, remaining inside the lobby while watching them climb into the cab that had pulled up outside the entrance. Once it pulled away, he phoned the member of his team who had been stationed at the airport.

"Make sure they get on the plane, and phone me when they take off."

~

Eva waited five minutes after leaving the hotel before taking off her ESO clothing. The others did the same, earning a strange look from the leather-faced cab driver, and all the bugged clothes went into a bag lined with aluminum foil she'd purloined from the hotel's kitchen the previous night.

Content in the knowledge that they could no longer be tracked, Eva instructed the driver to take a detour through the shopping district. She told him to pull up outside an enormous sporting-goods superstore and went inside with Sonny. They were back a few minutes later, each pulling a large suitcase behind them. These went into the trunk with the rest of the luggage, and they resumed the drive to the airport.

Eva removed the bugged clothes from the bag, hoping Wong would see the interruption as only a small glitch. It didn't really matter, but it was better than being brazen. As long as they got to the plane on time, Wong should have no concerns.

Traffic added fifteen minutes on to the trip, but they still got to the airport with a couple of hours to spare. The cab driver dropped them at the terminal, and, as Eva got out, she was accosted by a local.

"Miss Driscoll?"

Eva wasn't surprised. She assumed it was the ESO's way of letting her know that they would be all over her for the foreseeable future.

"Yeah."

"Follow me, please. Mr. Wong has asked me to ensure you get to your flight without disruption."

The others were already out of the car and emptying the trunk, and they all followed their new chaperone into the terminal. He led them through a door marked "Staff Only," and into the bowels of the airport. After passing half a dozen offices, the guide took them outside, where an SUV waited. They loaded it up with the bags, then got in for a five-minute ride to a hangar at the far end of the strip, where the plane stood on the tarmac, engines already spooling.

A flight attendant started taking the suitcases from the SUV and loading them into the hold, but Eva stopped him.

"I want everything inside, with me," she said.

The guide shrugged and instructed the attendant to do as she said, and the cases were taken into the cabin and placed in the galley at the rear of the plane.

"We'll be taxiing in ten minutes," the copilot said as he emerged from the cockpit. "Can I get you anything before we get underway?"

All three declined, and he returned to the front.

Fifteen minutes later, the Gulfstream was climbing through twenty thousand feet.

In the hold, the timing device inside the nondescript package began the countdown from 360 minutes.

~

"They're in the air."

Wong hung up and checked the screen in front of him.

After Driscoll and her team had left the hotel, he'd walked to his office a couple of blocks away and typed the plane's transponder code into a website that would report in-flight details, refreshing every thirty seconds. The display showed the outline of a small plane and recorded the height at just over a thousand feet. Half a minute later, it was at two thousand and turning south on a flightpath for the South Pacific.

Wong took out his phone again. It was just after eleven in the morning, so he set an alarm to be back at the computer by five in the afternoon. All he had to do now was wait for confirmation that the bomb had activated.

Eight minutes later, a text message arrived. It simply said: *Bye.*

Wong smiled as he put his phone away and locked his computer. He had a few errands to run before lunch, followed by a relaxing afternoon before returning to witness Driscoll's descent into the ocean.

~

Eva accepted the coffee from the flight attendant with a tinge of regret. The man was doing nothing more than earning a living, and in a few hours she would be forced to kill him. She suspected that the ESO had placed him and the pilots on the flight, but that didn't make her feel any better. If they were indeed ESO, they were mere foot soldiers, nothing more. She hated the idea of killing unnecessarily, especially innocents, but it was the only way to forge new lives for herself, Sonny, and Farooq.

When the attendant returned to the galley and closed the door, Eva leaned over to Farooq.

"Did you convert the money?" she whispered.

Because of the constant surveillance surrounding them in Shenyang, they hadn't had the chance to discuss his part in the plan in detail. While she and Sonny had taken on the more dangerous aspects of the mission, Farooq's role was no less important.

His first task had been to hide their money. No bank in the world was beyond the ESO's reach, so she'd been forced to turn her funds into something equally valuable, yet safe from their clutches.

"I put most of it into cryptocurrency, spread over a variety of coins. It's at a relatively low value now, so you might even make a profit over time."

Eva had looked at bitcoin a few years earlier, and while she didn't think it viable as an investment vehicle, she liked the fact that it wasn't controlled by any government or central bank. Farooq's decision to move her money into it was a wise one.

"What about the rest?" she asked.

"Diamonds and other precious stones. Payment has been made to a wholesaler in Amsterdam and the consignment is awaiting collection. I asked them to include a hundred grand in cash, too, in case you need instant access. It's a mixture of euros and dollars."

"Good work. And our rendezvous?"

Farooq took a GPS from his laptop bag. "The ship is eighteen hours out. By the time we get there it'll be twelve. Sorry it won't be there to meet us, but it was the best I could do."

"That's fine," Eva said.

It was actually better than she'd expected. Getting a boat to make a run four thousand miles into the Pacific at such short notice couldn't

Fight To Survive

have been easy. It would have been a huge undertaking with weeks of notice, but Farooq had been given only a few days.

"It wasn't cheap," Farooq added. "As you can imagine, there's not much of a market for clandestine trips into the middle of the ocean. It cost a million in the end. I found a company in the Philippines that was in deep financial trouble and offered a huge cash injection in return for them making a slight detour on their run to Hawaii."

"Are you sure no one will talk?" Sonny asked, leaning in to join the conversation.

"I don't think so. I gave half upfront with the remainder after we dock. The owner's being paid directly, and you can explain the situation once we're on board."

All that needed to be done now was to check the equipment they'd picked up on the way to the airport, something they'd do only after dealing with the flight crew.

~

Wong felt his loins stirring as the masseuse expertly worked her fingers up the inside of his thigh. Kim stopped tantalizingly short of the small towel covering his modesty, as she always did. It was a game she played to bring him to full arousal, knowing that he would take advantage of the other services she had to offer.

This time, though, Wong wasn't interested. The clock on the wall read four thirty, and he still had to shower before returning to the office.

The scantily clad woman in her mid-twenties slapped him playfully on the rump and told him to turn over. He did, and his erection was evident under the cloth. She unbuttoned her skimpy white uniform to reveal a leopard-print bra and panties, then removed the towel covering his groin.

"I have a cure for that," Kim whispered, leaning over him so that her ample breasts hovered near his face. She gently stroked his length to help him come to a decision.

241

Wong looked at the clock again. "Maybe next time," he said, and climbed off the bed. She looked disappointed, but he knew that was all part of her performance.

He would make it up to her on his next visit.

He showered quickly and dressed, then sent a text to his driver. By the time he left the massage parlor, his car was waiting outside.

Wong said where they were heading, and the chauffeur knew better than to try to engage him in conversation. Ten minutes later, Wong stepped out of the car and walked into the building that housed his office. He took the stairs to the second floor and pressed his finger against the pad on the wall. The door clicked open and he walked inside.

His two staff members were nowhere to be seen. He'd instructed them to finish up early and head home because he wanted to be alone to savor Driscoll's swan song.

Wong unlocked his computer and re-entered the transponder number into the tracking website. The symbol representing Driscoll's plane showed in the center of the screen, and he zoomed out to see the actual position. It was almost halfway to French Polynesia, right on schedule. The time in the bottom corner of the screen said it was three after five.

Driscoll had about ten minutes left.

He hoped she was spending it wisely.

Driscoll finished her glass of orange juice and nodded to Sonny before standing up and heading to the rear of the cabin. She knocked on the galley door and opened it, and the attendant smiled at her.

"Can I get you anything?"

Eva pointed behind him. "Just that big suitcase."

As the man turned around, Eva kicked the door shut, put her arm around his neck, and stuck her knee into his back, pulling him backward as she locked her other arm into place behind his neck in a chokehold, cutting off the supply of blood to his brain. The attendant's hands flailed as he fought to break free, but Eva had done this dozens of times to bigger, stronger men. It was a simple matter of maintaining the pressure until the lights went out.

Eva kept her grip for a minute after he went limp, then eased him gently to the floor. She took a sharp knife from a drawer and went back into the cabin, where she handed the blade to Sonny. "Your turn."

Sonny got up and knocked on the door to the cockpit. When it opened, he pointed toward the rear of the cabin, where the supine figure could be seen through the galley door.

"He collapsed!" Sonny shouted. "He needs help!"

The copilot leapt from his seat and rushed past Sonny, who casually backed into the cockpit, keeping an eye on the rescue attempt.

"You can't be in here," the pilot said. "Please return to the cabin."

Sonny turned to face the seated man. "Sorry, I wasn't . . ." His eyes darted to the window. "What the hell?"

The pilot's head swiveled to the left, and Sonny clamped a hand over his mouth and rammed the knife into the base of his skull, slicing sideways to sever the spinal cord. The man shuddered and went limp in Sonny's hands. He went back to the cabin to see that Eva had already dispatched the copilot.

"Grab the suitcases and get to work," Eva said to Sonny.

"I'll deal with the autopilot," Farooq said. "I've been practicing on a simulator for the last couple of nights, and I know how to insert a new fictitious airport into the system and set the autopilot to navigate to it. We place the airstrip a hundred miles from here and the plane goes down unseen."

"How long will that take to set up?" Eva asked.

"About twenty minutes."

"Then we go with plan A: flick the fuel dump lever."

His face dropped. "Oh. Yeah, well . . . I guess that would work, too."

"Great. I'll leave that to you once we've checked the chutes over."

Sonny dragged the first of the suitcases into the cabin and opened it. Inside were three backpacks. He took the first one out, opened it, and pulled out the contents. He took the nylon canopy to one end of the cabin, stretching out the lines until they were straight, then began folding it all up again.

"Is it okay?" Farooq asked.

"It's fine," Sonny told him, "but I never let anyone pack my chute for me."

He knew Farooq was worried about doing his first jump. If it had been for fun, it might have been a solo freefall, but in these circumstances, it was deemed best that he dive in tandem with Sonny.

With his own parachute repacked, Sonny checked the one Eva would be using.

"Jump zone coming up in seven minutes," Farooq said.

Driscoll checked her own watch. Six minutes after five, Shenyang time.

She went to the galley and retrieved the last of the suitcases. Inside was an inflatable life raft that had a depth-activated mechanism as well as manual pull handles. She took the last of the chutes and attached it to the large orange bundle with a carabiner.

"We all set?" she asked as she shrugged the parachute pack onto her back.

"Almost," Farooq replied. He'd put his backpack containing his beloved laptop and other necessities into a thick plastic bag, and was in the process of making it watertight. Once he finished, he went into the cockpit and threw the lever that would dump the plane's fuel. Immediately, the needle showing the remaining Jet A-1 began to drop. He walked back into the cabin and backed up to Sonny, who strapped them together.

"Shouldn't we have descended a little?" he asked nervously.

"Ideally, yes, but it would show up on radar. We'll just have to take our chances."

Eva stood by the door and gave the boys a thumbs up. Sonny returned the gesture, while Farooq only swallowed hard.

"See you at the bottom," she said, and hit the emergency release.

Their world turned upside down.

~

Wong lit a cigarette as the countdown on his watch ticked ever closer to zero. It currently read 1:13, roughly seventy seconds before the explosives in the plane's hold would send Eva Driscoll and her no-good friends to hell.

The symbol on his computer screen was still showing the aircraft at thirty-three thousand feet, maintaining its heading toward Bora Bora, the luxurious vacation destination they'd never reach.

What are you doing right now? Wong wondered. *Getting it on with that arrogant Englishman? I hope his last act is to give you syphilis.*

The timer reached nineteen seconds.

The screen refreshed. Same course, same altitude.

Wong extinguished his cigarette and waited for the computer to confirm the inevitable.

~

The moment the door flew out into space, Eva followed it. She had no choice. The air, seat cushions, an empty juice glass and the remaining occupants were all sucked through the small gap the moment the pressure became unequal.

Eva was three seconds from the plane when the C-4 shook the sky. Her perfect exit went to shit as flames licked at her feet and the blast pummeled her body. She managed to hold on to the life raft, but its boxy shape did nothing for her aerodynamics, and she tumbled end over end, alternately facing sky, then ocean, in a dizzying whirl. It was during this disorienting dash to the earth's surface that she caught the first glimpse of the Gulfstream disintegrating. She was spiraling out of control, and had no choice but to let go of the raft and seek equilibrium. After what felt like an age, she finally righted herself and took stock. Her altimeter showed fifteen thousand feet, which was still plenty. She flipped over onto her back and saw the trail of smoke that represented all that remained of the Gulfstream. A few hundred yards to her right and a thousand feet above her, Sonny and Farooq were already engaged in a textbook freefall.

Eva spread her arms as wide as she could to slow her fall, and angled over in the direction of her friends. In return, Sonny folded his arms in by his side and dropped down to the same altitude. When they linked up, Eva pointed at the life raft plummeting to the ocean. Sonny gave her the thumbs up, and they dived toward it together.

Eva grabbed hold of the raft at nine thousand feet. She pushed away from Sonny and Farooq, then pulled the cord on the raft's chute. It jerked out of her hands as the air caught in the canopy, and after steering clear of it, she pulled her own. The chute opened and she looked up to ensure the lines hadn't tangled. Perfect deployment.

Thanks, Sonny.

She tugged the guide ropes to point her toward the raft, and four minutes later she splashed down twenty yards from the other chute. By the time she'd shrugged off her pack, the raft had breached the surface, fully inflated. Eva climbed aboard and threw out the sea anchor, then held out an arm to help Farooq aboard.

The first thing he did was open his waterproof pack and ensure his laptop had survived the jump. He frowned when Sonny splashed it as he jumped into the raft. Finally satisfied that it was undamaged, he checked his other devices.

"What the fuck did you do to the plane?" Sonny shouted.

"Nothing! I just hit the fuel dump and that's it."

"It was Wong," Eva said, stripping down to her underwear. "The ESO must have ordered him to end us."

"Why?"

"They must have found out about Cheung. Or maybe we just out-lived our usefulness. Either way, they'll think their plan worked."

"Another five seconds on that plane and it would have," Farooq pointed out.

Eva agreed. She reached into Farooq's bag for a bottle of sunscreen and started applying it to her legs.

Whatever the reason, the ESO had inadvertently paved their way to freedom. No one would go searching for the plane's black box, that was for certain. And when Cheung returned to the world, there would be no searching for her team as their deception unfurled. The ESO would believe that the job was finished, and they'd move on to the next phase of world domination.

It also made her feel a little better about killing the crew, who would have perished anyway.

"Where's the ship?" Sonny asked, taking off his sweatshirt and smearing himself with sunscreen.

Farooq checked the GPS tracker. "Eleven hours, forty-six minutes away. Let me set the beacon and we're good." He found the device he was looking for and hit a button on the side. A light began flashing every few seconds. "Okay, all set. What do we do now?"

Sonny clapped his hands together. "I spy with my little eye . . ."

~

"It's done," Wong said into the phone.

"You did well," the voice replied. "We'll be in touch."

It was the shortest conversation he'd had with his masters, but by far the sweetest. His stock had risen, he'd made amends for letting

Driscoll make a fool of him, and the boorish bitch was dead. Watching the symbol disappear from the screen had been a moment of pure bliss, and for the foreseeable future he would picture her body being picked apart by the creatures of the deep ocean.

He imagined her screams as she plummeted to the sea, though he knew that in all likelihood she would have died instantly.

Even that thought failed to remove the smile from his face.

Wong closed down the computer and sent a text to his driver.

Kim and he had some unfinished business.

EPILOGUE

Three months later

Xu Wei lifted his heavy frame into the car and ordered the driver to take him back to the hotel. After five grueling hours of negotiations with PDVSA—the Venezuelan state-owned oil company—and the country's finance minister, he still hadn't managed to secure rights to explore the untapped fields west of the Orinoco Belt.

Xu Wei needed the deal to go through, but not at any cost. The Venezuelans were playing hardball, demanding ludicrous licensing fees in return for tiny percentages of any oil discovered. Xu Wei's exploration geologists believed that a rich reservoir of oil and gas lay undiscovered in the largely inaccessible region that the locals had no infrastructure to exploit, and his own experienced team would make light work of the terrain.

If only he could convince the Venezuelans to make it worth his while. For a country in financial meltdown, they seemed strangely reticent to embrace a venture that would earn them an estimated six billion dollars a year. That was, of course, only a quarter of the true value of the reserves, but Xu Wei had to make a living.

No one ever got rich by giving the little guy a break.

He hadn't expected the negotiations to stall, but it wasn't the end of the matter. He still had the big guns in reserve, and if the following morning's talks didn't go his way, a call would be made and the five-billion-dollar oil development loan the Chinese government had made to Venezuela two years earlier would be called in. The country was on the brink, barely able to scrape together enough to provide toilet paper for the public services it ran. Having to repay the money would gain the desired result.

The car pulled up outside the Cayena Hotel in the heart of Caracas, and Xu Wei eased himself out. Accompanied by his two security personnel, he walked through a huge red door that was four times his height, and took the elevator to his suite.

It was tiny compared to the luxurious rooms Xu Wei normally stayed in, but it was the best Caracas had to offer. A spare bed had been brought in for his men to sleep on, alternating as they always did so that one was awake at all times.

Xu Wei gave the room service menu to his bodyguard and told him to order the seafood pasta and a chocolate dessert. He didn't like Italian fare all that much, but it was all the hotel had on the menu. Most establishments went out of their way to provide whatever food he requested, but it seemed the chef at the Cayena was inflexible. Or, rather, undersupplied.

A knock came half an hour later. Lo, the smaller of Xu Wei's bodyguards, checked the spyhole, then opened it. A woman dressed in a waitress uniform of short skirt, white blouse, and black vest pushed a service cart into the room.

Xu Wei rarely noticed the common worker, but this one looked different from most. She had a figure to die for, and long blonde hair that hung down either side of her face, obscuring her features. He felt something stirring below his belt, but when she looked up at him, the face looked like it belonged on someone else. The nose was too big, the skin sallow, and she had a hairy wart on her chin the size of a grape.

Any carnal thoughts quickly dissipated.

The woman handed the bill to Lo, who signed it and gave her a small tip.

Xu Wei took a plate from the cart over to his desk, and the waitress left the room.

"Speak to the concierge," Xu Wei told Lo. "Have a woman sent up later. Brunette." He couldn't face a blonde now, not after seeing that crone.

Lo nodded and got on the phone to carry out what was a common order for his boss.

Xu Wei stabbed a mussel and wrapped it in spaghetti before putting it in his mouth. It was surprisingly good; not what he'd expected. He bit into a slice of garlic bread and signaled for his other bodyguard, Wang, to pass the bottle of white wine. Wang placed the ice bucket in a holder next to Xu Wei and poured him a glass.

"We have an early start tomorrow," Xu Wei said, while chewing his fifth mouthful of pasta. "I want the—"

He coughed, and again, and when it happened a third time, the food in his mouth shot onto the table. He grabbed for his glass and drank half of it, but another brutal explosion sent it shooting from his nose. Wang slapped him on the back, thinking he was choking, but Xu Wei was simply trying to get his lungs to cooperate. His throat felt as if it were on fire. He sucked in air, once, twice, then his diaphragm contracted violently and crimson shot from his mouth and nose.

Xu Wei panicked at the sight of so much of his own blood, but his torment wasn't over. He bent double as he lost control of his body. Vomit exploded from his mouth, strands of bloody pasta covering the tablecloth.

Lo, still on the call to the concierge, told him to send a doctor up immediately. After seeing the next emission from Xu Wei's body, he upgraded that to an ambulance.

Xu Wei tried to breathe, but while oxygen sucked into his body, it seemed as if it wasn't reaching his lungs. His throat felt like a straw that had been punctured numerous times along its length, and when he finally managed a big enough gasp, it produced a bubbling sound deep inside his chest.

Xu Wei coughed once more, and it was his last act on the planet.

∼

Eva walked out of the rear entrance of the hotel, past the trash cans, and vaulted the short wall into the neighboring parking lot. She got into the beat-up Honda, and Sonny took off.

"Any problems?" he asked.

"Yeah. He got off lightly."

The poison she'd purchased from a freelance chemist was the most aggressive he had in his portfolio, but even after he'd described the effects, Eva knew it wouldn't be nearly as violent a death as Xu Wei deserved. She'd originally wanted to cut out his kidneys and liver while he was still conscious, just so he'd know the pain of all those who had died to line his pockets, but that would have been a red flag to the ESO.

The little girl with the rag doll would have to be satisfied with the result, if not the method.

As it was, the note she'd left under the tablecloth on the room service cart would point the blame at the DVS, a Venezuelan social-ist activist group currently fighting the scourge that was capitalism. It claimed Xu Wei was the enemy of the people, here to strip the country of its assets for his own enrichment. Some of the group's members would be brought in for interrogation, but that happened to them every day, anyway. According to their website on the Dark Web, at least.

They drove for a couple of miles, while Eva removed the prosthetic nose and wart and cleaned the makeup off her face. She wriggled out of the hotel uniform and put the clothes in a bag, then slipped into her jeans and T-shirt.

Sonny pulled into an underground parking lot and parked next to their rented BMW. While Eva got behind the wheel of the German beast, Sonny removed the false plates on the Honda and replaced them with the originals. They went into the bag with Eva's disguise. The next stop would be to dump it all in an industrial trash receptacle on the other side of town.

Two hours later, Eva drove them through the center of Valencia, a neighboring town and home to Eva's makeup artist. After a few hours in the chair, she once again looked like the picture in her false passport. Sonny was already in his disguise, with the heavy brows, misshapen nose, and cauliflower ears of an old—and not very competent—boxer.

It was midnight by the time they reached Simón Bolívar International Airport. They collected their luggage from the trunk, handed the car in at the rental desk, then walked through the terminal, hand in hand, like any lovers would.

Only this time, they didn't have to pretend.

ACKNOWLEDGMENTS

I'd like to thank Nicola Mitchell for coming up with the title, and Alex Shaw, Leah Tonna, Joy Wood, Luc van der Heijdt, Andrew Bryan, Tracy Matthews, Vicki Wilkinson, Bella Doerres, Kat Dudley, Paula Thornhill, Ann Cohen, Debbie Lefort, Denice Lyn Jackson, and Lindsay Caglayan for providing their suggestions.

AUTHOR'S NOTE

If you would like to be informed of new releases, simply send an email with "Driscoll" in the subject line to alanmac@ntlworld.com to be added to the mailing list. Alan only sends around three emails a year, so you won't be bombarded with spam. You can find all of Alan's books at www.alanmcdermottbooks.co.uk.

ABOUT THE AUTHOR

Alan McDermott is a husband and a father to beautiful twin girls, and currently lives in the south of England. Born in West Germany to Scottish parents, Alan spent his early years moving from town to town as his father was posted to different army units around the United Kingdom. Alan has had a number of jobs since leaving school, including working on a cruise ship in Hong Kong and Singapore, where he met his wife, and as a software developer creating clinical applications for the National Health Service. Alan gave up his day job in December 2014 to become a full-time author. Alan's writing career began in 2011 with the action thriller *Gray Justice*, his first full-length novel.